For the Love of Ilsa

By Corri van de Stege

Creative Gateway

Paperback Edition: ISBN 978-1-908636-39-3
Also available in Kindle eBook

Typeset in Minion Pro Med 11/14
Cover and Interior Design: Creative Gateway
Published in Great Britain by Creative Gateway
Norfolk, UK

Acknowledgement

I would like to thank my husband, Roy Baldwin, for his support in undertaking the design and typography of the print and digital editions of this book. I also thank a good friend, Alan R. Massen, watercolour artist and author, for generously allowing me to use one of his original paintings of the north Norfolk coast at Blakeney as the basis of the cover. Finally, but not least, I thank friends and family who have read and commented on the final draft of this book and who have encouraged me to carry on and persevere to publication. Nevertheless, all remaining errors and mistakes are entirely mine.

I dedicate this book to long-lasting friends across the world, in particular: Linda, Angie, Susie, Rob, Terri, Sue and Lida.

Corri van de Stege
Summer 2016

One: London 1968

The demonstrators surged ahead, good-natured still although Ilsa heard someone say that the police were beating up protestors in one of the squares ahead. She craned her neck but all she could see were the backs of heads, long haired, shortcuts, hatted, straggly and bald and shiny, and also some side views of faces that were turned, friends shouting and laughing at each other, but also some angry ones. Flags were waving, a girl with long streaming blond hair was sitting on the shoulder of a stocky man, cradling his head with its long and unkempt black hair in her arms, as if she was at a music festival and she was craning to see the band and singers on stage from her vantage position, music that was far away and barely audible in the noise around her, as if this was not this anti-war protest, a celebration of the joint condemnation of power and of the wanton killing carried out in the name of policies and politics that the crowd rejected and abhorred. Ilsa was not at all sure what she was doing here either, just like the girl seemed to have made a mistake about the venue she was supposed to be, but then Ilsa was not sure of why she was anywhere nowadays, not since Jonathan had dragged her into his life and out of her safe environment, old fashioned but free of the need to make a stand, where parents decided what was best, and what might lead to no good, a world that was going crazy and people who challenged everything that they had always accepted as normal and right. If her father knew she was here he would kill her, for sure. Jonathan had convinced her though, had said it was important to be part of it, but why did she listen to Jonathan? Someone pushed her forward, she stumbled and grabbed Jonathan's arm to steady herself and he grinned down at her. 'Great isn't it?' he shouted. She could be his daughter or his sister, whereas she imagined that she could just about be his girlfriend. His face was red, and he had a glare in his eyes. He had bound his straight dark brown hair into a tail at the back and wore a black and white patterned scarf around his neck, was it Arabic, something worn by tribal people in Saudi Arabia perhaps, she wasn't sure, his short jacket open over a tight dark red jersey. He bent over to her as he spoke so that she would hear what he said, then shouted something else away from her to one of his friends, but she couldn't hear the words, just the gravelly boom of his voice mixed in with all the other shouts of the hundreds of people around them, all raising their voices to be heard over everyone else. Jonathan was enjoying this, she could tell. She felt proud to be with him, to have been chosen, was still wondering about him asking her to come with him and his friends, she only a school girl, he a student, and how he had arranged it so that they met up well away from their homes, but she didn't really want to be here. A friend of his, someone called Pete she thought, was behind her and steadied her back, as if they were intimate. She pulled away from him, as if stung.

'I want to get out of here.' She had to repeat it twice at higher pitch up into Jonathan's ear and he looked incredulous.

'You can't,' he shouted and tried to pull her along, along with the others, but she'd had enough.

She shook her head, the long dark blond hair flaring up as if in anger, her eyes half closed, she pulled herself loose from his grip and slid sideways, was nearly knocked over by a heavy set man with a flag who didn't even see her as a policeman grabbed hold of the pole and tried to pull it away from him. Was he crazy? She held out her elbows and fought her way out to the side and then moved backwards, battling a path into the opposite direction away from the surging crowds. They ignored her, pushed past her, forwards, laughing, and shouting, holding hands or linking their arms. Most of them in this part of the crowd were young people like her and like Jonathan. They wore caps or bandanas or wore their long hair in ponytails like Jonathan or shoulder length, straggly and unkempt, whilst the girls had bobs or had their long hair fall lose over their shoulders, their white faces shouting the anti-war slogans, the anti-Vietnam battle cries 'Ho, Ho, Ho Chi Minh' and 'Victory to the Vietcong,' they jibed at police and politicians and anyone in authority. Was that what Jonathan had been shouting? She hadn't heard clearly whatever it was he had been bellowing out, along with his friends, mainly male friends as well as a few girls, from his university. They all knew one another but she wasn't part of them and she wasn't really sure anymore why she was there. She hated crowds and she hated fights and, yes, she also hated war and that was why Jonathan had convinced her to come. Yes, she thought again, as she tried to disentangle herself from the mob, if her parents found out her father would tell her off and try to impose punishments, even though she was now seventeen and he really had no right to touch her but then her father had always slapped them, her and Marja, when he disagreed with what they did and wanted to assert his authority. She couldn't remember a time that he hadn't. He would impose house arrest or threaten that he would take her out of school and into a job. Her mother would tell her off and forbid her to ever talk to Jonathan again, in that voice of hers. She shuddered.

She scuttled through, ducked when someone held out an arm, kept going until the crowd thinned somewhat and then walked on, started to run, until she was well away from the protest and saw the sign of an underground station. She went down the hollow stairs into a smoky, dank corridor with that vague smell of urine, smoke and something sour and when she got to the platform she fumbled inside her red plastic handbag. She had thought she'd look smart with it until she had realised that girls didn't carry that kind of handbag in a demonstration so she had clung to it, and now she found the crumpled packet of cigarettes and a box of matches. A man held out a lighter as she tried to strike a match and failed, her hands trembling. He grinned at her when she inhaled deeply and she walked away from him and got into a carriage where a couple of girls looked up at her indifferently, worlds away from what was going on not far from them, their fishnet covered legs one over the other and their hair a halo of black and red around their white faces with eyes shaded by greens and blues and blacks. She sat down, still trembling and dragged hard at the cigarette, felt herself relaxing and when she looked again the girls had continued their conversation, they no longer noticed her.

She found her way back home even though she had to change three times when she realised she'd gone in the wrong direction and when she walked into the house her mother asked her where she'd been, she was home so late. She shrugged, 'nowhere, just hanging out with Jane. We went to the library and forgot the time. I've got exams next week, remember?' Her mother raised her eyebrows and turned away.

In the evening they sat, her father and her mother and Marja who was fifteen, two years younger than she was but also much more worldly wise, she was well into boyfriends, make up, miniskirts and whatever she could get away with, unlike

Ilsa, who'd always been the more serious older sibling. Her father expressed his anger at what they saw on their black and white television: the scrum on Grosvenor Square, and she shivered at the mud and stones that were thrown by the protestors, at the police. There were smoke bombs too and police on horses charged the crowds. She'd missed all that, thank God.

'Scum,' her father muttered. 'Really, all they want to do is have a fight with the police. This isn't about the war at all. They're hoodlums. Look at them. Students. Not an honest working man in sight.' He ignored the women.

People were arrested, they were pulled away from the crowd, and there were fights. 'I'd have gone and demonstrated,' Marja said. 'If only you would have let me.'

She looked accusingly at her mother. 'War is so wrong, especially what they're doing in Vietnam. They're right, the protestors.' She turned to Ilsa and asked, 'I wonder if Jonathan was there? Was he?'

Ilsa shrugged her shoulders. 'Nah, don't think so,' she said. 'He's too busy with his university lectures and studying and all that, and it'd be dangerous, wouldn't it? But then, what do I care?'

'Well, I would've gone with him,' Marja said. 'If only he'd asked me.'

Marja was in love with Jonathan. She'd almost said as much once when Ilsa teased her about her adoring looks when they passed him in the street. 'He's just so handsome,' Marja sighed. 'And so old! He's grown up.' They'd giggled, even though Ilsa knew that Jonathan was interested in her, Ilsa, not in Marja, only she would never tell Marja who would most likely go up to him and tell him off. She shuddered. After all, she wasn't even sure that she was in love with Jonathan, he fascinated her, yes, but that was different, wasn't it? He represented a world that so far she had only glimpsed at, unlike Marja, who was well into upsetting their parents, and trying to be part of this new freedom that everyone was talking about and that her parents tried so hard to avert.

Later that evening she told Marja she'd been there, at the demo, and swore her to secrecy. Marja was excited. 'You were there! Did you shout? Did you have a banner? Oh I so wish he'd asked me.'

Ilsa laughed and said she, Marja was just a baby; she would have been frightened, just like she, Ilsa, had been. And after all, she and Jonathan were just friends, kind of.

They had known each other for years. He and his parents, his twin sister Diane and younger brother Robert had moved into their street when Ilsa was twelve and Marja just ten, and they were quite friendly, sometimes hung out talking, and Jonathan, Diane and Robert went to the same school that Ilsa went to and later Marja also, only he and Diane were two grades higher than Ilsa was and Robert was in the grade below her and one higher than Marja. They just knew each other, but because they'd never been in the same grade they'd never become close friends, not even with Diane, who during term time had a large circle of classmates she hung out with and who considered herself far too mature for someone like Ilsa. Lately, however, after he'd left school and he had left home to go to university, where he lived in a student hall of residence, and after Diane had enrolled into some kind of secretarial college and was still living at home, Jonathan had shown an increased interest in Ilsa, she just knew, felt him looking at her. Not at Marja although Marja did her utmost to attract his attention and was forever trying to engage him in chats, was funny and lively. When he came home for a weekend, he would hang around outside and Ilsa just knew by the way he looked her up and down and then grinned and made a comment 'Still at school then? Can't wait for you to grow up. You should come to my uni, when you've passed your A-levels.'

She wasn't sure though about what he wanted. He never really asked her out, and that's what he should do, shouldn't he? Except for last week when he'd casually suggested that she should come along, to this demo and fool she was she had felt a glow and liked it that he was showing attention.

'It would be a good intro to uni,' he said. 'We need to show solidarity,' whatever he'd meant by that.

After her A-levels this year, she wanted to go to university herself, she wanted to study English Lit, become an English teacher perhaps, and then travel the world, do some teaching abroad, perhaps write a book. Her father had reluctantly agreed that she would go to university, couldn't really hide his pride in the fact that she was so very clever and got such high grades, but he'd said nevertheless 'only if you make the grades that the teachers say you will get.' He added that if she did go to university she would have to stay at home, look for a college that she could travel to on a daily basis, and it would have to be one of the London colleges. She didn't mind, was sure that sooner or later she would escape the tedium of her parents' life, but she needed qualifications, she needed to be able to get a job that would allow her to escape.

She hung out with boys of her class in groups, sure, but she also knew that she didn't want to be tied down to anyone or anything because that would make going to university more problematic, wouldn't it? Besides, she wasn't a slag; she'd never let boys do to her what some girls let them do. She kept aloof and hung out more with girls than with boys, as opposed to Marja, who was always leering, Ilsa thought, but who also seemed to have a lot of fun and would make up all kinds of stories about staying with friends so that their parents wouldn't find out what she was really up to, parties she went to, films she saw.

Ilsa didn't really want a boyfriend, unlike Marja, who giggled and blushed and tarted herself up when she went out, secretly, so their mother wouldn't notice. No, she, Ilsa, just wanted to get her A-levels and go to university. She wanted to escape, not only from her home but from all of her background, start again, a different kind of life, one that would not be working class, the way her parents were, always grumping at people that had an education, that were beyond them, according to her father.

In the end all her plans, all her firm intentions, it all went wrong, as if she'd been a spring coiled the wrong way somehow. Rather than finishing university she'd ended up with a baby before finishing her degree. All Jonathan's fault, she would think later, although she sometimes wondered about herself.

He'd never stopped showing an interest in her, not from that first time she went on the demo with him, even though at times she'd seen him around with other girls who seemed more mature, not schoolgirls anymore, and he pretended not to notice her, and then she convinced herself that he was no longer interested in her, not after she walked away from him at that demo.

Then, one stupid party in her first year of university she'd had too much to drink, couldn't really hold alcohol well, and he'd been there waiting for her, and telling her how he'd always been in love with her, and she'd ended up in a room upstairs and she remembered how he'd kissed her and held her and then before she knew what happened she'd given in, loving him she thought.

She'd ended up with baby Mark instead of with a qualification that would open up the world for her, and all her ambitions to forge her own life had come apart into so many dirty nappies. They got married, had to; she wouldn't let it be aborted even though Jonathan had suggested it and had even offered to come with her. He said he assumed she was on the pill, that she knew what she was doing, and he'd get the money together somehow. But she wouldn't hear about it and eventually told her mother who was even more horrified at the thought of an abortion than of a child out of wedlock. At least he'd had the decency to marry her, a shotgun wedding with her father and mother looking crestfallen and keeping their eyes focussed on the floor as if guessing what might be beneath it, rather than at the people who came up to them to congratulate, and her father looked as if he'd much rather be somewhere else than be a witness to this, their clever daughter who had always been so serious and so full of promises, here at her wedding with a big belly in a kaftan-like off-white dress that showed the outline of a beginning bump, and who was giving her vows to the man who had knocked her up, her father said.

And so she'd ended up looking after a baby while Jonathan had finished his degree and subsequently a PhD on university grants and with the help of his parents, all achieved with distinction. As Jonathan's sister Diana moved out of their parents' house Eliza and Jonathan had temporarily moved into Jonathan's bedroom and converted Diana's room to a baby room. His parents had been nice enough about it, much less condemnatory, but she'd been relieved when eventually they found their own place, a small two bedroom flat.

In fact, she'd been happy enough then, when Mark was a baby and she'd proudly shown him off to her friends and to Marja, who sulked for a long time when she realised that Jonathan was off limits for her.

There no longer was time for demonstrations or for a lot of the things she'd imagined she'd be doing, like getting her degree, a good job, being her own woman, unlike her mother had ever been. None of that happened, not immediately anyway. So much for 1968 and liberation and women's lib. It had all passed her by at the time although she'd managed to catch up later of course, but then her life once more became entangled and difficult, her own fault, and Jonathan's, in ways she wished it hadn't. But that was later, much later, after they'd had another baby and some more, when something of the shine disappeared from their marriage and it all started to go wrong.

Two: Norfolk 2010

It was one of those glorious autumn days, when the sky is blue with only a few white woollen clouds, when the wind is still mild although there's a chilly undercurrent of what's to come, and the leaves turn to yellow, red and gold and then start to drop off the trees leaving thick blankets of red brown paper-thin crisps on the lawns, the pavements and the paths and in the woods, until the inevitable autumn rain will transform them into slushy wet quilts of browns and yellows and slippery carpets waiting for someone to rake them and do away with them.

Ilsa came out of the clinic and as the automatic door closed behind her she opened the clasp of her large brown leather handbag, which was slung over her shoulder, and pulled out a crumpled packet of cigarettes. She stood on the step, momentarily blinking against the light of the milky sun. She noticed how her hands trembled, as if they were somebody else's, and she then thought they did not look like hers at all. How could they be? How could they be part of this person? It needn't be her, this woman, it could easily be someone else, just like these hands could easily be someone else's, they must be, that's how she looked at them. She would wake up soon and realise that this woman wasn't her at all, but an imposter.

She would deny everything, make it all go away. After all, no one even knew she was here, apart from the specialist of course and perhaps a nurse might remember her, oh yes, and the administrator who'd taken down her details so carefully and who'd looked at her, trying hard not to avert her eyes when she signed out and when she pushed the prescriptions in her bag, amongst the cigarettes and the lipstick and her wallet, some pens, an opened packet of tissues, a comb, her gleaming smart phone in that nice pure white leather cover that she'd recently bought on a whim, some loose coins that had slipped from her wallet and now lay scattered across the lining, as if lost.

Ilsa took a deep breath, walked down the step onto the leafy path that led from the clinic to the car park and pulled a box of matches out of one of her coat pockets. She'd lost her lighter and had decided not to buy another one as she would definitely give up smoking, just finish this last packet that was in her bag, and on a whim she had grabbed a box of matches from the kitchen drawer, there for lighting candles or for lighting a barbecue that never happened, before she came out this morning. It wouldn't make any difference now anyway. She shook her head, as if denying what she'd just heard.

'Is your husband with you? Or a close relative?' the specialist had asked, looking over his rimless clear glasses at her, and she'd shaken her head then as she did now. She'd confirmed once more that she was alone and didn't need anyone else with her. Why would she bring Jonathan anyway? He didn't even know that she'd made the appointment, for Christ's sake. They had been clear about their divorce, agreed that they were at the end of the road, barely talked to each other nowadays, so why would she tell him about this hospital appointment? She'd been convinced that nothing serious was the matter with her, couldn't be, it had just been a mess up in the scan, it had happened before. She'd been recalled then after the two-yearly scan and it had all turned out to be fuss about nothing.

Of course, she hadn't said any of this to the specialist, had only shaken her head and said brightly, 'he's out of the country, my husband.' And he was. For work, only for a day he'd said when he left early the previous morning. He'd be back early the next day, today, tonight, when they would go over the divorce paperwork. She hadn't told him about her appointment and the sudden pang of fear she'd felt before he left. Soon they'd be living in separate houses anyway and he would no longer be part of her life. She wondered if nevertheless he would want to know if something was wrong with her, but shook the thought away from her mind.

After a few attempts she managed to light a match, unused to the striking of a stick against the box, and she lit her cigarette. She threw the black bent match sticks into a bin that stood next to the door, took a long deep drag and felt the smoke softening her insides, as it always had, as it always did, the balmy narcotics settling in her brain and calming her. No use giving up now, was there? She'd never been a very heavy smoker anyway, she told herself, had gone without for years on end even, but always came back to them, the cigarettes, when she felt down or out of control, as she had been these last months, crunch time, everything running away from her and she had no control. She stood still, abruptly, and stared in front of her without seeing anything, while people passed her in both directions, along the path.

A man came up to her, someone in a uniform, 'No smoking here, not on the grounds, madam.' He wasn't unkind in the way he said it, but she growled, threw the cigarette on the greyish lumpy asphalt in front of her, on a leafless patch, and stubbed it out with the toe of her boot, then made to bend to pick it up

13

and stood quite still with the shocking pain somewhere deep inside her chest travelling to her abdomen, she was barely able to breathe. The man stood watching her and saw her face, 'you all right?' He said it kindly, concerned.

She had to get out of this place, away from this hospital, from these people, from the couple dawdling on the path before they climbed the steps to go inside, both looking at her curiously, she had to get away from the carelessly dressed woman in an ill fitting blue jacket and grey trousers that frayed at the bottom, who had a disapproving look and pulled along a small girl who nearly ran into her; she had to get away from the couple strolling up towards the entrance, hand in hand, talking and smiling as if this was the best day in their lives. How could it be? She should go home so that she could sit down and smoke as much as she needed to, shut out this world, and take deep smoky breaths. And think. Think about what to do next. Think about how to deal with this and with the rest of her life, whatever was left.

'I'm ok,' she made a gesture with her hand as if to wave the uniformed man away from her, and she carefully squatted, picked up the squashed cigarette and threw it in the bin. The man frowned, shrugged and sauntered past her inside the building, the doors swishing behind him. She continued her walk towards the car park, carefully now, as if she'd just come out of an operation and was learning to take the first careful steps.

A light breeze reminded her that it was November and despite the sun she shivered in her thick long camel coat, loose over a pair of smart brown trousers, an off-white coarse knit jumper, her knee length brown leather boots with leg-hugging trousers tucked in. Her dark blond hair, still not showing any sign of grey, was pulled back in a thin scarf at the back of her neck, hair that was thinning and would disappear altogether if she agreed to the chemotherapy, strongly recommended by the specialist. But she wouldn't, of course she'd refuse. What was the point? Just extend her misery? So that they could all watch her die? Feel sorry for her? Jonathan? And she certainly didn't want to upset the lives of her children, the three that were left, even if scattered across the globe, and who had plenty to worry about without having to be concerned about her. The specialist had told her to go home and think about her treatment, she would have to make another appointment, get further specialist help, he would assign a nurse. There might be remission. She'd not responded and he'd let her go, helpless in the face of her refusal to respond to his well meaning and kind words.

'I'll send an appointment letter, before the end of next week,' he said. 'That should give you enough time to think about your next steps. Come with your husband, I see that you're married, or at least with someone else who's close to you, children, a good friend?'

She scoured the car park holding her hand above her forehead briefly to ward off the now watery sun. The park was vast and overflowing and then she remembered where she'd left her people carrier, a Mazda that she'd bought when she retired from her teaching job, only last year, a present to herself. The car was too large; she didn't even like the model. She'd bought it because she and Jonathan had the money and she liked roomy cars, in case one of the children came to visit with partners and children and she might want to pick them up from an airport.

They hadn't of course visited, not for nearly a year now, not since that disastrous visit last Christmas. And why would they? After all, Jonathan had gone off and disappeared for the two days before Christmas Day and had returned late on Christmas

Eve, even though he knew bloody well that they were coming, Mark and Eliza and Mark's wife Samantha, and Eliza's new partner Gerry and his children. Stephan hadn't been there though, couldn't make it, he e-mailed, not that year, not all the way from Singapore. She suspected that Sander, his boyfriend, was less keen, because she hadn't been exactly forthcoming and warm when she and Jonathan had visited them in Singapore the year before. That had been a last half hearted attempt at making something out of their marriage, keep it together, and it had been a terrible mistake to try and do that in Singapore of all places. Her coldness during that week had had nothing to do with either Stephan or Sander and everything with the bitterness growing inside her, towards Jonathan, towards what she'd done with her life, towards her own miserable failures; after all, she couldn't put all the blame on Jonathan, could she?

She'd missed Stephan last Christmas, more than she would have missed either of the other two, Mark or Eliza. She still had that warm feeling inside, when she thought about him, her youngest, the child that would make everything all right, even if he hadn't, but the child that seemed to have needed her more than the others, when he was little.

No, last Christmas had been a disaster. A week before, as if he hadn't known all along, Jonathan announced that he needed to check out a software system in China and the client was important, he needed to keep him on board, even if it meant going away at that time of the year. He could just fit it in before everyone arrived, he said. Of course, it was none of her business, already they had known that this would be their last Christmas together, they would split up afterwards, tell them later. They already led quite separate lives and kept mostly to their own rooms in their sprawling house. However, if Jonathan had really wanted to keep up the charade as he said he did, that they were happily married parents and grandparents, he bloody well ought to have made an effort as well, whoever this important client was. He'd simply left all the arrangements to her, as if she didn't have her own commitments. But that was another story of course. By then she no longer really believed in the urgency of his workload, and she knew that work was simply an excuse to hide behind every time he disappeared for days and sometimes weeks on end, and wasn't this suspicion of hers exactly one of the reasons they were now set to separate, her belief that he had always been keeping things from her, that he led a double life? That he'd led a double life since the day they married, or perhaps not immediately, but certainly after he landed a job that meant he would need to travel, often abroad, and then later, of course, later, instead of walking out she'd come back to him, to Jonathan, wanting it to work, this marriage of theirs, their happy family, her long-term objective, the reason she had given up all her earlier dreams.

At the time, later on confirmed, she suspected that, rather than a client needing him urgently just before Christmas, it was more likely he'd spent the time with that nice looking colleague of his, Alea was her name, while she, Ilsa, had wrapped the presents, had bought and prepared food and had been cheerful with Mark and Samantha and their two children, Jonathan's and her grandchildren, and then on Christmas eve when Eliza and her Gerry and his two children arrived around lunchtime, she'd been the model and caring mum and grandma even though she resented that Eliza had brought these strangers. Just a partner would have been enough, but his children as well? But she hadn't of course shown any of this to Eliza, she wanted Eliza to be happy again, after all that business, after she'd left Tom and been so depressed. Besides, she now lived so far away that they rarely visited anyway.

When Jonathan had come in eventually, late on Christmas Eve, just in time for dinner, he apologised profusely to everyone and carried a bag full of expensive toys for Caroline and Jasper, and even for Gerry's two, so thoughtful.

'Father Christmas gave me these presents in the airport,' he'd whispered to the children. 'He was just on his way back to Lapland.'

And they'd loved him, of course, loved all of his boisterous and hearty laughing self as he threw them up in the air and made them giggle throughout that bloody awful Christmas while she ran herself ragged trying to keep everyone in food, drinks and presents. Well, sort of. Mark, Samantha and Eliza of course helped quite a bit, they always did. Even Gerry did his best to be gallant and helpful, pouring the drinks, clearing tables, filling the dishwasher and making sure his children were polite. But the house had been full and noisy and even if she had loved the closeness of them all, misery had enveloped her every time she stopped to think.

'Mum, you've got to either believe him or, if you don't, ask him right out. He probably doesn't even realise what you are angry about. Because that's what you are. Aren't you? Perhaps you believe he's cheating on you again, I mean.' Eliza had said, looking embarrassed, as she kissed her mother goodbye, that day after Boxing Day. If only she'd known the half of it, she'd simply guessed that something was wrong, which had not been that difficult.

How had they become such strangers, she and her children? She'd always been so close to Eliza when she was still at home; Eliza had always been on her side, when something was wrong, when she and Jonathan quarrelled like every couple would quarrel, she'd usually taken her side, even though Eliza loved her father and firmly believed he told the truth, always, that he wasn't a cheat, that he was just a bit unthinking sometimes. Eliza adored her father and would probably be the most upset when she found out that they were in the middle of divorce procedures. She was sure that Eliza firmly believed in their integrity as a couple, her mother Ilsa and her father Jonathan, that she thought they were the pinnacle of achievement, a happy family, one that she wanted to emulate. Wasn't that why Eliza had split up with Tom? Tom hadn't come up to her standards, had he? Not up to the standard of a happy family where the parents have a solid relationship, in which they share and tell each other everything. A relationship without secrets and Tom had failed in Eliza's eyes. So now she had taken on Gerry and Ilsa had to do her best not to show that she wasn't that keen on Gerry, that she would have preferred it if Tom had been there, the Tom she'd known for such a long time now and who had become part of the family, unlike Gerry.

Mark simply didn't care, or perhaps that was unfair, he just didn't think about his parents in that way, they were just there, Ilsa thought, and he was too busy with his own life, he didn't want to find difficulties and it was easier to assume there were none, except for an odd quarrel or disagreement, but then, didn't all couples have those?

If only they knew. Why had she put up with it all for this length of time, why had she tried so hard to make it work, this charade? Why had Jonathan? Why had they decided to carry on in their sham marriage, with all that hopeless history and pain? Even after Anthony? Even though they had both known it was all so hopeless, that they were on a road to nowhere? And now this, even if she wanted to she wouldn't now be able to take a different direction, to try and resolve some of this, to stop being dependent. She couldn't make any of it any better now, it was all too late. Everything was too late.

Ilsa drove away from the hospital car park and stopped at the chemist's, which was on the way home. She needed the painkillers the specialist had prescribed, if nothing else. She parked on the opposite site of the road, so that she didn't have to turn, and could carry straight on home. She slammed the car door closed behind her and started to cross the road, without looking sideways, deep in thought and unaware of the old red Ford Fiesta that came round the bend in the road at high speed. Someone screamed but it wasn't Ilsa, she just felt the sharp and quite extraordinary force of a hard collision and then everything went black.

Three: Singapore 2010

Stephan, sitting in the back seat, lightly tapped Sander's shoulder in the front, smiled at Sander when he turned and said, 'you deal with that. Paying the driver, I mean. I'll take us in and find the table.' He gingerly stepped out of the back of the taxi and held the door open for Sander's parents, his elderly father and much younger mother. 'Sander's good at that. He gets everyone confused, especially with these Indonesian rupees,' Stephan said to them.

Sander's mother Beatrix laughed her girly laugh, as if she was sixteen and being wooed by this much younger man, her son's lover, who held the door open for her. Her husband Martijn struggled out from the other side of the taxi. He was very tall and stooped low to avoid hitting his head. Even when he stood up straight he stood slightly bent, due to a lifelong attempt at appearing less tall than he was and avoiding banging his head into low door frames and even ceilings.

The early evening Bali heat was still overwhelming. Beatrix tugged at her loose sleeveless pale blue blouse and white linen trousers, plucked the thin and now slightly damp material away from her body, wiped a tissue across her glistening forehead and shook out her short cut brown hair. Despite all this she looked attractive and had managed to keep both lipstick and light makeup in place without smearing either.

Stephan, his bare feet in a pair of expensive looking leather sandals, was dressed in knee length tan shorts and a blue cotton short sleeved t-shirt, crisply ironed; he appeared cool as if the heat had no effect on him whatsoever. Not to the extent it seemed to affect their guests at least. Stephan loved these trips to Bali, away from the overpowering noise, the bustle of cars and people, the tall buildings, taxis, buses and people streaming into and out of the underground stations, and, as far as he was concerned, away from the much more debilitating heat of Singapore where he and Sander worked their high paid but intensely demanding jobs in the travel industry and airline businesses. Having Sander's parents over for a visit from their native Holland was as good an excuse as any to have organised a long weekend away in Bali. They were cool, these parents. They were totally at ease with Stephan and Sander being together, as opposed to his own mother, Ilsa, who had never recovered from that first shock when he'd told her and Jonathan that he was gay, when he'd come out, how old was he then, seventeen? Eighteen? Whatever. He knew, had always known he was gay and was surprised his mother had not cottoned on before. She was usually so very cool and collected and, he considered, very worldly-wise even though she led such a dull and secluded life, teaching at a school, rarely going anywhere exciting. She hadn't actually screamed and shouted at him or cold-shouldered him, but he felt that she'd never lost that edginess when he'd brought someone home, a man, and not a girlfriend who might produce grandchildren. His sister Eliza told him that he simply had imagined this reluctance on their mother's behalf and that there had been a time when Ilsa had been unhappy in her own marriage, that the relationship between her and their father hadn't been too good, but he thought the two were unrelated, his mother's personal unhappiness and her view of him as a gay man.

Sander's parents were good though. Moreover, they still functioned as a married couple, unlike Ilsa and Jonathan who never seemed to talk to each other anymore and when in company ignored each other, as if the other was an avatar, someone not quite human. It was embarrassing. Bloody parents, they fuck you up, as the poet said. But then, hadn't someone said that kids fucked up their parents just as much? He should give more credit to Jonathan, who'd been fine that time they'd visited in Singapore. Ilsa was the one who had been a bit obnoxious and had insisted they'd stay in a hotel, 'Not to impose on you two. The apartment is so small.' He was glad he lived well away from them now, even though he loved them, after all they were his parents and he'd had a kind of happy childhood, in a solid middle class family. It just seemed too difficult now, his parents' marriage, as if something had broken somewhere on the way, and actually not really that long ago. He suspected it had something to do with Anthony, but all that was water under the bridge now, so long ago, what was it, six years soon, too sad. It should have brought them closer together as a family but it had had the opposite effect, almost as if Jonathan and Ilsa blamed each other, as if one of them ought to have prevented it, even though it had been a stupid accident. Stephan missed Anthony, still, but wished his parents had not become so reluctant to talk about him, as if it had been something so dark and unimaginable and painful that it was better left unspoken about, even Jonathan wouldn't really talk much about Anthony anymore and changed the subject when anyone as much as mentioned anything that had to do with Anthony.

Stephan led Beatrix and Martijn, he called them Beatrice and Martin as he could not get used to the Dutch pronunciation of their names, through the crowded entrance of

23

the restaurant, where waiters and eager guests peered over table plans and menus that were spread over a large desk in the entrance hall as well as pinned to the wall behind, and once they were inside a thick hot noise of the music of a heavy rock group mingled with loud voices and laughter greeted them. Groups of people were seated at long tables and young waitresses and waiters dressed in black shorts and sleeveless black vests with a small red logo on their chest, weaved their way through the crowds balancing trays full of drinks and food or dirty plates and glasses. The maitre'd, a woman in a very short black skirt with a small microphone attached to headphones planted on her long straight black hair, and who smiled warmly as if they'd been expected, asked their names and then pointed to a table in the corner, away from the main dining area. Cushions were strewn across the hard wooden bench and covered the seats of the chairs, made of a solid wood that looked hard and uncomfortable without some padding.

'My friend will be coming in a minute,' Stephan shouted over the din at the maître d', who in fact looked like all the other waiters and waitresses except for the way she gave instructions through the microphone attached to her earphones.

'Also, we're expecting another couple, so there'll be six of us altogether. We've booked a table in the main dining area, I think?'

She held her head turned towards him to catch what he said, then spoke rapidly into her microphone and before they had time to arrange themselves on the cushions, two waitresses in shorts and bare legs were kneeling next to their low table and asked them what they would like to drink.

Stephan bent over towards Martijn who'd sat down in one of the wooden chairs with comfortable arm rests, pointed at the drinks menu and shouted to make himself heard, 'Mojito's all round? We'll have wine with our food.' And to the waitress he said, 'Four of these. Oh wait.'

Sander was at their table, with Kevin and his new girlfriend, a petite Chinese looking girl. 'Susie,' Kevin mouthed and pointed at the girl, who had a fixed smile on her face, baring perfect white teeth. She nodded respectfully at the parents and after another round of introductions they finally succeeded in ordering the drinks.

'He had a fight with the taxi driver,' Kevin said. 'Just as well we came along and rescued him. He was making a fuss about, what was it, fifty pence?' He laughed and explained, 'The guy, the driver, charged the equivalent of two English pounds or something like that for your ride and he here,' pointing at Sander, 'said they'd agreed on thirty-thousand rupiahs whereas the taxi driver said they'd agreed on forty-thousand. That's about fifty pence difference.'

Sander smiled, shrugged his shoulders and said, 'It's all these thousands. It always confuses me and I thought I was being ripped off.' He sat down next to Stephan and they smiled at each other. 'You twat,' Stephan said. 'You pay at least double the amount for one of them drinks here.'

'It's my Dutch nature,' Sander said. 'I count pennies and have always been told to live within my means.' He smiled at his parents, who clearly couldn't hear what they talked about, over the din in the room, and smiled back vacantly.

'Ha-ha and how does that fit with your image of being an important region director for Singapore?' Kevin asked. 'And if I remember correctly, you weren't so stingy when we were all living in London. You took cabs whenever you could find one, without asking what they would cost, rather than take the bus or the tube. Those were good times though.' He turned towards

Beatrix. 'Did you know your son was so hard on the locals? He really doesn't trust anyone.'

Beatrix smiled fondly at Sander, who sat back and slung one arm over the back of the bench behind Stephan, completely relaxed and enjoying the banter. Stephan took his phone out from his pocket, looked at it and apologised. 'There's a message from my brother. I felt it vibrate. Just let me see what it is. He doesn't usually contact me unless it's something important.' He scrolled down the screen, his eyes pinched and the smile left his face. 'It's my mother,' he said. 'Oh God. Something's happened. I think he's saying she died.' He looked up, pinched his left ear between his thumb and index finger and then grabbed the glass from the table in front of him and took a large gulp, emptying it. The telephone slid down from his knees onto the floor between the table and his feet, as Sander hugged him.

Four: Germany 2010

In Germany, Mark looked up from his phone as his daughter pushed the plate of food away from her. 'I don't like this,' she said in English. 'I don't like green veggies, you know that.' For good measure and emphasis she added contemptuously in German 'Mag's nicht!'

'For god's sake Caroline, just behave yourself. I haven't got the time for this nonsense.' He looked at the empty seat where Samantha should have been but wasn't. She'd gone upstairs to see if Jasper had woken up and to check whether he was fever free so she could try to feed him some dinner. They'd thought they heard him call, but everything was quite silent upstairs. Caroline started to sniff and pulled down her mouth, ready to cry, working up the tears. 'And no need to cry, it won't help.' Mark said. 'You won't leave the table until you've finished.'

Wrong, of course wrong. He should just take the plate away and take her to bed. She was clearly ready for a fight, sensed the unease in the house. Perhaps it was better to tell her, this silence just wasn't working. Jasper having come down with a fever didn't help either. They were all on edge and Caroline just didn't understand.

'Listen, darling,' he said. 'We're worried and we're a bit sad because Grandma isn't well. Not well at all. Can you be a good girl? Eat your food. We may have to go to England, to see grandpa.'

Wrong again. He was being stupid, treating her like this. There was no longer a grandma, although she still had her German 'Oma'. Grandma was dead, however, and he needed to decide what to do, not just how to tell the children but also he should book a flight; he should go over to England now to see Jonathan, immediately. He'd texted Stephan and although Jonathan had said he'd spoken to Eliza she bloody well hadn't been in touch at all, not even after his, Mark's, various messages and she was not picking up her phone either. No, Eliza had gone AWOL again; she always did when there was trouble. For a split second he wondered whether she would already be with Jonathan and was too upset to even talk to her brothers. What was he thinking? He shook his head and Caroline said, raising her voice, 'What? What Daddy?'

'He's gone back to sleep,' Samantha came back into their large kitchen where they usually ate their supper with the children. 'Cary, you've got to eat your food, otherwise you'll wake up hungry. Come on. You're a big girl.'

Caroline looked at her mother, swallowed back the howl she was about to produce for her father's benefit and picked up her fork. She pulled back the plate from the middle of the table and fished through the food with a fork, picked out a piece of potato and brought it to her mouth.

'Sam,' Mark said. 'I've got to go to England, now. I should be there. Help Dad. Eliza is probably already there. We need to find out what happened. No one is communicating and Jonathan just said he didn't want to talk over the phone and I should come so we could talk face to face. I'm sure he's in a bit of a state, although coming to think of it that isn't like Dad.' He was talking gibberish, trying to find reasons and explanations where none were needed.

Samantha pulled the elasticated band out of her hair at the back of her head, shook it so that it hung sideways down to her left shoulder, wound the curly brown mass round her hand and slid the band back in place. Her face was red and puffy and she looked tired, with deep blue rings under her green eyes, which seemed to have lost their sharpness. She hadn't slept much the night before with Jasper crying out every hour or so, then coming to their bed and he, Mark had disappeared into the guest room and slept through whilst Sam had tried to calm Jasper who it turned out had an ear infection. The emergency doctor in the hospital saw him early in the afternoon and prescribed antibiotics, said it was a nasty infection and sooner rather than later he should have gremlins put in. Late in the afternoon, once the medicine started to work and she'd given him some painkillers, he'd dozed off after a long and cranky day that had followed the sleepless night.

'I've texted both Stephan and Eliza but only Stephan has responded. He's catching a flight from Singapore on Tuesday, the earliest he could get one. Apparently, he was in Bali when he got my message. He flew back to Singapore today, cutting short their weekend, but then hasn't been able to get a flight for Monday, tomorrow. So he's flying on Tuesday and won't get to England until Wednesday morning, early, what with the time difference.'

'Your poor mother,' Samantha said. 'I do feel for her, even though she doesn't know anything now of course. It's just so sad. And then, what's all this about her being ill? Did you know she had been having tests?' Sam looked at Caroline, not wanting to use the word in front of her daughter, who suddenly sat full of attention, listening to their conversation, pushing small bits of food into her mouth, her ears on red alert.

'Is Grandma ill?' Caroline asked. 'Can I go see her?'

'Oh my love,' Samantha said. 'Grandma won't be there when we go next time. Grandma is very ill.'

'But I want to see her,' Caroline insisted.

'I've got to explain to her,' Samantha turned to Mark. 'I've just not had the time, what with Jasper, to talk to her about it. You take her to the other room and have a conversation, explain carefully. We have to decide what we do. Perhaps she should come to England, is seven old enough? For a funeral? Well, it's her grandmother. I'll ask Greta if she can come and stay here, to look after Jasper. He can't travel, not now, besides he wouldn't understand anyway and just be miserable.'

'Yeah,' Caroline shouted. 'I wanna go to England too. I will see Granddad and Grandma. Will it be like Christmas? Will we have presents?'

'Come pet, let's go to the other room so that Mum can eat something. I want to talk to you. Well done, you've eaten most of it and I won't make a fuss about the vegetables this time.'

He helped Caroline get off the chair and took her into the sitting room, closing the kitchen door behind them.

Samantha sat with her head in her hands, like a meditating giraffe, motionless. If only she didn't feel so worn out and exhausted. She briefly closed her eyes and felt tears welling up behind the lids. She bit her lip, then wiped hard and painfully across her eyes with a tissue. Poor Ilsa. Killed by a car and then this news that she'd been to see a specialist, a cancer specialist, in a private clinic, and she'd been hit by a car on her way back. Jonathan hadn't even known she'd had a checkup. How absolutely awful. What was going on? Why hadn't she told anyone? Why hadn't Jonathan been with her? She shouldn't have been driving on her own, not after that consultation.

Samantha remembered Ilsa the way she'd been when she and Mark got married. At that time Ilsa had been a much more bouncy person than the one of late, she'd been a woman who radiated health and optimism, who was full of energy and who clearly wanted to do a lot of things with her life; she'd been concerned about where they, Mark and Sam, would live, then later she'd been worried about Eliza when she broke up with Tom. Ilsa had been communicative then, even if not exactly overflowing, she'd never been overly exuberant, but she had not then been the silent and slightly cranky woman of these last few years.

At first when Stephan moved to London and then to Singapore, she took it all in her stride, even though it must have been difficult for her to accept that everyone was moving away, two children moving to other countries and then Eliza to the other side of England. Ilsa had coped so well with Anthony, the problem child, or rather problem teenager because he'd been fine as a child everyone said, it was only after he'd done his A-levels that Anthony started doing drugs and then, after she and Mark had been married for some five years, Anthony had died in that horrible accident. As far as Samantha knew that accident had been the final cause of Ilsa's change into an unhappy and withdrawn woman, that horrible death of her middle son. Sure, in reality she and Mark hadn't seen that much of either Ilsa or Jonathan during that time, they'd been in the middle of settling down here in Germany and their children had been quite small still, but once or twice, when they visited, Samantha had sensed that Ilsa was becoming bitter, she had changed dramatically, she was angry, she sneered at her husband, at Jonathan, when she thought no one was around as if she was digging for a fight with him. She became abrupt with her other children and then slowly reduced contact and would only rarely pick up a phone to talk to Mark and Sam, except for inviting them over for Christmas, as if a duty rather than something she'd be looking forward to? And then, with all her family around and everyone trying their best to maintain a happy and festive mood this last Christmas Ilsa had been cranky and cold with Jonathan, barely speaking to him, although both of them did try their damnedest to give their grandchildren a lovely time, and to make it seem that everything was hunky dory. She, Samantha, had known better. Something wasn't right. Perhaps Ilsa had known already that she was ill? But what a way of going about it, why not tell your own children? Why be miserable and cold as if whatever was bothering her was a hurt that had been caused by them, by her own family. No, Ilsa had not been right, not for a few years. Samantha sighed. Perhaps they'd find out now what had caused Ilsa being so miserably unhappy.

The door through which Mark had taken Caroline flew open and Caroline came running towards her mother, crying 'Mummy, Daddy says that Grandma is dead. She isn't, is she? Dead is gone, isn't it? Dead is dead, like Uncle Anthony is dead?' She tripped over the words, took a deep breath, pushed herself between the table and her mother to sit on her lap and threw her arms around Samantha's neck. And then they both wept.

Mark stood helpless. He felt his own tears and blinked hard.

It was Sunday but he'd telephoned his colleague, said he wouldn't be coming in for a week, briefly explained why, heard the condolences and the concern but it didn't reach him somehow, not inside. They were words and the enormity of what had happened to Ilsa still hadn't quite sunk in. His mother had always been indestructible, hadn't she? She was the core of the family, and he couldn't quite imagine what they would be like without her, whether they would still operate as a family. It was their father who'd always seemed the more remote of the two, as if never quite part of whatever was going on in the house.

He heard their downstairs neighbours slam a door, heard a loud voice echoing down the communal stairwell and then it was quiet again. Their apartment in this rather upmarket part of Neustadt exuded German solidity and finesse, the wooden floors, the large windows at the front looking out over the road to the park across and the apartment block to the side, similarly solid and well kept, windows with half open blinds, others that were blank canvases, and unless there was a light on inside the room, dark and slightly mysterious, as if unknown worlds were hidden within, lives and secrets, mysterious yet blank.

The streetlights below cast their shadows on the pavements and further down the park it was bluish dark with only an intermittent street lamp. Few people were out and about, it was Sunday after all. During the day, people took their children out to the parks, to the town, to visit family, to have a meal out and now it was bedtime and back to school and work tomorrow. Only they, he, Sam and the kids, wouldn't go back to normal tomorrow, he'd fly to England, with or without Samantha, that was clear, and Samantha would have to cancel her classes. Or perhaps she already had. He never knew, they hadn't talked about it. She was efficient in a way that he could only admire after the fact, arranging and organising his and their children's lives as if a perfectly oiled machine that would follow the preset code of her directions and instructions. Well, she was half German and completely at home living here, even though she'd been reluctant at first, to resettle back in Germany, after he had suggested it, the opportunity for him to transfer to the German based office in this new town in the former eastern part of German, away from the London stress.

And now this. What to do about Jonathan? Would he cope on his own in that big house in the country outside Norwich? What had he been up to these last years, withdrawn but cheerfully so, ignoring Ilsa's moods, silent about the loss of Anthony, although it must have hit him hard, surely just as hard as it had hit Ilsa and them, their other children? As a child Anthony had always been Jonathan's favourite son, Mark was sure of that, he'd even felt angry about it sometimes, resented the baby brother that had upset his own legitimate first place in the world. Eliza's birth hadn't done that, she was a girl and therefore different. Something had happened though in later years and it hadn't been only the accident, Anthony's death, something else had upset Ilsa, and Jonathan for that matter, to the extent that Ilsa had become bitter, almost accusing Jonathan, and as if it had all been his fault. Why? And now she was gone. They'd never know probably. But perhaps there was nothing to know anyway, perhaps they were just a couple that had not grown old well together, some didn't. He'd never thought that before, he'd always assumed that theirs had been one of those solid everlasting families with a dad who loved his mum and vice versa. But then, no marriage was perfect, he'd learned that much.

Mark sighed. He heard Samantha go upstairs with Caroline. They were lucky living on this top floor of the block where the apartments had an upstairs and downstairs, unlike the ones lower down, even though those appeared roomier somehow, when you came in, stretching underneath two apartments above them. But then, luck had nothing to do with it, had it? He wouldn't have moved into an apartment that was too small, not with two children. The company had been good to them and helped them find this place at a very reasonable rent. They'd kept the house just outside London, let at a very pleasant rate that easily covered their current rent in Germany and more, just in case they wanted to move back to England and they'd have something to move back into, or to sell and move somewhere else in England.

He sat down at the coffee table where his laptop stood open and searched for flights to London, they didn't fly to Norwich, not from here, he found a flight from Berlin to London and booked it, just a single return. Samantha would have to come a few days later, for the funeral; he'd get started on making the arrangements with Jonathan, support him.

He closed his laptop and went upstairs to tuck in Caroline, who was still sniffing and he kissed her wet face. He told Samantha he'd booked his flight. She nodded, 'that's ok; I'll come on Wednesday. The funeral will be on Friday, Jonathan said. I'll definitely come with Caroline, she's old enough I've decided and won't ever forgive us if she's not allowed to come; I'll ask my mum to come here and stay with Jasper. I assume we'll stay with Jonathan, at your parents'? I mean … oh shit, you know what I mean.' He nodded.

Five: England 2010

Eliza slammed the taxi door shut behind her. 'Keep the change' she mouthed through the window at the driver who held up a handful of coins, picked up the handle of her small wheelie case and ran into the station hall with it trundling behind her, the wheels never quite finding their footing. She searched for the notice board with departure times. The train to London would leave in six minutes and she had to get across to a platform on the other side of the station building, up the stairs along the gangway and then down again. Her mouth felt dry, her head was fuzzy and she needed a coffee before boarding but decided against joining the queue in the main hall. She'd have to get the slop on the train, even though she knew it was undrinkable most of the time.

'Excuse me,' she pushed past an elderly couple that stood blocking the staircase, peering at tickets the woman held up in front of them and then up at the notice board, and she ran up the stone stairs, hard and cold and unforgiving. There was a coffee bar on the platform and no queue. 'Ca … cappuccino please,' she was stuttering now, behind breath. 'You're alright,' the girl behind the counter said and handed her the coffee just when the train entered the station and she briskly walked along the platform to find the carriage number with her reserved seat.

The train wasn't very crowded and she found her seat and the one next to her appeared free so she pulled out the small tray, put down her coffee and then pulled the large grey leather handbag from her shoulder and dropped it on the empty seat. As the train pulled out of the station, she pushed her case on the rack above, took off her thick black knee length coat and wiped her forehead with her scarf before dropping both on top of her handbag all heaped up, bulky and ungainly. Only then did she sit down and it was as if the whole world was being pulled from inside out of her, leaving an emptiness that would, if let, collapse her into a blubbering mess. She quickly looked around but no one seemed to notice the tears that had started to blind her so unexpectedly and she pulled her handbag out from underneath the coat and found a packet of tissues, blew her nose loudly so that the man in the seat across the aisle facing her looked up from his book and quickly looked down again. She wiped her face carefully with another tissue, combed her shoulder length sharply cut blond hair back into some kind of shape by tucking it behind her ears, found her hand mirror and a lipstick and only after she had finished contemplating her reflection and had added the red across her pale lips, did she sit back and briefly closed her eyes.

She drank her coffee, hot and scalding on her tongue but that was exactly what she needed. Why had she refused Gerry's reasonable suggestion that he should come with her to Ilsa's funeral? After all, Gerry's parents had offered to come and look after Timmy and Joss, so why had she been so adamant? What did it matter now if Ilsa had maybe not liked Gerry that much; she knew this, of course she'd sensed Ilsa's silent rebuttal, her body language, her silence, more than if she'd said out loud 'I don't like this man, what is he doing here?' adding perhaps that she disapproved of her, Eliza having handed in her notice in London and left Tom and gone to live with Gerry all the way up in the north of England and that, God forbid, she even helped to take care of his two children. Ilsa had not trusted Gerry, Eliza thought, but she was dead now, wasn't she? Her mother Ilsa was dead, gone. How was she, Eliza, going to deal with that, all on her own, without Gerry?

There'd been a few missed calls from Mark, and then his text message when she didn't ring him back. Why had she avoided contact with all of them after that awful Christmas time last year, even now when they needed each other most? Ilsa had made it clear that she didn't consider either Gerry or his two children part of the family but neither Mark nor Stephan were to blame for that, were they? Or her father? After all, Jonathan had seemed perfectly all right. What had it been with her mother, all her sniping and grumbling, her short temperedness, had she known then that she was ill and was simply reacting in this unreasonable way? But why had she not talked about it if that was the case? And more to the point, what had happened to the parents she'd known as a child? They might as well be strangers, the way they'd behaved, both of them. No, their marriage was, had been, on the rocks, she was sure of that. Perhaps her mother had resented the fact that she, Eliza, loved her father as much as she loved Ilsa, perhaps even more. She'd always been close to her mother though, unlike some of her friends.

What was it that as you grew older you seemed to become more distanced from your elders even though theirs had always been a good relationship, she was sure of that. They'd been a good and solid family, until something had unravelled. Had that unravelling been caused by Anthony's death? Had it been Anthony's drug taking? Had it been his secret marriage? Had Ilsa felt that Anthony had rejected all of them, including her, his mother and Anthony being so much the wonder boy in the family, the one who was always cementing them, as if they needed his watchful eye to make sure that they'd stay together,

38

and once he stopped doing that, first by openly declaring war on all of them and then by dying and so leaving them all with these unanswered questions they had, leaving them with a hopeless feeling that they'd all failed somehow because Anthony had failed, and that therefore they had failed as a family. She was unable to make sense of it. Had all of this gone through Ilsa's head as it now rumbled inside hers? Was that all there was to family, a slow disintegration when new units were formed and the old one became redundant? Look at Mark, he lived his own life, and so did Stephan, really, with his man, this Sander, and Sander was a lot more important to Stephan than any of them would ever be. And of course, there she was now, with her own readymade family that she had slotted into without having had to do any work for it whatsoever.

Eliza sighed and sipped the last of her coffee that had cooled down to a reasonable temperature. She stared out of the streaky grey striped window at the fast moving landscape beyond, the trees, overhead wires, farmhouses here and there, then a path along a ditch where a woman and a man walked a dog, and once they were gone, more clumps of trees, some houses. It carried on and on, these fast flying changes of boring scenery, and she closed her eyes again. The train would take nearly three hours and she'd better get some sleep as she had barely slept these last few nights, tossing and turning, drinking too much wine in the evening to soothe her brain, which then kept her awake with a vengeance, causing three o'clock nightmares that wouldn't go away.

Jonathan had been quite collected really, when she spoke to him over the phone, but she imagined that he was putting on a brave face, he just wouldn't break down over the phone, would he. It was Monday now and already Ilsa had been dead for three days, no not quite, nearly three days. Jonathan had explained in his carefully clipped tone of voice that amongst her, Ilsa's, belongings had been the prescription with the name of the specialist and that he had contacted the clinic. How could Ilsa not have told Jonathan? What had she intended to do? Eliza swallowed and bit her lips, she didn't want to go there but it was screaming at her in her head, big and bold, that question: had Ilsa walked under that car purposely? Had she wanted to die? But witnesses had said that she'd simply not looked, had seemed deep in thought, and that the car that hit her had been speeding on a 30mile road, dangerous at that particular spot. Ilsa had seemed surprised but there was nothing anyone could have done. 'She simply didn't look,' Jonathan said. 'She was on her way to the chemist, not out to have herself killed!'

'Of course not,' Eliza had said. 'Why would she? She had you, and as you said, she was at a very early stage and the specialist actually confirmed the prognosis had been good.'

All these conversations, he must have been in touch with the hospital over the weekend, or perhaps the police had, perhaps they'd also suspected suicide motives? She didn't know, and didn't ask, didn't want to go into forensic mode, this was different; this was her mother and not a case for which she had to find evidence.

'The specialist also told me that she didn't seem to believe him. She was in shock.' Jonathan said.

What was the use, going over this again and again in her mind or with Jonathan? Did her father need to? Of course not. Perhaps that's why she didn't really want to talk to Mark, or to Stephan for that matter, although of course she'd have to. They all would have to, wouldn't they, talk about Ilsa and about her being dead? Or could they simply ignore the questions and cremate her and be done with it? Then go home and grieve each in their own way. Surely not? Eliza sighed again and dozed off to the background monotony of the tack tacking of the train engine, her breathing heavy and laboured from the stale dry air in the compartment. Her eyelids fluttered a few times and she didn't notice the next stop and passengers coming and going, looking at her curiously, her mouth half open, snoring lightly.

The conductor tapped her gently on the shoulder. 'Madam, your ticket please, I need to check your ticket,' he smiled at her. 'I've come by twice already, we're approaching Peterborough. Just in case that that's where you want to get off.'

Her mouth was so dry now that when she swallowed it hurt. She took a second to disentangle herself from her sleep world, something strange and grey and dark, but it was gone now. She gave her ticket to the conductor, 'I'm for London.'

She remembered why she was here, travelling to see her father, to meet her brothers, to go to Ilsa's funeral, a cremation, her mother had always insisted that she would want to be cremated, no bones of hers going into any ground of any cemetery, ashes to ashes, to be scattered, only Eliza couldn't for the world of her remember where that would have to be done. Jonathan would know. Would they all do this together or would Jonathan just scatter them on his own, in a place that they had agreed on between them? But perhaps he didn't know either. You just assumed that couples shared these things with each other, but perhaps they hadn't.

She grabbed her mobile from her bag and pushed in Gerry's number. 'Hi, Liz,' he said. 'Are you ok? Where are you? You haven't arrived yet, have you?'

'Gerry, I've changed my mind. Can you ask your parents to come and look after the kids? Can you come? Tonight or tomorrow? In time for the cremation?'

He was silent for a few seconds. 'Of course. I'll get organised. Will have to ring the office. Am working from home today. But it'll be fine. I've no clients to visit this week and I can work on the train.'

'Thanks. Sorry to have been such a bitch. I just couldn't face any of it. I realise how stupidly stupid I've been.'

Gerry laughed. 'That's my girl. Stupidly stupid. Now I recognise her. But of course I'll come. Whatever, we're family, aren't we?'

'Yes,' she said. 'You're my family and I want you to be part of this, I want you to be with me. I feel terrible.'

'Course. Just let your father know. Perhaps it's better if I book a hotel, rather than all of us descending on him? There's that small hotel, quite nearby. I've always wanted to stay there. And I can keep in the background.' He knew, of course he knew, that her family mightn't accept him there, that he wasn't really part of them. She shook the thought away, slid her hand through her hair and let it fall forward over her face.

'Yeah, come tomorrow and I'll arrange the hotel for tomorrow night, for a couple of nights. It's walking distance to the house. You're not driving down?'

'No,' he said. 'I'll work on the train, as I said. I'll hire a car once I get there.'

Gerry would not be anywhere without a car. He hated public transport most of the time and she assumed that he'd get a first class ticket and wangle it on his expenses account with the company somehow. He'd probably arrange a meeting in the London office so that the trip would go down on expenses. Whatever, she didn't really care, simply felt hugely relieved that she'd rung him and that he'd agreed to come.

They talked a bit more about the arrangements, his children, and now partly hers too, of course they were after the eighteen months she'd lived with them, they had begun to treat her as if she was a much liked aunt, they liked her, she could tell.

Perhaps that was due to her total lack of desire to become their mother. There hadn't been much difficulty with them, even though they had missed their own mother terribly at first, Gerry said. Their mother had taken off, had left Gerry and the children, said she couldn't take it any longer, needed to be away from Gerry and couldn't cope with them, felt imprisoned. Gerry never talked much about what had happened between them, but Jemima had disappeared, first to London and then to Australia, with a new man and now she sent birthday cards to the kids and had left it to Gerry to explain the why's and the wherefores. Eliza couldn't quite understand how such a thing could happen, a mother just leaving everyone behind, two young children, a husband, and saying she had no need for any of them.

When Eliza met Gerry, just over two years ago now, she'd been going through a bad patch of her own, she had just broken up with Tom after ten years of living together, and she wanted to move out of London, get a job somewhere less crowded, in a town or village where she would have a garden and where she could withdraw from the world and just focus on her job, her career.

Not for her family life, not for her cosy domesticity, she'd never wanted that anyway, that's not what she and Tom had been together. They'd been the professional couple who'd consciously decided not to have children, who said they were happiest when they could laze around on Sunday mornings and go to a concert or theatre whenever they wanted. Until it had all gone so badly wrong.

Before she had decided where she wanted to go to start again, a new life and a new career, she had met Gerry and he wooed her, enticed her to come and live with him in the north, he'd even suggested jobs in a few well known forensic science laboratories there, quite near to where he lived, and so she'd agreed, and less than a year after splitting up with Tom, she sold her tiny London flat and got rid of the ridiculous mortgage she was paying and moved into Gerry's sprawling ramshackle house just outside the town centre. The house needed repair and the gardens were unkempt even though the large patio at the back had a wonderful view of a pond and a rockery. When she first saw the house she'd been shocked and somehow couldn't imagine living there but Gerry promised refurbishment 'never got round to it but it's always been in the planning. And before you move in I'll have a lot of it done,' he had promised. He was as good as his word and when she moved in the house had a newly painted and tiled bathroom with a modern shower cubicle as well as the old ramshackle bath in the corner 'sometimes people prefer baths' Gerry had said, which had brand new taps and the kitchen had been fitted with a new cooker and also had freshly painted walls in an off-white colour and she, Eliza, had a room newly decorated and totally empty of furniture 'to put your own stuff in'. A gardener had been found who would, bit by bit, tidy up the garden and mow the lawns and fix fences and clean the patios of the moss and the weeds.

Of course, once she'd moved in Gerry thought it was only fair that they both contributed financially to the doing up of the house and she hadn't minded at all, of course not, she had a good job and they were a modern couple sharing their living accommodation because it suited them.

Nevertheless, at times she did wonder what on earth she'd done, why she'd been in such a hurry, as if one failed relationship wasn't enough and why she had been in such a hurry to get herself entangled for a second time, but as far as she was concerned it had worked out, despite the kids and despite Gerry being away quite a lot, on his work trips across the country, advising banks and financial institutions, writing up reports, wrangling with legal requirements on behalf of corporate clients. His elderly parents, who lived a few streets away, had taken on a large share of the caring for the two boys when their mother left and were clearly relieved that Eliza had moved in, even though she could hardly be expected to become a stay at home mum, she had told Gerry before she moved in. She was a working woman, and wouldn't give up her own career. His mother had continued to be around a lot of the time when neither Gerry nor Eliza could pick up the children from school, or even make them a meal in the evening before Eliza got back from work. Nevertheless, Eliza would be at home most nights even if Gerry was away so his parents no longer were required to do the night duty, as they sometimes joked. Eliza was never quite sure whether they meant it light-heartedly or whether it implied a criticism.

Ilsa had been unhappy about Eliza's impulsive move, so out of character she had said, and once wondered out loud why on earth Eliza had broken up with Tom, what was so wrong with him? Then, that last Christmas Ilsa had actually been quite rude to Gerry, had hardly acknowledged he was there, and Gerry had been so helpful, considerate. Once when they met upstairs coming out of and going into the bathroom Eliza whispered to Ilsa that she was rude to Gerry, what on earth was the matter with her? But her mother had shrugged her shoulders 'your imagination is running away with you. I have no opinion whatsoever about Gerry. I barely know him. He seems decent enough.'

'Well, he is!' she'd sniped back.

What had happened to Ilsa, what had happened to both Ilsa and Jonathan after Anthony died? Or was it even before he died and was Anthony merely the final blow in a disintegrating marriage? Eliza shook her head, and then quickly looked sideways but no one in that train compartment took any notice of a woman shaking her head as if she was talking to someone. The man with the book in the aisle seat on the other side had disappeared at one of the earlier stations.

She stared out of the window again. Theirs had been a happy childhood, a good family background, she was sure of that, so why try and find something wrong? Ilsa had been a good mother, even if at times she would be impatient, sometimes distant, but never mean or cruel. She had secrets, Eliza was convinced of that. There were things she hadn't told anyone, she sometimes had that far away look as if she should have been in a different world. No, she, Eliza, was being silly, she was seeing things were there were none. It was simply terrible that she was dead now. She would never have that conversation with her mother, that somehow or other she had imagined she would have one day, clearing up the misunderstandings they had had these last years. She closed her eyes and let her head rest back against the seat. She had imagined that conversation when she would tell her mother about the hurt Tom had caused, about his infidelity and her shock and that this was the reason she'd broken up, she couldn't face up to the fact that he'd had a fling, couldn't forgive him even though he had said it would never happen again. She would have liked to convince Ilsa that Gerry really was the right man for her and that he was reliable, and was there when she needed someone to be around, without asking questions. That Gerry needed her as much as she needed him. That Tom … She dozed off. She would never have that conversation anyway, and the way things had been, her mother most likely wouldn't have listened.

Six: Norfolk

The house stood at the end of the lane and was invisible from the main road, hidden behind a few very tall chestnut trees, 'still protected' Jonathan said, and high shrubs and hedges. Jonathan manoeuvred his large dark BMW through the narrow gate and up the driveway and parked on the gravel in front of the house, next to a gleaming eggshell coloured Peugeot. Large well kept gardens at both sides of the house lay slightly forlorn in the grey November mist and it was difficult to see much further than the patio on the left of the house, facing the South. The wooden chairs were stood leaning against the table so that the water would drip down and not collect on the seats. Ilsa's work.

'Mum usually takes those chairs inside, doesn't she?' Eliza said as she opened the passenger door. 'What happened?'

She walked round the car to the boot and opened it, lifted out her small suitcase and carried it up to the front door while Jonathan turned to lock the car with a flick on the key and shrugged his shoulders. 'Didn't get round to it this year I suppose.'

Idiotic conversation. She had changed trains in London, taking the tube to Victoria, and Jonathan had picked her up from the local train station. It was mid afternoon, and the weather had changed into a chilly and uncomfortable greyness that hung over the roads and the trees and the landscape. She shivered in her thick coat and blew on her hands, she realised she had forgotten her gloves and had texted Gerry, hoping he'd get the message before he left.

'Mark's already here,' Jonathan said. 'He hired a car at the airport. Samantha's coming tomorrow. I've given them the large guest room. You'll be in Ilsa's workroom, on the sofa bed, and the kids can sleep in the small study upstairs. I've put the camp beds there. Not sure where I'm going to put Stephan, in my study most likely. I haven't sorted out Ilsa's bedroom yet and I'm not sure Stephan would want to sleep there? It needs tidying first and Jean hasn't got round to changing the sheets yet.'

'Don't worry Dad. Gerry's coming tomorrow and I'll book us into the White House, just up the road. Stephan can sleep in Mum's workroom. I think it's all a bit too much for you anyway. All of us staying, I mean.'

'Well, if that's what you want. I'm sure Gerry can sleep on the sofa bed with you and Stephan will be quite happy on a mattress on the floor in my large study. We converted all the rooms upstairs to workrooms and studies, but that doesn't mean they cannot be used as guest rooms when needed.'

'Stop worrying, Dad. We'll be fine.'

So Stephan hadn't arrived yet. That would give them some time, the three of them, she wasn't sure for what. Stephan was no longer a little baby brother, she reminded herself, and would want to be part of any serious conversation.

'I've ordered a meal to be delivered. Don't want to go out really. Can't face it. But neither can I face all the cooking and messing about.' Jonathan said. 'The cleaner, you remember her, Jean, will come tomorrow and she's agreed to stay on and do some more cooking. We'll just have to stock up at the supermarket, or perhaps you do, I'm not in tomorrow.'

He fumbled with the keys, still hadn't managed to open the door, which was suddenly thrown open wide from the inside. 'Hi Sis, nice to see you,' Mark said. They hugged and Elizabeth wanted nothing more than to stay like that with Mark, make it all go away, believe that Ilsa would appear from one of the doors behind Mark, smiling and welcoming them, and that they could revert to being the happy family they once were, only now they were all grown up. But Ilsa didn't show and Mark was no longer the comfortable older brother who looked out for her.

'The food will be delivered shortly,' Mark said. 'The restaurant rang. I said seven o'clock would be fine. I'm sure you're starving after that trip; I am anyway. It's been a long day.'

Upstairs in Ilsa's workroom, the sofa bed was pulled out and made ready for her with clean sheets and a thick winter duvet. Jean had been busy, not Jonathan. She couldn't imagine her father even knowing where the sheets would be. He had seemed old, or perhaps she imagined it. Whereas last Christmas he had looked so vivacious, healthy and full of energy he now seemed slightly faded. He had large bluish rings under his eyes and looked as if he hadn't slept properly for weeks. He'd barely spoken in the car, driving from the station to the house, and had given her a short hug and said he'd been working that morning and had come straight from a client to pick her up. She'd raised her eyebrows.

'Well, I'm better working,' he said in explanation. 'This couldn't wait. What am I to do? Sit at home? And then what?'

'There must be an awful lot to arrange,' she said. How are you even able to work, she would have liked to say, but didn't.

'Jean has been very helpful, so has Alea,' he said.

'Alea?'

'Alea is a very good friend, I will explain later.'

She hadn't answered then, wondered if Ilsa had been right all along, that he really had been to blame for her unhappiness, that he had an affair, that he was going to leave her. She remembered how her mother had loathed all mention of Alea, last Christmas.

After that they both had remained silent. Eliza couldn't work out what was in her father's mind and felt too exhausted to change the subject.

She sat down in Ilsa's comfortable chair in the corner of her room, next to the large window overlooking the garden and set tight against the desk because of the space taken up by the pulled out bed. The desk was still full of her mother's usual knick-knacks. Her laptop, a fairly new Apple Mac of which she'd been so proud, stood there with its lid closed; the nice desk lamp that she'd found in a specialty shop in London; a pile of papers in a wired basket tray; a small diary, 2010 with gold lettering on a black cover, which seemed to suggest that despite the introduction of the technology and her use of laptops she was still wedded to the old fashioned way of recording events and appointments; a tall pot overflowing with pens and pencils of all colours and shapes; the speakers that were disconnected from the laptop. Eliza imagined that Ilsa liked to listen to her music here, straight from her iTunes library. It was as if she would come into the room any time now, as if she'd perhaps popped out for a bit of shopping, to get a cup of tea, or to tidy up something in the garden. Or perhaps she was downstairs doing the cooking, happy, as she used to be, all those years ago when Anthony was still alive and Stephan was in his room and they, she and Mark, were home for a weekend, and Ilsa would call up the stairs that the food was ready and they all had to come down, now. But that was a long time ago; the last years had been quite different and Eliza no longer knew how Ilsa spent her time, what her routine was after she had retired from her teaching job last year, and well after the last child had left home. After Stephan had left and when Anthony had become the problem child she seemed to have purposefully created a distance, hadn't she, not just with Jonathan but also even with her other, now surviving children?

Eliza pulled the diary towards her. Strange that it was here on the desk. Shouldn't it be in her handbag? She flicked through it, feeling guilty at being intrusive, but then hadn't Jonathan perhaps done the same and hadn't bothered to put it away again?

She looked at the almost illegible entries that didn't record times and tried to decipher the very short notes. 'Emma' she read, somewhere in October, and then two days running 'Clinic,' so small that she had to squint and hold the page under the light of the desk lamp that she switched on. No time, no name of a specialist, just 'clinic'. She shut the diary, and threw it back on the desk. They'd have to tidy all this away, all her mother's life, everything she'd been. How could they? Would Jonathan want to do this on his own? Would she, Eliza be expected to do it? She was the only sibling living in the country still; both Mark and Stephan would find it hard to come back for a few days or a weekend to help out. Mark might, or Samantha, but Eliza wouldn't want to go through her mother's things with Samantha, however much she liked Samantha. She felt protective of her mother's privacy, didn't want to lay it all bare for others to see. After all, she had been a very private person.

Outside it had started to rain, with the weeping drops slowly rolling down the windowpane, lit up by the light from inside the room and making the outside look mysterious and far away. Amazingly, some of the trees alongside the road to the house had seemed quite green still when she arrived, or perhaps she'd imagined this. It was more or less completely dark out there now but when you looked up close near the window the trees nearest to the house were still visible, with their branches sticking up and out into the black sky as if in prayer; they'd probably seen it all before, this weeping, this rain and this darkness, and ignored the world around them, stood stiff and still, with only the thinner branches slightly swaying in the otherwise invisible breeze that had come with the rain. Although it was quite dark now, at least the fog seemed to have cleared away. She got up and lowered the blinds and then pulled the curtains closed over them.

'Lisa, you're still up there?' Mark shouted from downstairs. Like Jonathan, he'd always called her Lisa, sometimes Lizzie, but rarely Eliza.

'Coming,' she called back. She looked around her and it felt as if she had defiled the room, just by raising her voice. The cream coloured curtains stared back at her. She was glad now that Gerry would come and they'd stay in a hotel. She wanted to flee. She did not want to recall any of this, wanted to be away again as she had been these last years, wrapped up in her own life with her own ups and downs.

*

Stephan arrived first the next day, by taxi, and shortly afterwards Gerry drove up in his rental car, a large Ford. Eliza and Gerry took their bags to the White House hotel nearby and Stephan went upstairs to look round the corner of the door of Ilsa's work room, saw the sofa bed that Eliza had freshly made up, and then announced that he would also rather stay in a hotel as he would need to do some work, contact clients, 'Can't just leave everyone in the lurch, can I?'

In the afternoon Eliza and Gerry went to the supermarket and Mark drove all the way back to the airport to pick up Samantha and Caroline. It was not clear to him now why he'd travelled ahead.

Throughout all of the arrangements and changes of plans, Jonathan moved around as if he didn't quite belong, as if he wasn't part of any of it. He disappeared for a while in his car but turned up again in the late afternoon, before dinner, when they all sat round the dining room table after Samantha had given Caroline, exhausted and whiney from travelling, something to eat in the kitchen and taken her upstairs.

In the middle of the table stood the food in dishes and on platters, prepared by Jean that morning and warmed up by Eliza in the microwave according to Jean's instructions. There was a lasagne, some vegetables, a salad, and garlic bread. And it seemed as if Ilsa might walk in any minute now, because all of this was only pantomime in preparation for her entrance and they would then all smile and laugh and be happy as a family, together after a long separation. But she never came and they looked bewildered at each other and ill at ease, almost strangers now with different lives and stories and secrets, and then Jonathan pulled the cork out of a bottle of red wine and poured them all a glass. 'Should have done that earlier,' he mumbled. 'Forgot to open it.'

'What happened exactly?' Stephan was the first to speak after they all sat and took a sip of their wine. 'I still don't understand. What was she doing, Mum, in that street and who was this fucking driver?'

He looked dishevelled, his shirt was creased and smudgy, his cheeks and chin and above his lips showed the stubble of someone who had not shaved for a day or so, his eyes were red shot through and Eliza wondered why he'd not bothered to have a shower after his twelve hour flight and then the taxi ride from the airport. She refrained from mentioning this out loud; he would only flare up, the mood he was in. He hadn't even changed his clothes, and said he'd had a snooze in one of the chairs in the room when Jonathan asked him. He'd been too tired to do very much else.

Jonathan now looked at Stephan, his eyebrows a question mark, whilst Mark shook his head and clicked his tongue. 'Not necessary, Stephan. Not necessary to be so aggressive,' Jonathan said. 'It was an accident, Mum crossed the road without looking.'

'Yes, just like Anthony's was an accident.' Stephan's face turned red and he swallowed another big gulp of his wine as if it was water. 'What is it with this family, do we all have to die in car accidents?' He should have had a shower, calmed down, had a proper nap. Instead he was sitting there getting himself and all of them worked up.

'Don't,' Mark said.

Samantha looked over at Mark and then took Stephan's plate and served him some of the lasagne, offered him the salad, 'here, eat something.'

'Your mother had parked her car and was on her way to the chemist. She didn't look where she was going and simply started to cross the road. Eyewitnesses confirm this. The car was speeding, but not that much really, doing 35 or so in a 30 mile zone, but the fact was that Ilsa crossed coming out from behind her car and this Ford was upon her before the driver realised that she was coming into the road. She died on the spot. Massive brain injury.'

'Why was she going to the chemist anyway?' Gerry asked. 'Did you not know that she'd been diagnosed with cancer?'

They all looked shocked at Gerry, for being blunt, for saying something they were all trying to avoid for the time being, but at the same time they felt relieved that it had been said out loud now and they could take it from here, no more beating around the bush. Jonathan shook his head and looked forlorn. 'I just cannot believe what happened. I honestly didn't know. She was not herself, these last weeks, months really. But, well, we didn't talk much, I have to admit, we hadn't talked about anything, not for a while … There were other things. We were going to tell you in good time. We were sorting things out.' He carefully brought a fork full of food to his mouth, which prevented him from saying anything else, and they waited.

Eliza who sat next to him put her hand on his arm. 'Dad,' she said. Then she looked round the table. 'Let's eat. Tomorrow's going to be tough. We'll sit around after dinner, but Gerry and I will go back to our hotel and now Stephan also, I understand. We can take you in our car Steph.' She turned to him, he had his eyes closed and opened them a fraction to look at her and sipped some more wine. He had barely touched his food.

'You can come with us, in our car,' she said again when he didn't respond and he nodded and closed his eyes again. 'I still can't believe what's happening,' he murmured. 'This feels even more unreal than Anthony's death, and that was bad enough.'

They knew what he meant, although Anthony had left them all well before he'd died. He'd walked out on them, had turned his back on them, and had said, actually told them when they asked, that he no longer needed them as his family, that it was all a lie and Eliza couldn't understand what he meant, whereas Mark had shrugged his shoulders, he and Anthony had never got on that well, and Stephan felt that Anthony had betrayed them because he had not wanted to have anything to do with any of them, as if they hadn't shared the same childhood, the same parents. Every one of them round this table grieved about Anthony, except Gerry of course, Gerry had never known him; the others had all tried to contact Anthony in their own way, even Mark, they had tried to speak with him, to see him, had wanted to find out what on earth was happening, whether they could help him, why he'd walked out of university high on drugs, why he'd then gone in the completely opposite direction and married this woman, a girl really, who had this crazy religious belief that, according to Anthony, forbade family interaction with non-believers, as if that had been not the most idiotic explanation they'd ever heard, as if that justified his behaviour. And then Anthony had simply stopped communicating with them, had married the girl, apparently had himself baptised into their fold and so he'd disappeared out of their lives, had no longer turned up for Christmases, had no longer picked up his phone or even responded to e-mails, to joke with them about a birthday party, or to invite himself over for a night's dinner and a bottle of wine, had no longer asked after Mark or even Stephan, his favourite little brother and so had hurt Stephan to the core, even if Mark by that time had been rather indifferent to anything that concerned Anthony, and Eliza had been too embroiled in her own life in London, her studies, the excitement of moving in with Tom, her career progression, her new colleagues, Tom's rise in importance in the art world. Anthony had simply gone AWOL, had extracted himself from the family and none of them could have done anything about it even if they'd tried harder than they had. And then, to top it all, they'd suddenly been informed that a stray deer, of all things, had killed him on one of those country roads. A deer had jumped straight across that road into his car and he'd lost control and hit a tree and was dead. That was the story of Anthony and their grief about him, who was part of their childhood, of their collective memories, gone as if he'd never been. Anthony had become the first shard in the shattering of their family unit.

Stephan couldn't bear thinking about any of it and with Ilsa now dead as well it all came at him full force. Anthony had let them all down and then he'd gone and died in a stupid accident that shouldn't have happened. And apparently he'd left two children, a nephew and a niece to his brothers and sister, and grandchildren to his parents. How could that be? And none of them he thought had ever seen these two kids. Or perhaps Ilsa had, but if so she hadn't told any of them. Or perhaps Jonathan had but then he hadn't ever mentioned it either.

Old sorrow welled up and Stephan felt exhausted; all he wanted was to lie down and apprehend this new grief of a mother lost, what was it all about? Ilsa was dead and all that was left of their previous family unit were the people sitting round this table, people who had over the years become near strangers to each other, who barely saw each other from one year to the next and so that as a unit it didn't mean very much anymore, did it? They were so wrapped up in their own lives, growing further and further away from what had once been such a stable and unbreakable family unit, 'their ménage' as he used to tell Sander. He wished Sander had come. He needed Sander now. Sander would understand and hold him and let him fall asleep. He felt as if he was going to fall asleep sitting at the table and wanted to put his head on his arms on the table.

'I've got to lie down,' Stephan said. 'I'm frazzled. I'll lie down on Mum's sofa bed after all. I can't face going anywhere now.'

He pushed his chair back, gave a wave with his hand and walked out of the room. They heard him close the door of Ilsa's room, and then everything became silent again upstairs.

He didn't even go to the bathroom, Eliza thought.

Seven: The Funeral

The last Friday of November, the day of Ilsa's cremation, was crisp and sunny and the fog and dreary grey skies of the previous evening and week had disappeared, as if to say, "Enough, enough of this grey misery, this reminder of death and decomposition. We need clarity for this important day, clarity and coldness and …" No one was quite sure what it meant, really, people just blinked and registered the change although they shivered and realised that the clear blue sky belied the cold biting wind and the car windows were frozen over after the first night frost of the year. So instead of grey fuzziness they noticed an opaqueness wrapped in blustery penetrating coldness rather than clarity and this seemed to confirm that no one could quite clearly comprehend what had happened and why, no one could form a clear picture of who Ilsa had been during her last few days and weeks and why she was gone now without leaving them any reassurance that she was alright, had been alright. Eliza shivered and pulled her coat around her, tight. The hotel car park was deserted except for their car and a black BMW nearer to the exit.

'No scraper,' Gerry said, looking at the windscreen of their car and then bent down again inside the car to look in the glove compartment. He'd already searched the door compartments and the back seat. 'Damn hire cars. I'll have to ask the girl on the desk if she can help.'

Eliza opened the boot and held up a scraper. 'You didn't look.'

Gerry wore his dark suit, a black tie and white shirt with a grey woollen coat. He looked smart, Eliza thought, and suddenly felt a pleasantly warm feeling towards him. There was something about Gerry, the way he moved his body, so easy within himself it seemed. Or was it that he was simply totally oblivious to everything and everyone around him? Her mind drifted away from the present and clung to irrelevant thoughts, irrelevant to what she had to face today, to what she had to come to terms with. She never had worked out why Gerry's wife had walked out on him, what had been so awful that she'd decided to leave him and their children. He seemed such a normal man, he was so accommodating, tried so hard to make the people around him feel comfortable.

'She was basically a very dissatisfied woman,' Gerry once said. 'I made the mistake thinking that she was simply looking for reassurance, at first I thought that and I thought also that I could satisfy all her needs, that I could make her happy, that we would be happy. And then she cleared off.' He added that Jemima had met someone else, had fallen in love and decided to move with him to Australia. She had not wanted to uproot the children, and, Gerry said, he would have fought her through the courts anyway if she'd tried to take them away from him.

Her thoughts drifted even further away from Gerry now and somehow Tom turned up and she wondered what would have happened if she had not walked out on Tom. Had that been different? Did Tom also think she'd simply walked out on him? Surely he couldn't. When she and Tom split up in 2007 after having been together for over ten years, she had moved out of their apartment, which was really Tom's anyway, and into a tiny flat in Willesden Green, very inconvenient for her daily journey to work, but it was all she could afford then with house prices in London rocketing. She did not want to share with anyone else and Jonathan had helped her out. Neither had mentioned this to Ilsa, but Jonathan had put down half of the deposit she needed for the mortgage. She was not too concerned about that, she knew that he'd helped out her brothers when they started off whereas she had simply moved in with Tom, during her time at university.

She looked again at Gerry who was now scraping away at the side windows, the motor on full blast, spitting hot air inside the car. What would Ilsa think of Gerry at her funeral?

Ilsa had been devastated about her breaking up with Tom; she had never kept it a secret that she had liked him and they, Ilsa and Tom, got on well together, always had. Sometimes Eliza had wondered whether Ilsa had always known about Tom's dalliances, that she perhaps thought it was part of the course that men neither would nor could be faithful to one woman. After all, she'd been sure that Jonathan had his affairs and had shrugged her shoulders about it, until recently. She'd talked about 'fighting for your corner in a relationship' and said things like 'Take your time before you throw it all overboard, there are always hidden surprises as far as consequences are concerned'.

Over the years, after Eliza had left home and during the time of her relationship with Tom, her mother had become more and more of a mystery to her. Whereas, when Eliza was still living at home with her parents, her mother had seemed natural and without guile, even if sometimes somewhat moody, and she could at times be impossible, they all thought, nevertheless she had always been a reassuring and supportive parent to her children, and, as far as Eliza remembered, there had not really been great disagreements between her parents. They'd been solid. At least that's what they all believed, she was sure of that.

Once they'd left, however, all of them, after they'd started out to make their own lives, Ilsa changed and it was as if she felt that she'd done her duty and that they now should fend for themselves; she was no longer always there to help them out or to give them advice, not voluntarily anyway; except, Eliza thought, when she'd had that slight look of disapproval when she'd broken up with Tom. Eliza wondered if her brothers felt the same, if they imagined that their mother no longer approved of them or of their father—that something had taken a wrong turn and she could no longer be bothered with any of them, especially not after Anthony's death.

Eliza had her mother's good looks even though not all of her character; where Ilsa had always been reserved and over the years had become moody and distant, Eliza had always been straightforward and, as far as she was concerned, there were very few cases where you couldn't classify events and behaviour or people and friends and family as either good or bad, rarely was she doubtful about where to file things in her head. Even as a child Eliza had always demanded clear cut explanations and would not be fobbed off, by a casual 'ah, you're too little, you wouldn't understand,' thrown at her in exasperation by parents or teachers and she would demand reason and proof for decisions and edicts that she didn't agree with or didn't understand.

She almost naturally studied biochemical sciences and eventually became a forensic scientist, and her character fitted precisely the character of the job, Tom once said, and he had inscribed a book, a Christmas gift or a birthday present, she couldn't remember clearly, of one of the Sherlock Holmes novels, with the epitaph 'for the woman who will always provide objective information on which she bases her decisions. Do not cross her as she subscribes to the author Conan Doyle's mantra that it would be a mistake to make conjectures before you have the concrete evidence and data, because if you do that you will inevitably try to make the facts suit your theories, instead of the other way round.'

Standing there in the cold of the deserted parking lot, shivering in another sudden chilly breeze which died down again as quickly as it had come round the corner, Eliza just stood and watched Gerry scrape off the ice from the side windows of the rental car. She was an attractive, slim and tall woman in her late thirties, her unbuttoned bottom half of her coat showing a dark green-grey dress; she wore sheer black tights and comfortable low heeled smart shoes. A black rucksack, which she had put on the back seat of the car, held a pair of smart black trousers and a casual lemon coloured jumper, ankle boots and thick socks. She knew she'd want to get into something more comfortable in the evening. She didn't normally wear a dress and sheer tights in this kind of weather, far too cold, and she quickly buttoned up the rest of her coat and pulled the scarf that was hanging loose from her shoulders around her neck. She wanted to look smart in honour of her mother, who had always been a keen dresser. She pushed her hair behind her ears at each side of her face, which was now white and almost translucent in the winter cold.

She slightly screwed her brown-grey eyes against the light of the cold sun and said, 'we'll have to stay another night, Ger. Dad said he wanted to talk about something tonight. He told me he expected all of us to be there.'

Gerry raised his eyebrows, his face red with cold, while scraping furiously across a thick layer of ice that wouldn't come clean off, whilst thick grey smoke continued to blast from the exhaust. The ice on the back window was melting now, but the windscreen wipers were stuck to the front windowpane still.

'I'll have to ring my mum and Dad in that case,' he said. 'I think they expect us back tonight, late. I'll have to tell them they'll have to stay another night. They won't mind, I'm sure.'

'We can't just leave him to it,' Eliza said. 'I just don't know what's going on. He hasn't said much these last few days. As if it's all passing him by. Or perhaps he's just hanging in until the cremation is over.'

'I think you're wrong,' Gerry said. 'He's trying to move on. He and your mother weren't in a good place together, take my word for it. That was clear over Christmas, I just know.'

'What. You think there was more to it than Mum being annoyed that Dad cleared off just before Christmas? Mum's been angry, I know. But then she could be moody, always was and that just wasn't a good time for her. Perhaps she already knew about her health, perhaps she suspected?'

'No, I don't think so. I think your parents were talking divorce. They were just keeping up appearances until we'd gone.' He sounded as if he was in the know. Infuriating and callous? But no, that was just Gerry. Always blunt and businesslike, and she somehow knew that he might be right, only she'd rather not know, now.

'Then why didn't they say anything? And why do you say all this now?' She felt a surge of anger as her face turned from white to red not just with the cold wind that blew around the parking area of the hotel. What business was it of Gerry's to suggest that her parents were not what they seemed to be to her, that there was something wrong between them, more wrong than an odd quarrel? As sudden as the anger welled up she felt ashamed and stupid. Of course Gerry had every right to think or say what he wanted, they were partners, he should be able to say to her what he thought without her flaring up every time, as if he was an outsider still, not really part of her family, not quite approved.

'Well, let's wait and see. First of all we've got to get today over and done with. Not looking forward to it,' she said.

Gerry nodded, gave a last hard scrape across the windscreen and said, 'done, that's good enough. Let's go.'

*

After it was all over, after they had wound their way back to the house, late that afternoon, Mark stood at the large kitchen window overlooking the back garden and watched a few pigeons and a magpie eying each other suspiciously, ready to pounce. The magpie made the first move and hopped towards the crusts of bread that someone had thrown out, Jonathan probably. Mark had seen him leave the kitchen through the utility room and backdoor carrying a mall plastic freezer bag with stale crusts of bread. A blackbird joined the gathering below the bird table and aggressively pushed itself forward and picked at the bread, the few pigeons shied away and observed the territorial battle between the two birds. The blackbird picked a piece and flew away, as if to let them know that he had what he'd come for and could not be bothered with their game any longer. The magpie hopped forward again and only after he also flew off with some bounty did the pigeons start their own battle for what was left.

Mark turned when Eliza came into the kitchen and asked if he wanted a tea.

'I'd rather have another drink, if I'm honest. I feel washed out and I'm not in the mood for tea. Is there any tonic left in the fridge or the pantry? I'll fix some gin tonics. I'll go and ask the others what they want.'

Jonathan, who had sat down in his comfortable chair in the large sitting room off the entrance hall, said he'd rather have a whiskey and that there were also some bottles of wine out in the kitchen on the rack, somewhere. Eliza who'd followed Mark into the sitting room shrugged her shoulders, looked over at Samantha who sat in the large comfy chair in the corner next to the window, still wearing the rather glam black dress and jacket she'd worn that morning, reading softly and very fast in German from a picture book, to a red-eyed and tired looking Caroline who had curled up to her in the same chair. Samantha looked up and shook her head and said she'd prefer a tea, it was too early and she would need to take Caroline up soon, the girl was exhausted and needed a good night's sleep. Also, she, Samantha, wanted to change into some other clothes first.

'Are there things we need to discuss Dad?' Stephan asked when Mark had left the room to get the drinks. 'I'd rather we did that today, I'm flying back tomorrow and need to do some work tonight.'

Eliza breezed, 'Can't you wait one more day? We hardly ever see you and it's as if you never stop working, even now, even this morning immediately after the ceremony you were at it, rather than talk to people.' She looked over at him, accusingly, as if he'd committed some serious crime, Stephan thought.

'Don't deny it. I saw you scrolling away on your phone and ticking in messages.'

'Just mind your own business, will you? You've no idea who I was texting and why.'

She wished she hadn't said it. It was none of her business, Stephan was right. She couldn't help it, had this urge today to fill up every silence with a comment, to avoid the realisation that they were at a loss, that neither she nor her siblings had any idea of what all this meant. They had lost something irreplaceable, they were no longer sure who they were in this context of their dead mother, now reduced to ashes that were stuffed in an earthenware jar with a stopper, one that had always had pride of place in her room, a memento from some holiday or other. They were here, a gathering of siblings and relatives who, in the normal state of things, would be minding their own lives and business, far apart from each other in countries across the world, but who now found themselves in this one room to try and get used to the thought that they'd come to bury an essential part of their past, an act that felt like the disintegration of their unity as a family. It had been their mother, it had always been Ilsa, around whom they pivoted, the magnetic centre which kept them floating around and connected with each other, she'd kept them, her children, together after they'd left, however much she had tried to distance herself in later years. They had all loved Ilsa, even if they were no longer sure whether they still loved each other, whether they had in fact anything in common anymore, without their mother. When still at home, as children they had known who they were and why they related because Ilsa had always been there to provide that security of an unbreakable unit.

They'd always come back to England, to Norfolk, because of their mother, because of Ilsa, and Eliza wasn't at all sure that Jonathan would be able to do the same: make them come together, make them belong. He'd been away so often, even when they were children and even if he somehow had always seemed to be part of their unit, but like them, he'd always been kept in orb because of Ilsa. It was because of Ilsa, their love for her that they would come back here as a family unit. No, Eliza wasn't at all sure that they were still part of one unit, not with their mother gone, not with a brother who had first disappeared and then died, and a father who, she was sure, would revert naturally to something he'd been before, well before they became a family, and he would return to a lost entity, and he would simply forget about keeping them together, the importance of it. Eliza couldn't help but feel that her mother's death was partly his fault, he should have been there with her and that horrible accident wouldn't have happened.

Stephan didn't bother to make a further response to Eliza's comment and instead turned to his father and repeated what he said before, 'Dad, is there anything you want to discuss with us? Really we need to talk now; we'll all be going off again, that's just the way it is. I assume that you'll carry on living here, at least for the time being? Do you need us to help you with anything, do we need to sort out anything?'

'Of course,' Eliza again interrupted him. 'Of course, he'll go on living here. Why wouldn't he?'

'Can you two just stop this idiotic conversation? Don't talk about me as if I'm not here, or as if I'm some complete wreck, or an idiot?' Jonathan said, barely audible. He pressed his lips together so that they formed two pencil lines across his angular face, which had slightly blushed over his earlier paleness. His hands were balled in a fist, but as they looked at him he unclenched them and took in a slow deep breath.

Jonathan had changed out of his funeral clothes and was wearing his blue fitting jeans and an expensive looking dark red woollen jumper over a red and blue checked shirt, the collars just visible. He looked smart and in control, as if he was on a weekend off in the countryside. He'd kicked off his shoes, which stood one on each side of his comfortable deep chair. On the small side table next to him were a coaster, an e-reader in a maroon coloured cover and his glasses. He picked up the glasses and put them on, looked at them over the top of the rims.

'Listen, I'm sorry. It's been a shock to all of us. All of this. I don't know how you're all going to cope with your mother's death. It's been just terrible. I don't know what you expect me to do or say, however, to answer your question, I can't see any reason why I shouldn't continue to live here, for the time being anyway. I can look after myself, always have done. I'm comfortable in this house; I have an office and can work here whenever I want to. Jean will continue to come in and keep the house. My business is doing well. I have no intention of retiring now, nor am I going to live in some small bungalow or whatever you may be thinking about.' He stretched out his arm towards Mark who'd come in with a tray full of drinks and took a thoughtful and measured sip of the whiskey Mark handed him.

'Sorry Dad, I missed some of that,' Mark said, handing a glass to Stephan, who sat slightly apart and alone on the two-seater and then another glass to Gerry, who sat quietly in a small wooden armchair next to a bookshelf, reading a newspaper. Mark and Eliza had seated themselves on the sofa and Eliza eagerly took a gulp of the white wine, as if she was drinking water. Although there had been plenty of wine at the reception after the funeral, she had only drunk water then but now felt desperate for a drink. She looked taut; her eyes were red and her face blotchy.

'It's not as if I'm incapacitated,' Jonathan said. 'I would appreciate it though if you would help me go through some of your mother's stuff, Eliza. Not straight now, but perhaps in a couple of weeks' time? When you could come over again?'

Why me, Eliza thought. I don't want to go through Ilsa's stuff. I can't resolve what happened, not by going through her stuff. Or perhaps I would and that is even more frightening.

'You're her only daughter. You two were close.' Jonathan added when he saw her raised eyebrows. 'I want you to have a look at her jewellery, choose what you want to keep. She would have liked that, make sure you also share with Samantha and Caroline. Also her clothes need sorting I suppose. I'd rather get it done sooner than later. Of course, she left a will, we both signed it and I will let you know as soon as I have been in touch with the solicitors.'

'Will you sort out her papers and workroom though?' Eliza asked. 'Her desk drawers are full of stuff. There are her work files, teaching plans and things like that, I'm surprised she still has those lying around, but there are also drawers with personal papers. I had a quick look when I was up there. When I arrived. And of course, there's her computer, telephone, iPad …'

Then, suddenly, without warning and as if in answer to a question that was not actually raised, Jonathan said,

'It's not as if we were still living as a married couple, your mother and I. We were only living together still in this house because it was convenient, for both of us, but especially your mother didn't want to separate before. She didn't want me to leave, didn't want to live alone in the house and neither did she want to leave and live somewhere else. She said we were too long in the tooth, even though we agreed that our marriage was over. Quite recently we also agreed that we would separate, we filed for divorce.'

Eliza nearly dropped her wineglass and coughed, spluttered some wine on her lap. She'd forgotten to make the tea that Samantha had asked for and sat still now, clenching the wine glass, looked up at Mark and then towards Gerry. Samantha got up abruptly and shoed Caroline ahead of her through the hall and into the kitchen saying that she would make tea and find some biscuits and fix something to eat for Caroline so she could go to bed. They'd be leaving again the next day. She looked at Mark with raised eyebrows and shook her head, pointing at Caroline.

Stephan turned from Mark to Eliza and only then to his father. He waited till Samantha had closed the door,

'What do you mean? Did you two go through a bad patch? Doesn't that happen in marriages? You were together for all this time, we were a family. Were you really thinking of a divorce? Poor Mum.' He had gone red in the face and seemed to have difficulty swallowing. He had also changed out of his dark suit into jeans and a grey sweat shirt and looked more or less his normal self compared to the day of his arrival, his face was clean shaven and his eyes had lost their redness, if not the bags underneath.

'Well,' Jonathan waited, took a deep breath and said, 'the truth is that we were living quite separate lives, have been for the past few years really. We discussed divorce a few times, but as I said neither of us wanted to leave the house for the time being and so we kind of continued to live here in the same house without seeing very much of each other. We occupied separate parts of the house, at least when there was no one else around. You see, I have my office and work and Ilsa had her large workroom. She started to write, I don't know what, some work related stuff, she found a publisher. Besides, she kept a part time teaching job in the village, did some supply teaching, and didn't want to move away. Neither did I, not for the time being, anyway, but that changed recently.'

'But why?' Eliza said. 'Was that why Mum was so unhappy last year? And the year before? Why didn't you talk about it?

71

Why did you two pretend all this time, keep up a charade? For Christ's sake, we're all grown ups. Why didn't you tell us? We could perhaps have helped? What happened? It was Anthony, wasn't it? Something happened. It wasn't just his death. You two disagreed about something.' She stopped.

She felt flush with hostility, a helpless and unfocused fury that encompassed everything and everyone in the room. She felt immensely sad and in addition to the creeping anger at her father now felt angry about the loss of the happy family image that she had always nurtured, angry that it was soiled and dark and dirty. She felt incontrollable fury about the parents she thought she had and who didn't actually exist, hadn't existed for a long time, that their childhood had now become a big lie. Then, immediately she felt a deadly tiredness settling over her. Of course, Gerry had been right. She'd simply not wanted to know, hadn't wanted very much to find out the real reason for her mother's unhappiness. How important was it to know all this? Really it simply was all water under the bridge, irrelevant to them now, just the past of two people who were their parents, one now dead, the entanglement and disillusions of two people who hadn't managed to live their marriage to a happy end. What was so strange about that, what was so different? Hadn't she herself split up with Tom? Hadn't Gerry divorced his wife? The difference was of course that Jonathan and Ilsa had children who had totally believed in them and their marriage, had never doubted that it would be everlasting 'till death us do part', and so whatever they had done and discussed would affect them, their children, somehow; their memories would have to be adjusted in some way. Why bring it up? It shouldn't be necessary for them to know all this, to drag all this up. Why not simply let her mother rest in peace? She shook her head, wordless. It was all too complicated and she felt too tired to try and make sense of this.

'You've all been gone a long time,' Jonathan said. 'There was no reason to involve you in our quarrels and disagreements. We were two people who were drifting apart.'

'Quarrels?' Stephan repeated. His eyes were screwed up and his nose was wrinkled as if he tasted something sour. 'Why do we have to talk about all of this now? Why can't you pretend for one more day that you two had a happy marriage and that you're really sad that Mum's dead? I assume that you aren't really sad. Is that what you're trying to tell us?' He was hostile now, as aggressive as Eliza had been.

Jonathan sighed. 'There's more to it than that. But, yes, of course I am utterly and truly devastated at your mother's death and at what has happened. We weren't enemies you know. I don't know how she felt when she was diagnosed. I can only imagine how utterly lonely she must have been. I can only say how sorry I am that I didn't know and that I wasn't able to help. She died in an accident, however, and there is absolutely nothing I can do about that. However, it's best if you know and I don't want you to expect me to fall apart or be incapacitated with grief. Our marriage was long over. Of course I'm sad. Very sad.'

It slowly dawned on them. He was explaining to them of course why he'd refused to take the lead in the ceremonial address that morning, why he'd asked them, the children, to decide who would take charge, why he'd agreed that Samantha was the best person, the most capable, the least bowled over and so able to provide a professional address, rather than weepy accounts and stumbling half finished sentences. She'd done a great job, they all agreed, she'd written it up the day before, helped them chose the slides and music and had

73

brought real warmth to the address, so that people had come up afterwards and commented on the lovely way she had managed to convey to them the kind of woman Ilsa had been, how loved and loving. Eliza and her brothers had sat, red eyed and were grateful to Samantha for doing what none of them felt capable of doing, saying goodbye to their mother, Jonathan's wife.

Jonathan took another small sip of his whiskey while they sat and looked at him and then away, no one said anything. But they weren't waiting with bated breath, they were stunned. There was something hard in Jonathan's eyes, they thought, and they realised that they hadn't seen him cry or even wipe away a tear throughout the cremation ceremony and reception, nor during the previous few days. They had assumed that he was quiet and withdrawn because of shock, they hadn't known how to approach him, how to make him come out of himself. When Eliza had hugged him he'd hugged her back and then turned away to busy himself with something or other. Within all the commotion and arrangements and trying to put together a ceremony that would be right for Ilsa and write a farewell speech, decide on which photo should be placed on the coffin, none of them had been able to have a conversation with him, separately, seriously. They'd been taken in by his ability to maintain his composure. They'd known him as a flamboyant and gregarious man but during these last few days he had been quiet and reserved, as if a different person, or as if he was putting up a good show, burdened by grief, or so they assumed.

Nevertheless, during the ceremony he'd been dry-eyed and afterwards had seemed almost businesslike with people who had come in large numbers to offer their condolences, shaking hands, letting them kiss his cheeks, hugging them if that seemed to be required, an actor at the height of his performance in a sad and tragic play. To each other they'd commended him on how well he'd managed to maintain himself, how courageous, how admirable even, and it had given them strength as well, had steeled them not to succumb to wailing and crying, as they wanted to, but to act in quiet dignity. That, after all, was what Jonathan did, so they, his children, should be able to do the same. After that late morning ceremony with Samantha's beautiful address and quiet dignity and subdued grief they had all walked up to and past the coffin, on which stood a large portrait picture of Ira laughing at them and a single bouquet of many-coloured flowers, whispered their goodbyes and they had walked to one of the large low-ceilinged function rooms, where wine and beer, soft drinks and teas and coffees and a light lunch were served by staff dressed in crisp white shirts and blouses and dark green suits. A very large number of people had turned up wanting to give their condolences, former colleagues, friends, neighbours, distant and close relatives, some previous pupils and also some current pupils, the head teacher of the school, the chair of governors, so many people that they didn't know and Eliza had been astonished and happy at the warmth with which so many people spoke about her mother, how they had loved her, how she'd contributed to the village life, always ready to help out, to support one charity or another, come out for a coffee, listen to a neighbour. Ilsa had been loved and admired and people spoke kindly about her.

All through the ceremony and the reception afterwards Jonathan had spoken very little, looked smart in his dark suit and tie, his sharply boned face pale but composed, his eyes clear but deep set and his eyebrows seemingly even more bushy than usual. A woman, Eliza assumed it was a colleague or a business partner of her father's, had come up to him and kissed him on both cheeks and they had whispered something to each other, but she had quickly withdrawn when she noticed Eliza looking at them and starting to come forward to greet her. Jonathan hadn't introduced them, however, and the woman had disappeared before Eliza reached them. Jonathan had turned towards another guest and more or less ignored Eliza. She had felt slighted and wondered why he wouldn't introduce her to someone who presumably knew her mother? Perhaps he thought it was a bit of a waste of time, after all, they would never meet again, most likely. Neither she nor her brothers had been part of her parents' life for such a long time. And even when her mother was still alive they hadn't exactly been in each other's pockets and knew little about day-to-day life of the other.

At the reception Eliza had felt busy anyway, talking to relatives, people she did know, to her mother's sister Marja who had come from Chichester and who said she would return back home by train that same afternoon. She'd been naturally upset and wanted to talk to Eliza about Ilsa and said how close they'd been as children and when they were young girls, and how they'd grown apart after Mark was born. They had married such very different men, Marja a banker, who was pompous and reluctant to travel any distance and who hadn't come with Marja to the cremation but had given some kind of excuse about not feeling well at all, having flu. Eliza remembered that before Marja's wedding Ilsa had married Jonathan, flamboyant and attractive, 'a real firebrand' Marja said almost wistful looking over at Jonathan who hadn't yet acknowledged her presence; Jonathan who'd become successful in business, a keen traveller and entrepreneur who'd had little time for either Marja or her boyfriend and then husband apparently and who had made that clear on numerous occasions even to his children, he would do an imitation of 'John the banker', wagging his fingers at them whilst Ilsa tried to shush him and said that he shouldn't do that, not in front of the children.

Jonathan's twin sister and his younger brother, both as outgoing and successful as Jonathan was, in their own and different way, had been there. They'd all been in touch a few times before the ceremony, had offered support, had offered to arrange a dinner somewhere 'for close family', but Jonathan refused and said that he wanted to spend the evening with his children and that he would see his siblings some other time.

'Eliza,' Gerry stood next to the sofa, holding up his glass. 'Are you still with us?' He grimaced. 'You seemed miles away there. You want another glass of wine?'

She shook her head. She hadn't realised she'd drunk all of it and felt dizzy with exhaustion. All she wanted was to get away from them, away from this house and its uncomfortable atmosphere, she wanted to go back with Gerry to her own life, up north, far away, and mourn her mother in her own good time, she wanted to disentangle from what she considered a very sordid confession of her father's, at this time. She wanted to defend her mother but wasn't quite sure against what and how, but she wanted to shout 'we love our mother. For the love of Ilsa, don't make it worse than it is.'

'Let's go for a short walk,' Gerry said. 'Then we can come back and see what else there is to do.'

*

Stephan slammed the door shut behind him, dropped his laptop with a bang on the desk and sat down on the sofa bed. He fumbled in his trouser pockets for his phone, and then realised he'd left it downstairs but didn't want to go back down. He looked around the room, his mother was everywhere and he felt imprisoned by her memory, which was mixed with a feeling of utter sadness, fury and helplessness. What was it with his father and with Mark and with Eliza, keeping their distance, as if they felt uneasy with each other? Eliza was choked up with grief, you could see that, but all she did was nag, just like old times, and she was clearly hurt by what Jonathan had said. What did it matter now anyway? He wished Sander had come; they could have stayed in a hotel and to hell with what the neighbours said, or what his father said for that matter. He didn't seem to be with it anyway and clearly wanted all of this over and done with as soon as possible.

Stephan thought he knew his father pretty well, but couldn't help thinking that he behaved odd and out of character. For three days now, the man had been utterly composed and quiet, almost as if he was a distant relative, not their own blood father, not the husband of the woman who had died, his wife, no, Jonathan was not the father he remembered, the man who would throw him up in the air when he was a child, the man who was happiest when he had his family around him, when there were lots of people, the man who enjoyed taking people out to dinner, who enjoyed having drinks out on a terrace somewhere, who loved to play tennis, or to take his family skiing in winter, high up in the Alps. That was a long time ago now and of course Stephan hadn't expected his father to be bouncy and jovial, of course not, but he was definitely out of kilter and cold to people around him, and not just because of what had happened to Mum. He had withdrawn inside a shell, as he used to when he wouldn't or couldn't cope with what was happening, when he wanted to distance himself and make clear to everyone around that whatever was happening had nothing to do with him.

It was just like that time that Jonathan had seemed lost for words when he, Stephan, had come out, when he'd come home from University one weekend with his then boyfriend, Tony.

He'd forewarned his parents, of course he had, over the phone. However, when they had come in through the backdoor there had been a quick shadow over Jonathan's face, but that might even have been pure imagination. He, Stephan, had after all been hyper sensitive at that time to any show of disapproval or even hesitation. Perhaps he'd just imagined it; perhaps Jonathan had been OK about it, you couldn't always tell with him. He'd certainly never made any comments, not then or since, and had basically ignored it when his son would turn up with a boyfriend at parties or celebrations; unlike Eliza who'd be almost too welcoming and too nice as if to make sure that no one could accuse her of being petty or disapproving or, God forbid, homophobic. Nevertheless, Jonathan had also always made sure that he'd book them into the local bed and breakfast if they'd intended to stay the night, always with some excuse or other, that the rooms were all full because someone else was staying over, or because the heater was not working, or ... He was sure that Jonathan had not really liked it that he was gay, not under his roof anyway and he'd been old-fashioned about it, or perhaps it had been something else. Nevertheless, he'd not been similarly negative about Eliza and Tom staying a night, even if not married, although it was clear that he didn't have much time for Gerry. Poor Gerry. No one seemed to like him much, except for Eliza.

In contrast to his parents, Sander's always were quite natural and friendly and open with them. Perhaps he was just imagining things though, after all, he'd also suspected that Ilsa had been critical, but now he thought that perhaps she hadn't been, that it was all his father's fault, this coldness that had come about, this distance that had been created these last years. Then again ... Oh blast, he was being unnecessarily morose. After all, they'd all moved out and no one had after all tried very hard to keep in touch, or to have regular reunions or family gatherings. The reality was he'd been glad to leave home and then the country. Ilsa had become more and more distant, already when her children were teenagers and even more so when they became adults and moved out.

During his last few years at home, and then when he went to university, Ilsa had been aloof and the whole Anthony affair hadn't helped, had it? She'd been quite distressed when she found out that Anthony was on drugs and subsequently arranged that strange disappearing act, by swinging the other way and getting himself hooked to some religious freak, so out of character with everything he had been before. Ilsa hadn't talked much about it, not with them anyway, and after a while he, Stephan, had given up trying, and then he'd gone through some kind of depression, had seen a shrink even, to help him come to terms with the loss of Anthony in his own way. He'd not told his parents, nor his siblings how bad he had felt and how he'd nearly cracked up. By that time he'd met Sander who'd helped him through, and rather than running the risk of his parents being aloof or obnoxious to Sander he'd simply avoided visits and it came as a kind of relief when they were able to move both their jobs to Singapore, in order to do what some of their friends had done, earn a lot of money, pay little tax, have a good life and save up for their future London dream home. Not that that would happen soon, with the inflated house prices in the capital and the economy going down the drain, still, they had a good life and it was much better than they would be able to afford here in England.

Stephan got up, walked from the sofa bed to the window and stood staring at the darkness beyond, not seeing much more than his own reflection and the projection of the room behind him. He wanted to get out of this house, out of England,

and go back to his life in Singapore, back to Sander, pick up where he'd been a week or so ago, go back to Bali, have a good weekend. He would mourn Ilsa in his own space and in his own good time, rather than here. He felt suffocated and tears started to run down his cheeks.

He smoothed his hair back with his left hand whilst he furiously drew a smiley on the window with the index finger of his right hand, as he and Eliza used to do when they were children. He liked his sister well enough, she was solid, always ready to help, and she was honest, definitely honest, whatever everyone said or thought about her. That she now was with Gerry was just a matter of serendipity as far as she was concerned although he did also think that Gerry was a bit of a jerk; they had barely exchanged a word these last few days, but Gerry seemed damage proof and if his sister was happy with him then who was he to question that?

He wiped his face dry with a tissue and continued to draw until the pane was covered in smiley and not so smiley faces; he thought the straight lipped ones represented Mark. That's how he and Eliza used to draw Mark. Stephan had never quite figured out Mark, who'd always been distant and the ten years age difference between them had been too much for them to bridge even as children and later, once Mark went to university and then left home, well they'd just gone their own ways, and years could pass by without them contacting each other. Mark was the eldest son; he'd often been held up as their example, and he seemed to have grown into that expectation and had become the successful older brother who, as they had been told, would be successful in the same way their father had been successful in business.

Stephan stared at the smileys and wondered if it had been taken for granted that Mark would go much further than any of them. If so, he and Eliza had proved that supposition wrong, hadn't they? They'd all done well in what they'd set out to be, Eliza the respected forensic scientist and he, Stephan, financially much more successful than any of them, even if none of them quite understood how successful he was. None of them had any idea of how much money he actually made, how much he had already stacked away and how, with Sander, he now lived the life of well-to-do expatriates in Singapore, financially secure in their future as well as in the present. He'd once tried to convey this to his mother and although she professed to be happy for him, she had been preoccupied with what had happened to Anthony, and so having a younger child who, against all odds and despite her and his father's doubts about him, was a success; no, this hadn't really aroused any kind of joy or happiness, not at the time, overshadowed as it had been by the dreadful loss of a child. What had happened to Anthony at the time had knocked the life out of her and she clearly couldn't bring up the energy to focus on any of her other children or, by that time, grandchildren.

Their brother Anthony had always been the one out of step, he'd caused havoc whilst at the same time he was also the brother that Stephan desperately missed, the brother who would have been his lifelong friend, he was sure of it. He'd loved Anthony more than anyone else in the world. Before it all went wrong Anthony had been his ally, his mate, he'd been fun; as teenagers he and Anthony would go out together. Anthony had always known that Stephan was gay, even before he dared acknowledge it himself, that he was different from the others, but he'd been totally cool about it. Eliza had never made any silly comments either, or even frowned, and she'd been openly happy about his relationship with Sander when he'd announced that they were moving in together and then to

Singapore. But whereas both Anthony and Eliza had been cool about it all, Mark had continued to ignore his relationship with Sander and never even asked after him.

Stephan closed the blinds and then the curtains, obliterating the smileys and the darkness outside. None of it mattered now, did it? His life was in Singapore and with Sander. He didn't need to try and rebuild bridges with this family of his. As he thought this, he felt a deep ache, somewhere low in his stomach and belly and he wanted to scream. He would get over it though, he knew. He'd remember and continue to love Ilsa for who she'd been, his mother and very close ally when he was a child. He'd remember her for everything that had been good in his life. He was proud of her and she would forever retain that special place deep inside him.

He walked out of the room, went downstairs and retrieved his telephone from the dining room table. A text message from Sander said 'Miss you—come back soon! Hope it's not all too awful and sad. Love your family for me. Xx'

*

When at last they sat down for supper, a meal that had been prepared by Jean and warmed up by Mark and Samantha, they didn't talk much that evening, as if the wind had been knocked out of them. They missed Ilsa, she would have made them talk, would have asked questions that only mothers ask when she hasn't seen her children for a while, she would have chatted with her granddaughter who sat looking forlorn between Mark and Samantha. She would have asked Eliza about her latest case, Mark about the prospect of buying a house in Germany, and about his future plans, and Stephan about his long term plans and how secure his job was, and she would have ignored Jonathan as she had over Christmas, but then Jonathan would have talked with Mark or with Samantha when Ilsa was talking to Sander and to Eliza and Gerry would have talked to whoever asked him anything or included him in the conversation.

Ilsa wasn't there, however, and they fumbled and started one conversation and then got tired and dropped it for another, but none of it really mattered or would make any difference to their feeling of abandonment and loss. Mark raised a glass, 'to Mum, to Ilsa. We love you.' And they all sniffed a little and wiped tears away from their eyes.

They didn't talk much the next day either when one after the other they said goodbye to Jonathan, held his hands, dry-eyed, hugged him briefly and then disappeared to the airport, to the railway station, in different cars, scattering back into the world from which they had been so rudely recalled less than a week ago, to come and say goodbye to their mother and grandmother. The urn, Ilsa's beautiful pottery vase that she'd once bought in Greece, Eliza belatedly remembered, and now filled with her ashes, stood forlorn on the desk in her room, as if she might come by to collect it herself and dispose of it. Eliza had intended to talk about where to scatter the ashes, and so had Jonathan, but both forgot and Mark was already on the telephone to Germany to rearrange one of his meetings, whilst Stephan would first go to London for a business meeting and then to Hamburg for a conference. Arrangements were complicated and they all re-entered their busy lives even if they still felt hollow inside and they wished they could say goodbye to their mother and expected, irrationally, that she would turn up again after all, perhaps all this was some kind of mistake, something they had dreamed up and could now forget.

When they had all gone and Jonathan surveyed the house he felt an ache and he tiptoed up the stairs as if he was afraid he might wake her up, the wife he was going to divorce, and he looked round the corner of the door into her room with the smileys on the window, barely visible, the bedding disorganised and a ball of dust slowly slipping away in the draft created by the opening of the door, and he carefully shut it again. He walked back downstairs and picked up his telephone from the side table and dialled a number.

'Come over tonight or tomorrow,' he said. 'They're all gone. We can talk about where we go from here. Yes, as soon as possible.' And then 'I miss you. If you can come straight away, so much the better.'

Eight: Notebooks

It was February, nearly March, before Eliza travelled down to London on a Saturday to help Jonathan clear out Ilsa's room and belongings. The room had not been used again after Ilsa's funeral and felt airless and dusty. A few boxes had been left in the corner and contained CDs, DVDs, some cooking books, a few prints, handbags, shawls and other random personal effects that had been collected downstairs and dumped here. Jean had tidied away as best as she could, the bed was reverted back to a sofa after Stephan's departure, the desks were tidied, the blinds half closed, letting in subdued light.

Eliza folded away clothes and put them in bags for charities, she cleared a few things that had been left behind in the large family bathroom, she took the knick knacks from desks and windowsills and out of cupboards and desk drawers and left a pile of folders and notebooks, some work related, others personal journals and letters, in the middle of the room. There were bank statements and invoices and school papers as well as bundles of letters that she put in a box and left for Jonathan to destroy, and she destroyed other work related papers and folders that looked like lesson plans and coursework and put them through the shredder that Jonathan had left for her in the room. She hesitated about what to do with the laptop and the more personal and writing journals that Ilsa had left neatly stacked in low cupboards on shelf after shelf.

Eliza thought that Jonathan most likely wanted these destroyed but she couldn't help feeling curious about all this writing her mother had done, indicating that she had been a much more prolific writer than any of them had ever realised. Jonathan had said she'd been writing some non-fiction work, a number of related essays and perhaps a book, but going through Ilsa's room and belongings Eliza realised there was much more. She'd looked through some of the journals kept in a separate pile away from work related folders and realised that a number of these had very personal entries and dates going back to the time Mark was born. In addition to these handwritten journals, more recently she had started writing directly on her laptop in folders that were headed 'personal'. She couldn't simply delete and destroy these, neither the handwritten notebooks nor the personal folders, surely? Ilsa wouldn't have written all of this just to be to be destroyed? She must have had a purpose in mind, must have wanted to do something with these notes and entries. Why would she have kept these journals all these years if she hadn't wanted anyone to read them? More likely it was Jonathan who would rather it was all destroyed, who would rather no longer be reminded too much of a past that was no longer of interest to him.

As before, Jonathan had picked her up from the station; however, when they arrived at the house the front door was opened by the woman Eliza had spotted at her mother's cremation ceremony, 'Hi, I'm Alea. Nice to meet you at last.' As if Jonathan should have prepared her. He had simply busied himself with her weekend bag.

*

Two days later she was glad to be back home in the north, away from Jonathan and Alea, even though she couldn't help but admit that Alea was a pleasant and kind woman, that she and

Jonathan clearly got on very well, that they were so much more at ease together than she remembered her parents being these last years. At the same time, she hated Jonathan for this intrusion and she'd fired off a curt text message to her siblings, the first contact with them after the funeral, 'Dad is now living with a new woman—she was at the cremation. Her name's Alea.' Neither of them had responded. What had she expected? It had been a stupid message anyway, childish and unnecessary.

She sat at the kitchen table with Ilsa's laptop and a few of the notebooks that she'd smuggled out. She looked over out of the window.

The weather was unusually spring like for the end of February and everything was getting ready for a new season of growth and colour. Clumps of snowdrops were visible on the rough patches of the garden at the end, underneath the trees, snow piercers they were, but no snow in sight, and she remembered someone telling her that snowdrops were for graves, that they were the markers of the dwellings of the dead. Her mother. Yes it had been her mother, Ilsa used to love these first signs of spring. They still hadn't scattered her ashes, she reminded herself. The vase stood on her desk and she'd intended to remind Jonathan but couldn't find the words somehow, not with Alea there as well.

Her mind floated, trying to hold onto something about the snowdrops until she remembered that in old times snowdrops were reputed to have been a magical herb, the herb that acted as an antidote to Circe's poison and it was believed that it had saved Odysseus' life. She smiled. Her mother liked that kind of thing, *useless but interesting facts and suppositions*, she used to call them.

In the flowerbeds the daffodils had started to come up, the *narcissus* of Greek mythology, the name of the boy who fell in love with his own reflection. Another useless but wonderful fact, she thought. Even Wordsworth had thought it worthwhile to write a poem about daffodils, referring to them as the crowd that flutters and dances in the breeze. She couldn't wait, she wanted it to be spring and she would take her mother's ashes and whether or not the others agreed, she would put her to rest amongst the spring flowers, if necessary here in the north of England.

Despite the winter not being over by any means, even birds were half heartedly beginning to collect twigs and grass and one of them, a large wood pigeon, flew off with a beak full and crashed into the hedge at the back, the twigs too long to allow it to fly inside the green cover easily.

Eliza smiled. She loved to watch the busyness in the back garden, even if it was still brown and wintry and needed a lot of work. At her asking, Gerry had erected a birdhouse and now insisted on placing nuts and food on plates underneath so that sometimes there were wars between the blackbirds and some wood pigeons, whilst the small redbreasts and finches looked on and hipped around as if to say it had nothing to do with them, these fights.

She looked down at the notebooks and the laptop, sighed and stirred the frothed milk in her cup of cappuccino as she picked up the notebook in front of her, placed it back on a pile of papers and other notebooks that were strewn over the table. She'd taken the afternoon off because she wanted to go through her mother's papers carefully and deliberately, without anyone around, but she couldn't make up her mind that she was actually going to do this, read her mother's papers and journals. In the end Jonathan had said it would be fine, he definitely didn't want to see them, and she suspected that Jonathan had put a line under it all, wanted to focus on the future rather than the past, the future with Alea. She, Eliza had not liked her being there however nice she was, she wasn't ready yet for someone else taking Ilsa's place, in that house that had been Ilsa's as much as Jonathan's.

Jonathan said the papers and notebooks should be burned and he would do it himself but thought she might be better doing it in her back garden 'which is large enough for a bonfire, isn't it?'

She'd said she would do just that, knowing that she wanted to have a peek at some of them, that she wanted to find out more about her mother, so she was disobeying his orders really, but she didn't feel guilty about it. After all, he'd admitted he and Mum were no longer together, not really, and if they had separated then she, Eliza, would have had the say-so over her mother's effects, or Mark, but definitely not Jonathan.

She loved Jonathan, of course she did, but now also wondered again if he had been a difficult person to live with, whether Ilsa perhaps would have liked him to be different from the way he was, more helpful, more considerate of her needs, less flighty, less social, less boisterous, less …

Eliza drank her coffee, licked the chocolate powder off her spoon and put her right hand flat on the pile of papers, crunched her eyebrows and then resolutely picked up one of the notebooks from amongst the pile in front of her. The book she'd picked out was hardly used and it was almost empty, even though some of the pages had yellowed slightly, there were just a few entries on the first five pages or so. She had a lot of those, half filled notebooks and for a moment she wondered if Jonathan was right perhaps, and that none of these were intended for scrutiny by others, not even her own daughter, that it was stuff she might use for a book, but definitely not to be read verbatim. She shrugged away these thoughts.

She scanned the sentences, then her eyes shot back to a paragraph to check that what she read was really there. She checked the front page again; it was not clear what year this was written as only dates were given in terms of days and months. A few entries for February, one for April and then a few more for May, all fairly short. But what she read made her sit up, she shook her head 'surely,' she muttered. Who was this Hans she was writing about? This must have been written some time during 1978, before Anthony was born, when she and Mark were little. The sentences were cryptic, "I miss Hans and just don't know what to do. Tell Jonathan? And then what?" What was it she couldn't tell Jonathan—that she had fallen in love with another man? That she wanted to leave him?

"It wouldn't make sense," the notebook continued. "It won't work out, Hans won't stay anyway. And I don't really want him to stay, do I." and then, "what would happen to Mark and Eliza? What if Jonathan wouldn't let me keep them? I've got to remind myself that it'll never work out with Hans anyway; he's wedded to his Holland. Be reasonable!"

Then there was something about feeling lonely and finding it difficult to look after two small children, whilst pregnant with a third one "that should never have been" but that she was already in love with.

What was all this about Anthony? Ilsa had been very fond of Anthony, naturally of course, but nevertheless she, Eliza, had often felt jealous when they were small, without knowing why; later she'd assumed that it had just been the usual baby envy of a toddler, a child being replaced by a younger baby, didn't they all feel like that? Then, some years later Stephan had been born and it was as if all Ilsa's attention was transferred to the latest baby and they had all had to get on with it, to a certain extent, even Anthony.

Or not? She cannot be sure now, it was all so long ago. And wasn't it the case that people misremembered their childhood, even things that had happened only recently? Witnesses in the cases that she dealt with at work rarely remembered the same thing, and you needed hard evidence.

What she remembered was that they were just an ordinary family, parents and four children who'd played together and fought each other, nothing unusual there. They'd been happy as children, she was sure of it. There were ups and downs, and she remembered there were times when Jonathan seemed to be more away than at home, but then he'd always been the travelling dad, the dad who had a job that involved seeing clients in countries all over the world and who had provided a well to do environment for them. When he was home he was special, he always came with little gifts, as if to make up for his absence. There had been some help for her mother, someone who kept the house clean and Eliza had studied 'to finish my degree' once children were at nursery or school and she'd had that determined look on her face. Later, at the time she, Eliza, was doing her A-levels and would go to university, Ilsa had got her Masters degree at last, had done a teacher training qualification and then got a job in a private girls' school. Her jobs were always part-time when they, the children, were still at home, but more and more as they'd become self-sufficient, the older ones helping out the younger ones, Ilsa had become more engrossed in her career away from home. They'd never questioned their mother's right to do what she wanted to do. Eliza remembered that even as a young child her mother used to tell her that she was going back to university to become 'independent, just like you will have to be.' She'd not really understood what Ilsa meant by that and later, once she'd left home, she couldn't see why her mother had been so obsessed by this. However, there must have been other things going on.

What was it that had thrown Ilsa so badly, that had made her become angry and withdrawn with Dad, even more than she'd been before? Surely, she hadn't always been that unhappy. Eliza had imagined that the turning point had been Anthony's death, and that, rather than her parents growing together in their loss, they'd become, well, yes, they'd become enemies, but why she didn't know. It just seemed to happen that when couples, parents, suffered a loss or went through a trauma they ended up separating and divorcing. As if the pain was not one they could ever share, but rather one that they dealt with in opposite ways, whatever that was.

Eliza put down the notebook and pushed it back in the pile. She should have burnt these as Jonathan had suggested; she now wished she'd not taken them. She didn't really want to read any of this, didn't want to know. They'd moved on. She wanted to remember Ilsa the way she was, a loving mother, not always easy and definitely not perfect, but a woman who had got on with what life had allocated her and had made a good job out of it, as far as Eliza was concerned. She was admirable in that way that she had 'made good,' a woman who knew what she wanted and was not going to be defeated by babies and household chores and who'd instilled in her the importance of a career, that she should not be satisfied with anything less than what the boys aimed for.

Eliza stopped in her tracks as she remembered the man at the funeral amongst the crowd of people that she didn't know, someone she hadn't met before but who, unlike some of the others, had stopped to talk to her, and to Mark too. He'd introduced himself as a former colleague of her mother's, way back in the seventies, or rather not a colleague, he said, but one of her tutors, and he spoke with an accent, either Dutch or German, she wasn't sure. She hadn't caught his name, not his first name anyway, something like Veebeek or Vabiek. She'd been too preoccupied, didn't want to talk and smile with strangers, listen to people who'd want to know who she was, the daughter, there had been so many hands to shake, people she didn't know, to take much notice and she tried to remember whether he'd also given his first name, he must have, but she hadn't really been listening to him, had looked over to where her father stood and Alea, had seen how these two had almost naturally found each other there in the midst of the reception of strangers.

The man had followed her glance and had turned away when she was merely responding politely, mumbling something about being grateful he had made the effort to come. He was tall, taller even than her father but heftier as well and slightly stooped which made him look shorter than he really was. He had bushy blond eyebrows and she thought his face looked familiar, but couldn't work out why. Then she had thought that perhaps he looked a bit like Anthony, the same green eyes, the facial features, the nose, the same tall posture even if bent, but she had immediately rejected the comparison as stupid. Hadn't they always said that Anthony looked like their father's twin brother and a bit like the sister, their aunt whom they so rarely saw? Now, suddenly, she couldn't be so sure.

She didn't want to go there, didn't want to let her thoughts take her into a direction that she wouldn't be able to deal with. She was being stupid and in her forensic mode. Damn her inquisitiveness, damn her desire always to want to know exactly the ins and outs of everything, to 'find the truth that lies out there' even if not immediately obvious. Ilsa was dead and what was there to gain by imagining things and delving into a past that probably had nothing to hide except her, Eliza's, wild imaginations on the basis of her mother's desolate scribbling in a notebook when she was pregnant? And even if there had been anything why would she now want to even know about it, what good would it do to any of them. Even Anthony was dead, wasn't he?

She sighed again, made another coffee, dawdled at the window, and then sat down again, staring at the notebooks. She had enough on her plate, it was much more important to make the best out of where she was now, with Gerry, her job, her new life here in the north, and to remember her mother without all these idiotic suspicions that were floating through her mind. Gerry was her family, even though of course she'd keep in touch with Mark and with Stephan, but wasn't it the case that siblings when they lived so far apart, even if she'd previously imagined that they would naturally continue to be the close-knit family of the past, she was well aware that they'd never be that, probably had never been anything of the kind, that this close knit family of her girlish imagination had not really ever existed.

Look at them. They'd all flown the nest, drifted away and apart, Mark to Germany, Stephan to Singapore, and she herself lived here in the north of England now, far away from her father and the parental home that was in Norfolk; it was still there though it no longer felt that way. Not with Ilsa gone; and not with Jonathan already making the changes that would make the house unrecognisable, she knew. He'd got builders in to revamp the kitchen and had made alterations downstairs as well as upstairs. Bedrooms had been turned into work spaces a long time ago, a large room for Ilsa, a study and a workroom for Jonathan, one his office, one his 'den'. Stephan's bedroom had become the guest room. It had been as if their parents had been waiting for the younger two offspring to clear out as well so that they could at long last live the way they wanted to, in a house that had extra rooms, spare rooms. All their belongings, whatever had been left behind, hers and Mark's from the previous London house and Stephan's and Anthony's from the Norfolk house, had been taken up into sprawling attics and her father had said that he would throw out anything that they didn't claim within the next six months. What was the hurry all of a sudden? Either he was making alterations so that the house would become unrecognisable, no longer reminding him of what it had once been, or he was preparing to sell.

Suddenly Gerry was in the kitchen next to her. 'What. You're still sitting here?' he said. 'Don't tell me you've been sitting here the whole afternoon, rather than getting rid of these papers? I thought you were going to burn them, not read them.' He laughed. 'I suppose you deserve a break. Too many crimes to solve in that brain lab of yours I guess.'

He tended to made fun of her work; as if he couldn't quite fathom what it was all about, this 'forensic peeping' as he called it. It sometimes irritated her but then she reminded herself that he meant no harm, it was just his slightly offbeat sense of humour.

She was a forensic scientist and worked in the local small private laboratory that supported the police and the judiciary in their crime investigations. She loved the work; she would become quite engrossed in the meticulous investigations into substances and materials that might throw up a lead that would help resolve a crime or even a murder mystery. She liked discussing with her colleagues the careful analyses of evidence, never prejudging, never letting your imagination roam free, but always following the small threads of factual evidence that you had to work on. Recently there'd been a murder of a young woman near a lake not far from where they lived; the woman's husband claimed that she'd been shot by someone who stopped them on the road and who'd demanded her jewellery, which she had refused to hand over. The story had been all over the local papers. It seemed strange that he hadn't driven off as fast as he could, but rather had parked the car at the side of the road and claimed that the gunman had shot him in the arm when he tried to help his wife. It all sounded suspicious but of course they couldn't let themselves be led by suspicion, rather, they had to examine whatever they could find, bullet casings, DNA, fingerprints. Eliza was part of the team working on 'the lady by the lake', as they called the investigation, and relished the challenge. She knew that her boss relied on her heading up the team and had recently commended her work to one of the directors. However, Gerry liked to joke about it, or rather about what she did and he said that was because he thought she'd rather be a policewoman, preferably with a gun license, so she could shoot the criminals and make them pay for what they did. She took it all in good spirit and assumed that underneath it all he was actually quite proud of who she was and what she did.

She told Gerry about her find in the notebook, the reference to someone called Hans in her mother's life a few months before Anthony was born. 'Just so strange, this. Never heard the name before. She certainly never talked about him, yet there he was at the funeral. I'm sure it was him. I now wish I'd paid more attention. What was he doing there? How did he find out that Mum had died, that she'd had an accident? Well, maybe he read it in the paper, but if he's Dutch …Were they in touch still, I don't know, my head is spinning.' She sighed. 'Was Mum in love with this Hans, was that why she'd agreed to divorce dad?'

Gerry shook his head, 'Leave well alone.'

*

Her instincts told her to stay clear and to get on with her own life, that there was probably nothing in it and that she saw mysteries where there weren't any. Of course, she couldn't help it, would like to know who this man was, this Hans, and what role he'd played in Ilsa's life, perhaps in all their lives. Ilsa had become so withdrawn and had distanced herself from her children, once they'd all left home. When at first only Mark had left and there'd been the three of them still at home, Eliza, Anthony and Stephan, no longer small children and able to look after themselves, Ilsa had broken loose, at least that's how it felt later; as if she had some catching up to do. Eliza tried to remember when Ilsa had started to work, part time at first but slowly increasing to full time once Anthony went to university. Her earlier studying, taking time away from home, had been gradual but once Anthony had left and then started to do drugs, she and Stephan, she was sure of that, had both felt forlorn and Ilsa had withdrawn herself from them. Whereas until then she'd always been there for them, even when they were obnoxious teenagers, she'd pushed Eliza as much as she'd pushed the boys, to go to university, to qualify, to be able to get a decent job, 'to be independent'. But there were gaps in what she remembered about Ilsa. Ilsa hadn't been a mum who'd try to be her 'friend' as some of her friends' mothers had. She was glad about that, even if Ilsa had been a very young mother and could easily, for a while at least, have been mistaken for an older sister. No Ilsa had never tried any of that, had always been aloof and never pretended to be anything but their mother. Of course, later they'd all slowly but inexorably turned away from the parental home and their parents, found their friends in universities across England so that by the time Mark got married they'd already lived dispersed across the country, doing their own things and living their lives, well away from each other and the parental home. She, Eliza, had been the first to move away for good, to study and then when still doing her PhD had moved in with Tom, and they'd stayed together, partly for financial reasons but as far as Eliza was concerned, it had been pure love and she'd expected to live her whole life with Tom. Once she'd finished her studies she'd found her first job in a lab in London. Now she thought she'd been a goose, naïve really, to move in with Tom and not give herself a chance to be independent, but her mother had never said anything against it, nor her father for that matter, they'd only been concerned that she wouldn't get herself pregnant too soon, she remembered. Her mother insisting that she'd go on the pill, even before she went to university, 'just in case'. She'd felt embarrassed, but later on was grateful.

Soon after, Anthony had dropped out of university, after two years of being obnoxious and, as she found out later, taking drugs and being in trouble a few times with the police. There would be a hush in her parents' conversations every time Anthony was mentioned and then he'd turned down the invitation to Mark's wedding, said he couldn't come. Never even explained why he couldn't come, just turned his back on them. Mark had been upset, of course. But then Anthony had been a troubled child, hadn't he, always, even before he went to university, and she remembered when he was sixteen and was brought home in a police van, drunk and incapacitated and the policeman had said they were lucky that he'd found him and picked him up, another copper might have taken him in and charged him, but then he knew them, their family, from the village. Then, later, when there had been the drugs Jonathan had threatened he would no longer be welcome, especially not as Anthony had filched money, and then stole some more, and when found out had created some very ugly scenes with Jonathan.

*

Gerry said again, 'You really don't want to go there, really Eliza.' And then, 'I know what you're thinking, about Anthony and this Hans, whoever he is. You don't know what you might find and Jonathan would not be very pleased with any of it, you can't do it without telling him. Leave well alone, is my advice, unless he tells you to investigate, but I doubt that somehow!'

'I wonder if Dad ever suspected that Anthony might not have been his son? Anthony was always different, a troublemaker, as if he was in the wrong house. You think that's why Dad and Mum became so distanced, because Dad found out? A DNA test would easily tell the truth. Or perhaps he knew from the beginning.'

'Don't' Gerry said again. 'Really, you're making things up. Don't get involved unless your father agrees to it. And as you say, perhaps he already knows anyway. No one is going to feel any better if you drag it all up and find out now that Anthony was your half brother. Besides, I thought he was estranged from your parents and the rest of you anyway, when he died? It's all water under the bridge now, surely.'

'Not for me,' she said and got up, picked up the pile of papers and walked out of the kitchen to take them up to her desk in her home office, that had a no-entry sign on it for everyone else in the house. He shook his head and called after her 'don't do it Eliza! I know you can, but don't.'

Gerry wasn't one for taking any risks, she thought. She opened her eyes wide and shook her head. Why was she so surprised, she knew that he was risk averse, that he would always rather let sleeping dogs lie, and what was the other cliché he used, not disturb the neighbours or something like that, and not upsetting the applecart? He variously emphasised that he was for being careful, for not disturbing what he considered to be perfectly calm waters; all that had been clear from the beginning so why would she think that he'd give a different response now, that he would say something like, 'oh yes, good idea Eliza. Go ahead and mess up everyone's life and your own at the same time. Dig up whatever dirt you can find.' Is that what she expected him to say? Gerry dealt in clichés, she'd always known that. That's what she'd loved about him, uncomplicated, straight and often laid back, that's why she'd moved in with him, to feel safe and for being calm. What was she doing now, criticising him for being who he was, would always be? He was reliable, unlike Tom, he was trustworthy, unlike Tom, he knew how to make her feel good about herself, unlike Tom, well, unlike Tom recently, he admired her work, but Tom had as well, even more so than Gerry, she sometimes thought. But what was she on about all of a sudden? She shook her head again, this was something she had to sort out herself, and it had nothing to do with Gerry, so why would she ask him? She needed to ask her father about her mother, or Mark, or Stephan, or all of them, but not Gerry, he had barely known Ilsa anyway, and Ilsa probably hadn't really liked him that much, but Eliza had never said this out loud to Gerry. Gerry probably knew anyway.

*

Once, not so long ago, when Gerry came back from work and she sat on the sofa watching some news on the TV and the boys were in their rooms doing she didn't know what, he said, 'Perhaps you should read to them, you know, in the evening. It'll make you closer.'

Eliza wasn't at all sure that she wanted to become much closer to them; she had never intended to become a second mother, had she? She had come for Gerry and it had only slowly begun to dawn on her that being here for Gerry included being part of the family, of his family, his children and yes, even his parents who were always there to help take care of the boys.

She was sure that the children were fine with her, even if they perhaps weren't to start off with. They had been reluctant to talk to her at first, barely wished her a good morning or a good night and rarely talked about what happened at school or during the day, even if she did remember to ask. That had changed over time and she was sure that they now accepted her as part of Gerry and so part of them as a family. They still seemed more at ease with their grandparents though, but that was hardly surprising.

'Why should I read to them? They're not babies anymore. They can read themselves. I bought them books for their birthdays.'

'Kids always like you to read to them,' he said.

She was not convinced, they seemed much happier when they watched something on the telly, although they were only allowed an hour a day at most. Gerry was strict about that, and their grandmother not any less so. She rarely interfered with any of that.

She never thought much about bringing up children, what was right or wrong, or better or worse for that matter. She didn't have children, and neither did the London friends she had had with Tom. She had observed Mark's children over Christmas, but barely knew them. She remembered Samantha would sit and read to them endlessly even though they were also quite capable to read books themselves, at least Caroline was, surely? Or perhaps not, not then anyway, and perhaps that was because Samantha would read to them in German whereas Caroline went to an English school, or did she? She was surprised how little she really knew about them.

Nine: Email and Telephone Calls

A sudden midnight thunderstorm woke Stephan from a restless sleep. He stretched out his arm across the damp sheet and touched the reassuring heat of Sander's back, moist also. They were both naked and Sander had kicked the sheet back in an effort to cool down. The Singapore heat was relentless even in the middle of the night and no matter whether it was midwinter in England or high summer in Asia, the temperature never changed; their current sweaty discomfort was their own fault though for having switched off the air conditioner and leaving the bedroom window open which now let in the sudden rush of thunderous air. Rain splashed against the panes and the curtain billowed against the rattling blinds, a smell of damp and heat pervaded the bedroom and Stephan slipped out of the bed, padded around to the other side to close the window. He stared out across the city where lightning came down in violent waves, shooting arrows at the skyscrapers and then disappeared in the blackness of the ocean beyond. The lightning was followed by heavy thunderclaps, or was it the other way round? Boom after flash had taken over the night sky but then as sudden as it had started it quietened down and disappeared in the distance. Rain continued to slap down, hard and fast. He closed the windows, then the blinds and the curtains and felt his way back to his side of the bed, found the monitor on the side table and turned on the air conditioning. The soft hum and breeze were a welcome relief.

Sander turned, restless, and he grumbled in the dark. Stephan switched on his bedside light, a low dimmed bulb that shed a yellowish glare across his side of the bed and he pulled up the thin summer duvet that lay half folded at the bottom of the bed and spread it carefully over Sander, then slid under it and rolled close to him.

His mind was whirring with non-stop flares and psychedelic shapes and as he switched off the light his head turned into a glowing and painful ball where a dark shadow slowly unfolded itself. He remembered, although he didn't really want to, Eliza and what she'd read in Mum's notebooks. Eliza who had thought it necessary to inform them, him and Mark, by e-mail of what she'd found and her suspicions that Anthony wasn't Jonathan's son, and about the possible affair that Ilsa had in the distant past with someone called Hans. Why did she do this? What was it in Eliza that made her act like a terrier with a bone, that she felt the need to tear at anything that was a bit of a mystery to her? It was callous. Why did she have to know the exact ins and outs of everything and everyone and then lay it out like a spreadsheet with details carefully entered in every single square and on every line? Why not let Mum, and them, be in peace in her death, why rake up all this stuff about Anthony. Anthony who he still missed more than anyone else in his life, more even than Mum? Could that be so? They'd been so close, he and Anthony. Anthony had always known that he was gay, even before he'd known himself. Anthony had tried his best to make him feel good about himself, when he was sixteen and Anthony had caught him with this guy whom he'd really rather not remember. 'Don't worry about who or what you are,' he'd said. 'Just make sure that you don't try and prove something by pretending indifference to your own feelings.' And he'd added 'don't forget that we all love and like you as you are. Even if they seem stupid enough not to realise that you're gay. Just grow up and get out and do your own thing.'

Anthony had been totally indifferent to whatever anyone gossiped about or said about him. But that had been the Anthony before he'd gone to university and become distant and before he started doing drugs, before he'd started to push everyone and also him, Stephan, away. And then all of a sudden he was going to marry this girl, who clearly didn't want to know about any of them. At least that's what they all assumed. Some kind of religious thing. He, Stephan, didn't do religion and neither did any of his siblings as far as he knew. Perhaps their mother had kept some distant memories, she knew all about religion but never ever brought it up.

Sander grunted beside him. 'R you awake? Go back to sleep. You're tossing and turning. Come here. I'll hug you back to sleep.' He laughed softly.

He let Sander hug him and curled up behind his back when he turned over once more to fall asleep.

The next morning, the wooden balcony floor was soaking wet with a dark brown sheen, but their big potted plants looked revived and greener. It was Sunday and although they'd previously decided to have a quiet day, tidying the flat so the cleaner could get on with it the next day when they were out and to prepare some work for the following week, when the sun all of a sudden appeared and wiped away all the remnants of the thunder of the previous night, as if all that had been a mistake, they decided to take a taxi to the East Coast and have lunch in the Seafood Centre, drink a beer and look over the beach and the ocean. As they sat and relaxed, cyclists pedalled past on their rented bikes with baskets on their handlebars that held their cameras and bottles of water. 'Want to go for a spin after?' Sander asked. 'Get rid of your agro?'

Stephan looked at him, his eyes hidden behind his small round sunglasses, took a sip from his small bottle of beer. 'You know, I'm so fed up with Eliza and what she's come up with. All this stuff about my mother. I know she wasn't always pleasant to you, my mother, but she wasn't always like that. She changed after my brother died. And I'm sure she would eventually have come round. She just wasn't like that, prejudiced I mean.'

'Is that a no?' Sander asked. 'It might do you good, a spin on the bike in the heat. Just to get your thoughts in order, sweat it out.' He turned towards a waiter who was clearing up tables behind them. 'Can we have some water please?'

The waiter nodded and walked off. Sander turned back to Stephan. 'You know. From what you've told me, your sister sounds like a real snoop. To be honest, I wouldn't want to know all that stuff about my parents. In the same way that parents of course have no idea about our lives, about what their children are up to, about what we do, when and where. It's unhealthy, I think. Besides, your parents just like mine grew up in the sixties. Wasn't that when there was all this group sex that everyone engaged in, swapping partners? Ok, most of it was heterosexual as well as gay stuff, but not that different from what some of us have been up to before we got settled.'

That's what Stephan liked about Sander, his matter-of-factness, a typically Dutch characteristic he thought, down to earth about who they were, and about himself, that somehow there were no real secrets about their individual past lives, just that certain things weren't made explicit. And why would everything have to be made explicit? Nevertheless.

'But I'd want to know if you were doing that now, though,' he said. 'Picking up others, having it off with others and I'd want to know about it. I wouldn't want you to do it, I'd be jealous.'

'Of course you wouldn't, neither do I. And of course I'd tell you. But things were different then, just for a short time. At least that's what I understand happened in the sixties and early seventies. And they all knew because they did it all together. When was Anthony born?'

'1978, so that doesn't quite match your timeframe. It was Mark who was born early seventies. I think people were having second thoughts about all that sleeping around by the time Anthony was born. England was a different place then, there was inflation, there were even riots and that was the beginning of the Thatcher era, wasn't it? I get some of my history muddled up—it was such a boring era, really. The seventies. Besides, I somehow cannot imagine my mother having been part of that sixties crowd somehow, what you read about it, the sleep-ins and the wife swapping, she just wasn't that kind of a person, I'm sure. She was too straight somehow. My father though ...' He stopped. Shrugged his shoulders and carefully balanced a prawn between his chopsticks and slid it into his mouth. 'Delicious,' he said. 'None of this is relevant though. They're both dead, my mother and also Anthony. And I loved them both. I also love my father, or at least I feel affection for him. I don't want all that ruined by raking up irrelevant dirt from the past that will simply get everyone upset and miserable. I'd much rather continue to believe that Anthony was my brother, which he was anyway, whether a half brother or a full brother who cares, and that my dad was the dad of all of us, whether genetically as well as in practice I don't care, and that we were a happy family, once.'

108

'But what if your father knows that he isn't? That he wasn't the dad of Anthony, I mean. Perhaps he's always known but they decided not to tell any of you.'

'Eliza didn't say. I don't even know if she's told him that she's been snooping around and that she's made this discovery. Although he gave her Mum's papers, to destroy I presumed, rather than chucking them in the bin straightaway, or burning them. I don't really know why he did that. Knowing Eliza that was taking a risk, I can tell you.'

The waiter arrived with a carafe of water clinking with ice cubes and Sander poured them both a glass and emptied his in one big draught, then refilled it. 'God, it's hot. Sometimes I just loathe this relentless heat and the stickiness of it. I know it doesn't seem to affect you as badly. Nevertheless, it's better than bloody miserable and grey Holland or England for that matter. For now at least. Do you know actually that our relationship, a male homosexual relationship, is still illegal in Singapore? Not that anyone cares much, I think. But you can't get married here, not you and me anyway. That is, if we wanted to.'

He wiped a tissue across his forehead, which was glistening in the hellish light that was tempered by the parasols all around them. A slight breeze ventured their way from the ocean and for a while they sat wordless looking into the distance where the large shipping vessels, the ocean liners and the sleepy containers moved silently as if toys floating in a big grey blue basin of water, undisturbed by the world around them. There was only a vague smudge of a line between what was sky and ocean. Closer by, across the path where strollers and cyclists moved back and forth in continuous streams on this weekend day, and across the stretch of stony beach, the water was murky and paddled back and forth across the boulders, stones and pebbles strewn across the sand, inching its way forward and then moving backwards again, too tired to assault the land in the way the sea would assault the beaches in Holland or in England. There in the autumn the foul grey white heads of violence would throw themselves at the dark yellow sand that was murky and slippery under the onslaught, or at the rocks that lined some of the Norfolk coast. Each of them knew their childhood coasts in different ways. The contrast with what they saw here was too much to linger on for long.

After the rain of the previous night the day had woken up sunny but already this afternoon clouds were re-forming and provided a hazy shelter against the oppressive heat. Quite likely these woolly sky shapes would accumulate, reform into something grey and dark and there would be another sharp and heavy shower before the day was over. This was Singapore after all. Or perhaps it would just stay dry now for a few days, after the storms had wreaked their havoc the previous night. You couldn't tell. The forecast would forever predict 'showers', just to be sure and most people going to work didn't even consult the weather forecast but simply took their tiny umbrellas as a matter of course, tucked away at the bottom of a briefcase or rucksack or handbag, just as here in Singapore people were never without their mobile phones or, increasingly, not without their tablets. Their own phones lay on the table next to their plates but they had agreed to switch them off whilst they ate. Around them people were laughing and talking and held phones as if an extensions of their hands, as if they would be incomplete somehow without that additional feature, scrolling up and down whilst talking or holding them up to take pictures of their companions or to make selfies. At least they, Stephan and Sander, didn't have the earplugs in their ears whilst they were in company of others, not yet, anyway. In the metro, on the MRT trains and on buses people would sit or hang in the rails with earplugs in and staring ahead of them or on their screens, intently listening to whatever these small devices procured for them, music, most likely, or perhaps they consulted the stock markets, or holiday destinations, and games and films and videos they'd made and wanted to revisit. The possibilities were endless and this companion helped them stave off the boredom and the tiredness that lay on their faces like a permanent layer of makeup and they could ignore the overcrowding around them, the halo of a mobile afforded them their private space.

'Oh Christ, look who's coming there. Our Charley, with a different waif. Another local? Chinese by the look of her, definitely not Indonesian or Malaysian this time.' Sander murmured, keeping his voice down.

Stephan turned to look. A very tall thin man with a baseball cap and wearing flip flops, looking hot in a bright yellow sleeveless t-shirt over a Hawaiian themed pair of knee length shorts, walked in their direction, waving and calling out, 'hi Fellows! How are you two? Great to see you.' A tiny girl, who only just reached halfway his chest, carefully balanced alongside him wearing red, high heeled open toed shoes, dressed in a blue kaftan that came to her knees, and who held on to his other non-waving arm. She smiled wide as if she knew who they were, but Stephan was sure they'd never met before.

'This is Tina, my friend,' Charley said when he caught up with them. 'Shall we join you for a beer?'

'We're about to leave, we've just eaten. But we can hang on for twenty minutes. Good to see you. How are you?' Sander said.

Tina's smile stayed on her face like rictus and she pushed her very large and dark sunglasses on top of her small head

111

revealing the Chinese look and eyes covered in a green shadow that somehow enhanced the blue of her kaftan. How did she do that? An English girl would have looked tarty, she simply looked childish and yes, fun.

'Tina's a fashion designer,' Charley said. 'She's Singaporean and she's showing me the nooks and crannies of real Peranakan culture, we've just had a stroll around Joo Chiat, not too far from here, but it's too bloody hot today, so we took a taxi this way.' He took out what appeared to be a real old-fashioned handkerchief from one of his pockets and wiped his forehead. When neither Sander nor Stephan responded he added, 'you know who the Peranakans are, don't you? The real Singaporeans, the ones who've always lived here. Not intruders like us.'

Tina looked at them and then at Charley, 'Sure they know, ley?' She spoke English with an American accent but couldn't help adding the 'ley' as she would when speaking Singlish, the Singapore patois, with her friends. She seemed ill at ease despite her broad smile.

Stephan couldn't quite remember how and when they'd met Charley, an English language teacher who came from Leeds, for the first time. But then they all seemed to meet sooner or later, all the temporary residents, especially the young and childless couples or singletons, that came to Singapore to live the expat life on generous salaries and low taxes, who lived in gated condominiums with swimming pools and gyms or, if that proved unaffordable as Stephan imagined that it would be unaffordable for someone with Charley's income, they would rent a small room in a communal flat with a shared kitchen and bathroom in less expensive areas somewhere near the central district, so they could go out of an evening and frequent the numerous bars and hawker centres, and they probably imagined they were part of the real Singapore by spending most of their time out and about, eating and drinking, and meeting friends and acquaintances wherever they happened to be. Singapore was just full of these happy lost souls but lonely people, Stephan thought.

They imagined, coming from cold and damp Europe, that in Singapore they could live the dream and in a way you could of course, as long as you made enough money, but someone like Charley would probably not last longer than a couple of years and then pack up his bags and go somewhere else that he hoped would bring him the paradise he was looking for. Until, that is, he grew old and realised that he belonged nowhere and everywhere.

Stephan wondered sometimes how someone like Charley imagined his future to be, wasn't he worried he'd end up lying in Waterloo station with a blanket and a saucer for the pennies that passers-by dropped onto it? Sander and he knew why they were here and what they were going to do eventually, which was to pack up what they had accumulated and take with them all their hard earned savings squirreled away in bonds and savings accounts, for a deposit for a house in London. That's where they really wanted to live, or somewhere near London anyway, in a large house with a small ornate garden and with beautiful furniture and art on the walls and with a dining room that could entertain their handpicked friends, guests and family. They'd ask their firms to relocate them, and if that failed, they'd find another job or set up their own business. For the time being they would stay put, however. They would definitely try to sit out the economic downturn across the world, which so far appeared to have had little effect on their own lives and incomes here in Singapore.

'Have you got tickets for the Grand Prix yet?' Charley asked, when neither of them picked up on his conversation, but instead scanned the area around them for the waiter. 'I've not actually been yet, to the Prix. I wasn't in Singapore last September. It's expensive, isn't it?'

'We went last year,' Sander said. 'Yes, we'll be going again. I haven't actually thought about it, it's only March, but, yeah, sure. We'll go again. Perhaps we'll see each other, most likely we will if you're going.' He turned to Stephan who nodded and said, 'Anyway, what are you up to these days?'

The waiter came round and Sander asked for the bill whilst Charley ordered a beer, 'Just a water for me,' Tina said. She smiled again and put her sunglasses back over her eyes so that all they could see was her small nose and her lips framing her sharp white teeth. Her face was pale and her sleek shoulder length and shiny black hair was tucked behind her ears. She was quite pretty, Stephan thought. Where did he dig them up, Charley? He wasn't such a big catch, really. Always trying to scrounge off what he imagined were his friends. He was probably fishing for an invitation the way he talked about the Grand.

'We really got to go now,' Sander said after they paid their bill and Charley and Tina carefully sipped their drinks.

'Wanker,' Sander murmured as they walked away. 'I'm sure he's a member of some kind of dating agency and he only holds on to them for one fuck and one night out. Then they've cottoned on and drop him like a brick.'

Stephan laughed out loud. 'Come on. Let's go for that bike ride.'

'Yes, I could do with some exercise. I've been sitting in meetings all week and next week isn't going to be much better. The week after I'm going to Germany, remember? I might include a short visit to my parents in Holland. They were quite upset when you had to suddenly leave us in Bali that time. Can't you arrange a business trip and come with me to visit them? My sister is expecting her first, and I'd like to see her. You could even try and visit your brother Mark in Germany?'

Stephan shook his head. 'Afraid not, I'm over my ears with everything and am needed here in Singapore for that conference. Besides if I go to Europe I'd have to visit Dad and I'd want to talk things through with Eliza. However, it just can't be done at the moment. We need to talk about going together next Christmas though, to visit all of our families. That'd be fun!' He laughed and pulled up his eyebrows. 'Not, I think!'

They sauntered towards the bike hire place, holding hands for a moment and Sander pulled him over closer, 'Don't worry too much. It'll all work out. You've got to hang on to your own memories of Anthony and your mum. You loved them and they loved you. That's all that matters.'

*

Mark slammed the front door behind him and stood in the hall, breathing heavily, forcing himself to calm down. Bloody Eliza! To ring him on his mobile and tell him she thought she'd discovered that Jonathan wasn't Anthony's father. What the hell was she up to? His idiot sister.

'I'm doing it for Mum,' she said. 'I need to find out what was the matter with her these last few years. I need to know. I'm doing it for the love of Mum.'

'For the love of Ilsa,' he scampered. 'Don't give me that crap Eliza. You're just snooping into things that you have no right to. What does Dad say about all your so-called findings? I'm sure he's pleased that his daughter is calling a witch hunt on him now that Mum is dead.'

'I can't help it Mark. I just found these papers. Dad gave them to me, remember? To be honest, I think he knows anyway. Just got that feeling. Why did he give me that notebook, and the others? It would explain a lot of things. He wanted us to find out so he needn't tell us himself,' Eliza said.

Mark came off the tram when she called, back from the station and a meeting in Berlin, and he now wished he'd asked her to call him back later, but once she'd started he could hardly stop her. In the end he managed to interrupt and said he would ring her back; that he was in the middle of the street and needed to get home.

He took another deep breath before he walked into the sitting room, where Samantha was reading to Jasper. Caroline was busy gluing something on the dining room table. Sam looked up. 'You're early,' she said. He bent over her and ruffled Jasper's hair as he gave her a kiss.

'Yes, meeting finished early and I managed to catch an earlier train. A bit difficult as of course I didn't have a seat booked on that one, but I found one.'

'What's the matter?' Samantha asked. 'You look as if you've had some bad news. Everything OK at work?'

'It's not work,' he said, pulling off his jacket and loosening his tie. 'I'll go and change first. We can talk later, after dinner. It's not something I want to talk about with the kids around.'

'We're just fine, Daddy,' Caroline said. 'You can talk.'

'Oh really,' he said. 'But I want to tell Mummy a grown up story. Sometimes it's better that you don't hear those. Now I want to see what you're making and you can tell me all about school while we set the table.'

He went into the bedroom and changed into his jeans and a sweatshirt. He felt better already, just changing. Somewhere far below he heard the downstairs neighbour practising her saxophone. Bloody loud instruments they were. To be fair, she'd come up and knocked at the door and had asked whether they minded if she practised at an hour that would not be too disturbing for anyone, say late afternoon, and she'd kept to her promise. But these chords and endless out of tune scale sessions were just painful to listen to, even through the walls. He went into the bathroom and looked at himself in the mirror. He was still the same Mark, he thought, irrationally. As if Eliza's suggestion that Jonathan might not be Anthony's father had any bearing on how he himself should look or feel. Or had she meant to check on all of them? She better not, he would not give permission. What had she done, found Anthony's DNA somewhere, just happened to lie around, a scarf, a hat? Unlikely. He was curious. And how had she got hold of Jonathan's. Had she obtained it without his permission, sneaked into his bathroom and taken away a toothbrush or a comb? She was mad, really. What was she trying to do, now? Anthony was dead and so was their mother and he thought that he missed Ilsa more than he could express to his siblings or his father. Sam knew. Sam always sensed his emotions and had held him when they had returned from the cremation and were back in Germany and he had started to cry, just like that, in the middle of the bedroom, half undressed. He'd collapsed on the bed and Sam had held him as if he was a baby. He had been surprised at himself. He couldn't remember when he had cried last.

'I miss her,' he said. 'I wish I'd gone over to see her. That we'd gone over to visit. She would have liked that, even if she appeared to be indifferent and cold. Something was bothering her. Things weren't right. You remember that last Christmas, when we visited? I so wish I'd made the effort to try and find out whether I could've helped her, whether we could help her.'

'Shhh, I know,' Samantha said. She sighed. 'It wasn't always easy and you only have limited holidays, remember. And you needed a break, badly. You were overworked last summer, under a lot of pressure. We had to go somewhere comfortable for you. Staying with your parents and running the risk of a rain sodden holiday indoors was just not on. Besides, we asked your mother to come with us to Greece, but she wouldn't. She said she wanted to have some time off in England, see some friends. Didn't she go to see her sister?'

He couldn't remember what Ilsa had done in the end, she hadn't talked about it much and they had been full of stories about their own holiday on Crete, and once back their own work routines and school schedules had taken over again. But why hadn't he insisted that she'd come with them, or that they'd both come along, Jonathan and Ilsa? They could easily have rented a larger villa. After all, Jonathan was hardly hard up and could well afford a holiday, and his mother had her own comfortable income as well, but Jonathan had been busy last summer, said he couldn't take it off in the middle of the summer. He, Mark, had simply assumed that Ilsa wouldn't come because she didn't want to go without Jonathan. But that seemed hardly likely now, not after what Jonathan had said, about them living separate lives and heading for divorce.

He'd always loved his mother, unreservedly, from when he was a small child. There'd been a short time when he'd tried to be grown up and impress everyone that he was indifferent to women and especially his mother and he wouldn't have wanted to be seen with her, but that had passed, as with all boys. Didn't they all go through these phases? He always knew that his mother cared for them, that she loved him and that she would always be there for him. And she had. Only perhaps he hadn't returned her love in the same way, had perhaps taken her too much for granted. Had he? It was silly though to start self-recriminations where there were none necessary, after all it wouldn't change anything. And it was definitely silly to start digging into her past as if they were on a criminal investigation! He would have to tell Eliza. None of it was going to be of any help to any of them and what difference would it make? He wanted to remember his mother the way she'd been in his own mind, loving, caring, a good mother, a woman with ambitions of her own, his father's wife and a mother who had always been there for them as far as he was concerned.

Later that evening, after Jasper and Caroline had been put to bed and the dishwasher was churning away in the background, the water pipes humming slightly when the water was pumped in and out, Samantha asked, 'So, what was all this about? When you came in earlier?'

'It's Eliza,' he said. 'But I've already decided that she can't do what she's setting out to do. Destroying our memories of who or what we are, especially not those of Mum and Dad.'

'What's she doing? Why are you upset?'

He told Sam about the notebook Eliza had found and that she said she'd carried out a DNA test, which appeared to show that Jonathan wasn't the father of Anthony. 'Imagine doing that without any of us knowing, without getting agreement, probably not even from Dad,' he said.

Samantha pulled a face as if to say she didn't believe what she heard. 'How can you do a DNA test on someone who's been dead for years? Who's well and truly buried? Even Eliza couldn't pull off that one.'

'The thing is. It won't do any of us any good at all,' Mark said. 'What's the point? What are we going to do with that information? It's not going to bring back either Mum or Anthony, nor is it going to help us in coming to terms with

Mum's death, in the same way that it was difficult to come to terms with Anthony's death, what, eight years ago now.'

'Have any of you spoken with Jonathan? You or Eliza or Stephan?' Samantha asked.

'I certainly haven't. There's something strange going on I think. Why did Dad give those papers to Eliza? He must have thought that there was nothing in those papers to suggest any of the stuff that Eliza says is in them. I just cannot imagine Jonathan would have given them to Eliza with the idea that she would find out and do a paternity test on him and on one of his children, behind his back.'

His mobile rang suddenly, loud and impatient. 'Christ. I said I'd ring her back. I completely forgot.'

It was Eliza. Sam shook her head as if to say, don't pick it up, don't answer, but he already stood with the phone to his ear.

'Sorry Eliza, it's a bit late I know. But then, there's family and dinner and bed time stories and all that, as you know.'

Sam could hear Eliza's voice, loud but calm, as if she was setting out a case, as if she was speaking to a jury. She wasn't sure about Eliza, never had been. Eliza had always been distant, as if she didn't quite trust her, Samantha. As if she'd stolen the family silver when she married Mark soon after they'd met. But then, she'd deny it and it mightn't be true anyway. Eliza was just too wrapped up in her own life to care much about anyone else's. Except for her family, though. She did care about her mother and her father, and she did care about Mark and Stephan and she'd probably cared a lot about Anthony. She still had tears in her eyes, half the time, when she spoke about him, as if she still couldn't accept that he was really gone. Had been gone for all of eight years.

Mark walked out of the room and she could hear his voice from the kitchen, rising in tone, angry and growling. There was a long silence and then Mark again, quieter this time, imploring. Samantha switched on the television so that she didn't have to listen to what she couldn't hear properly anyway. There was news on, another terror plot, politics, and the war in Syria where armed forces appeared to be attacking their own people. She never liked the news and when she heard Mark come back into the room, she turned it off again and asked, 'So what's up?'

'She's done this test and is adamant that we need to know, that she needs to know in order to understand what's been going on. She says she'll talk to Dad over the weekend, when she's going to see him to help him pack some of his stuff. Gerry's going with her, they're driving down. Apparently Dad's moving. Again, I didn't even know he'd sold the house! But he has and he hasn't asked any of our advice that's for sure.'

He felt hurt and could not understand what was happening, what had created this distance between him and his father, between him and his past and for the first time in his life he wondered who Jonathan was, if he wasn't the Dad he'd always imagined he was, uncomplicated, easy, somewhat distant perhaps; someone who was away a lot but who'd always turn up again, usually with presents and happy stories, and who'd disappear again as soon as he seemed settled back into a kind of family life; someone who had always travelled here, there and everywhere, who had always been busy, who had earned a very comfortable living for all of them. Before starting his own consultancy Jonathan had been employed by a large corporation, was a kind of consultant, an adviser who was a computer software wizard and who advised on high finance, later, once he had set up for himself he supported companies and individuals streamline their businesses, he was much admired and had important friends. For all of Mark's childhood they had lived in a large house with a garden just outside London, until he and Eliza had gone to university, when 'home' had been moved to the present large house just outside Norwich, 'out in the sticks', Ilsa had said. 'We like the peace and quiet and we have got cars if we want to go anywhere. It's not as if we have to drop you off at schools and events anymore.' It was still a pile of a house, he realised, compared to Samantha's parental home, which was more modest although very comfortable. And now that house was sold and his father was moving to another place, alone or with someone? Perhaps he'd at long last decided to live with that woman, Alea was her name, he thought. He'd forgotten to ask Eliza.

Mark and Samantha sat in silence at the enormity of it all. The house, Ilsa's house as much as their father's house, had been sold.

'What's happened to your mother's ashes?' Samantha asked suddenly. 'I thought about that today, as a matter of fact. I thought we were supposed to plant a tree or something? A kind of ceremony with all of us there? In the garden?'

But that wouldn't now be very appropriate, would it? Not if Dad didn't really want her around? Anyway, the house was sold and there was no reason to bury Ilsa's ashes in the garden of a house that she'd never lived in. Mark shrugged his shoulders, 'I really don't know.'

They were quiet then until Mark said

'I really need to go over and talk to Dad, as well as Eliza. There's too much that needs sorting. Dad took the urn upstairs to Mum's room and I assume it's still there. I have talked to him a few times, over the phone, but he's completely wrapped up in his work, or so he says. Now I'm not so sure. Perhaps he's just avoiding the past and us as best as he can.'

'Perhaps you should go over this weekend, when Eliza is there too. Just take the Friday off and fly and come back on Sunday night. I can drop you and pick you up. From the airport I mean. There must be flights.'

How easy it was to just slide back into your daily lives, to be busy with your work, your family, the school pick up and drop down routines, the out-of-school arrangements for the children, the shopping and the visiting of friends or having a night out and all the arrangements around that. How easy it was to let the hurt settle deep down and quietly mourn your mother's unexpected death and after a few months life would be running again the way it always had. Only deep inside you were aware that you wouldn't go over for Christmas to see your mother, you assumed that you would invite your father to come over and celebrate it with you but even that seemed somehow unlikely now. At least unlikely that he would accept. You thought that perhaps you could arrange a short week away for everyone, when Stephan would be in Europe next and they could all go and see Dad and have a proper remembrance day of your dead mother, in the house where she used to live. None of that would happen, he realised. Families just didn't work like that anymore. And in all honesty, he hardly had the need for any of that. He had his own family, he'd grown away from all that had seemed so important when you were a child. He was an adult himself, with his own responsibilities, no longer tied to a past that had become irrelevant to daily life.

Samantha got up from the sofa when she heard the beep of the dishwasher, announcing that the cycle was complete. When she came back into the room she said, 'we should arrange a ceremony for Ilsa's ashes to be either buried as they are or scattered. That's only right. I'm sure Eliza and Stephan would agree. And your father would. Isn't Stephan planning to come over around Christmas? That would be as good a time as any, although my parents have asked if we want to come to them this year, they always love to have the children around, you know that.'

'Christ, I can't think of all that now, it's only March! Talk of Christmas is just mad. I've got to get up early tomorrow; I have a two-hour drive to go to a client. I'm going to get my case ready, and my clothes. I'll sleep in the spare room, will set the alarm for 5.30, don't want to wake you up.'

Mark walked out of the room and carefully closed the door behind him. Samantha sighed and got up to empty the dishwasher.

The following evening Mark returned late, after the children had gone to bed and told Samantha that he had spoken with Jonathan and that he had booked a flight for Friday morning ten o'clock.

'Dad was reluctant to speak over the phone. Said it was a good idea if I'd come as well as Eliza because he needed to talk a few things over with us. He also said it was a pity that Stephan couldn't be there at the same time but that he'd let him know that Eliza and I will be there.' Mark got up and came back with a glass of water. 'Do you want some?'

Samantha shook her head. 'I'll take you to the airport. I'll have to drop you early though as I have a class at eleven.'

'You know I've been thinking about Mum and about who she was. You take for granted you know your parents and you assume that their lives on the whole have been fairly straightforward, especially if they never say anything differently,' Mark said. 'But you know what? Mum could be quite strange at times, I told you before. She was very warm and then sometimes it was as if she glazed over, as if it was all too much of an effort. She'd become distant. Not cold or indifferent, more as if she was on a remote control that wasn't working properly.'

He got up from the chair, restless, and walked to the window, stood there staring over at the park that was shrouded in darkness with only intermittent balloons of light that made visible short stretches of the path that ran alongside the main road beneath. A late tram chuntered past, but the double glazed windows shut out most of the sounds so that everything outside seemed unreal and disconnected. A few cyclists raced the tram and caught up with it, and then they also disappeared from the frame. He drew the blinds and sat down again.

'I never knew your mother that well,' Samantha said. 'She was always very friendly but, well, we didn't see that much of your parents did we. Not even when the kids were small. Your mother always worked, and so did your father of course, it was always my parents who jumped in to help with babysitting or having the kids over for a holiday. Your parents just lived too far.'

'Don't apologise,' Mark said. 'It was their choice as much as ours. Mum always assumed that she'd have plenty of time to do "more caring," as she used to call it. She was just glad to have time for herself and her own career. Even if that came very late or rather, because it came so late for her.'

She'd never worked when they were small. He remembered that she used to sit at the kitchen table or at the dining room table with books and notebooks and pens 'trying to get my degree, about time.' By the time Stephan was halfway through secondary school she'd got a degree in English literature and a teaching certificate and started to teach at a private all girls' school. Then he seemed to remember an MA but couldn't really place it in a timeframe. She'd been very preoccupied for a while and he'd always thought that her spells of aloofness had been part of this obsession to make good what she hadn't been able to finish because of his, Mark's, birth. At first she hadn't been bothered, he thought because she was happy looking after them and then Anthony had come along, a good five years after Eliza was born, and he was seven, Eliza had still been young, only twenty-eight, younger than he was now, and Dad must have been doing well because even though Mum didn't work there'd been help around the house, a few days a week, someone would come in and take care of them or do some cleaning and tidying whilst Eliza would sit and study or go out for half a day, sometimes a whole day 'to college', or 'to the library'. It had taken her a long time though, he thought. But at least she'd persevered so that once Stephan was of an age she'd started her own career. He'd always been quite proud of that, his mum, becoming a teacher and then a head of department, respected and, as he thought, showing herself to be an independent woman. It couldn't have been easy for her, not with four children and a husband who was away quite a lot, often at critical times. But that was the way it was. Sometimes he thought that in fact they'd been quite lucky, that only Anthony had gone off the rails, taking drugs and then that strange marriage.

'Mind you, we were actually quite a strange family,' he said, as if Samantha had heard his thoughts.

She looked at him, 'what do you mean?'

'Well, when I look back, Mum was a good mum and we all loved her and she made us feel good about ourselves. But there was something quite weird, with Dad being so at a distance sometimes. There was always an au pair or a nanny of course. There were days, weeks, my parents seemed to barely talk to each other, although they were polite, to put it that way. As if they were living separate lives together, even then, as if they were there as a couple just for us. I don't remember violent quarrels, just sometimes you could hear them argue downstairs, when they thought we were all asleep, or away.'

'Well, all parents quarrel some time or other,' Samantha shrugged her shoulders. 'I don't think it'd be healthy if they didn't. We do.' She looked at him. 'We disagree sometimes,' she repeated, as if for emphasis or to dare him.

He wanted to say, but I try not to do it in front of the children. He realised that he didn't want to emulate his parents' marriage, whatever that had been like for them. There had been something odd about their relationship, something that wasn't quite right. You shouldn't want to know about your parents' marriage or love lives anyway, he thought, and he really didn't want to know. He wanted to get on with his own life, he liked his job, he had good colleagues, he was happy with Samantha, happy with his two children and he wanted a good life for them together, as a unit, not being a distant father like his own Dad had been. He was always careful to get back at a time that he would still see them before they went to sleep, and would then perhaps work on later, at his laptop, whilst Samantha watched television or did something of her own, corrections, preparing lessons.

'It's no use,' he said. 'I don't actually want to know. I wish Eliza hadn't started all this. Why can't we just get on with what and who we are? Without raking up a past that hasn't got anything to do with us, unless you think you cannot be who you are without knowing? And I don't think that.' He felt angry. 'I'll go and see Dad and try and help out with clearing the house, but I'm not going to allow Eliza to stir up a past that may turn out to be murky and can only upset us. I just don't want to know.'

Ten: Family Visits

Mark and Eliza sat next to each other at the large wooden table in the kitchen of what was still Jonathan's house, their previous family home. It was unusual, the frequency with which they saw each other this last year; first at the funeral and now again, even if it was just the two of them this time, there were no other members of the family present. It was strange because even though they were so very familiar with each other they had grown apart, inevitably. They were nearly middle aged themselves now, and they felt slightly uneasy at being thrown back together into a no-longer appropriate familiarity.

Mark showed the beginning of fleshy cheeks, a slight thickening around the middle, a few streaks of grey hair here and there, lines were forming where previously the bone structure had been smooth and angular, and Eliza, well Eliza still had that nearly translucent white and soft skin but nevertheless you could see the crows around the eyes, a soft line around the mouth that would, like her mother's become deeper and pronounced over the years, she was still a very attractive and youthful looking woman who liked it that no one at work believed that she would be thirty seven soon. Brother and sister were adults now who were living their own lives, well away from what had once been the parental home and which as a matter of fact, didn't feel like that anyway, a previous home, as it had never been the house they grew up in when small and had only been their refuge for the times, when at university and living away from home, they had felt that pull to go to what had become 'home' because that's where parents and younger siblings had moved to; but the house had never settled inside their psyche as the place that was home, it had already begun to unravel even then.

The house wouldn't be Jonathan's for much longer as he would hand over the keys in a week's time to the couple with two children who had come to see it and loved it and who'd offered more than the asking price just to be sure, according to Jonathan, and despite the slow down and the financial crisis that had hit the world and England. It showed that people still had money, some people did anyway, and the house had been sold after only having been a very short time on the market. Mark suspected that despite his father's reassurances he had probably sold it below the asking price, which had been well above what he'd paid for it when he bought it. The sound of a late passing car came in through the window which had been opened to let out some of the cooking smells when Eliza had turned off the fan because it was 'too noisy'; then the darkness settled back quietly around the house.

'Actually, now that both of you are here it's a bit of a shame that Stephan's not here as well,' Jonathan said as he handed round plates that he'd warmed up in the microwave.

Eliza got up, closed the window and opened the oven, took out a large dish of lasagne and put it in the middle of the table.

'Sit down Dad, it's all ready. Just pour us a glass of wine.' She handed him the bottle that stood opened on the side. 'Gerry won't be coming in till later, he arranged to see a colleague of his, couldn't let the opportunity pass, he said.' She frowned slightly and added 'well, it gives us some space to talk, I guess, just the three of us.'

'What have you been up to today?' Jonathan asked. 'Have you managed to clear your mother's room?'

'There's a lot of stuff to go through,' Eliza said. 'You clearly haven't touched much of it all this time. It's as if she's still living here. I find it difficult. I miss her.' She gave a lopsided smile and just for a moment looked like the little girl she once was and as if she was going to cry, then she shook her head and took an eager sip from the glass of wine that Jonathan handed her.

'Except for some of the papers and notebooks, I took those last time. But there are many more papers and files in her drawers. You need to look at those; some are letters, dating back to the eighties and nineties, as far as I can see. Strange to think that people wrote real letters and now we have to decide what to do with them. Well, you have to decide. I'm sure she would have destroyed everything, if ...' Eliza set down the glass, hard, and turned to Mark and then back to Jonathan. It was as if she couldn't make up her mind who to address or who to ask, whatever it was that she wanted to ask. She wasn't sure herself. Perhaps she should have just put the lot through a shredder or burnt them, as Jonathan had suggested, or she could have put them in the boot of their car to destroy later.

They helped themselves to the lasagne and the salad that Mark had made. He'd joined Eliza in the kitchen when he arrived. Eliza had confirmed that Jonathan knew all about what she'd found out about Anthony and that he'd merely said she could have saved herself the trouble of the DNA test story as he'd always intended to tell them anyway. Suddenly, Jonathan started to talk, ignoring Eliza's questions,

'As I told Eliza, yes, Anthony was your half brother, he wasn't my son, I knew, but I've always considered him to be a son of mine, have never looked at him in any other way.' He

130

stopped. Then continued, 'Your mother and I, we decided to keep it from all of you, we wanted you to grow up in a normal family, not make it more complicated, especially as we wanted to stay together and it would be something you wouldn't understand, not when you were children. We told Anthony before he went to university. He was very upset for a time and angry, especially with your mum, but also with me, for keeping it a secret, for not telling him.' Jonathan held up his hands as if he was begging. For what? For their sympathy? Was he saying that he knew Ilsa had been sleeping with another man, and he simply had accepted it all as if it was just a minor divergence in their family life?

Mark stared at him and looked down when Jonathan repeated, 'Anthony was angry.'

I would be angry, he thought. I'm even angry now for you telling me, like this. Why do people, even your parents, deal in so many lies all the time, what was wrong with being honest?

'I never treated Anthony any different from the way I treated you or Stephan,' Jonathan said. 'There was much more to it than that of course. When it happened, I mean. Your mother and I, well, we went through a bad phase. Your mother went through a very bad patch, the year before. Anyway, to cut a very long story short and without all the ifs and wherefores, we had a brief separation, I'd met someone else and we, your mother and I, talked about getting a divorce. It was a bad time. She threw me out. I think she implied to you that I was on a long work trip abroad, or something ...'

The year before what? Eliza wondered about the words she heard, words that made up sentences that tried to convey something that was incomprehensible, and she wondered about the reliability of the words strung together to give them his account of what Ilsa was like, all those years ago, of who she was and what she had done. She couldn't help it, this scepticism. It was ingrained, the distrust of witness statements, too long after the fact. She knew that what Jonathan said was only so much of his own truth, an account of his own unreliable memory, whatever certainty he tried to bring to his tale. All she had was the DNA test which, she knew but didn't think anyone else did, could not confirm what she had suspected, but then Jonathan had confirmed that part anyway, he'd not batted an eyelid, had he, when she confronted him with her so-called findings, had only made a slightly weary wave with his left hand and had stopped himself from answering her or saying anything at all. She could see it. He was determined not to irritate her or his other children, he wanted the air cleared and move on. Callous, she thought. How can he be so callous? Why didn't he show any emotion, why didn't he grieve for Ilsa? The way she and Mark and of course Stephan grieved? After all, she was, had been, his wife, their mother? She had separated from their father and must have fallen in love with another man, got pregnant by him. And then what? Why couldn't she remember any of it? Surely she should remember, Mark should remember? Why had it never come up in their conversation? They must have had a sense that something was wrong, that their parents were quarrelling, even as children. Why had they never brought it up? She looked over at Mark who was fixed on the kitchen window somehow, half turned away from them, a grim look on his face.

The enormity of it all began to sink in. Sometimes, these last few weeks, she would wake up in the middle of the night, barely able to breathe, as if all foundations had been knocked from underneath her. She hadn't felt this bad when her mother had died, when they'd cremated her, and it was only when she'd realised what she'd found out about Anthony that she'd collapsed, and cried every evening for days on end, with Gerry trying to soothe her, the children at a loss about what to do or how to behave, uneasy. Gerry had packed them off to his parents and it was only when her boss told her that he might have to take her off the case she was working on if she didn't pull herself together, he wasn't callous but he'd simply tried to pull her out of the useless torpor that, as sudden as she'd collapsed, the tears had gone, the helplessness had gone, she'd focussed on the case of the murdered woman, on the evidence and what that told her and her colleagues about the perpetrator. It had been a relief, to be so completely absorbed once more by the investigation. The trial would be soon.

'I'll take care of your mother's letters,' Jonathan said. 'They are personal, private. I expect I know what they are. They need to be destroyed, and I'm not sure you'd do that …'

'Dad!' Mark interjected.

Eliza ignored what he said, 'who was that man at the cremation? The man who sat towards the side, as if he didn't want to be seen, not really. He looked quite smart. Was it someone you invited?' she looked straight at her father, daring him. 'He came up to me briefly but I was distracted, thought he was a colleague or someone she'd worked with before. He left almost immediately afterwards.'

'I don't think I noticed,' Jonathan said. 'I'm not sure who you're talking about. There were so many people and I didn't know all of them. Some were colleagues of your mother's, people I didn't really know, very well.'

Unlike Ilsa, Jonathan had never bothered much with the people who lived in the village. He'd moved to Norfolk because he liked the house, the seclusion, and the opportunity of living in a large property with a garden away from the pressure of London. In his heart he was still a London man, however, and he had his own small flat there, where he would stay when his work demanded it, very often staying away for weeks on end. In contrast, Ilsa had become the 'local,' someone who was well known and liked because of her job at the exclusive girls' school in the nearby town.

Only Stephan and Anthony, still attending sixth form colleges, had had their own rooms in this sprawling house with its six large upstairs rooms and an office built as an extension at the back as well as a small downstairs study. Anthony's room had long ago been converted into a kind of library space, soon after he'd moved out.

The house was far too large, Eliza thought. The two of them must have been rattling around in it like peas in a pod but perhaps it had been ideal if you didn't really want to see too much of each other anyway.

The rooms were being emptied out now and already the house had taken on a look of abandonment, it had stopped being a family home, Eliza had said when Mark asked where he would sleep. 'We're staying in the hotel, Gerry and I,' she said. 'There's no point creating more work for Dad, or rather for his cleaner. I don't think he actually does anything around the house, never has.'

'You disapprove?' Mark raised his eyebrows and smirked. 'Come on Eliza, why should he? I'll find a room; there must still be beds in some of them. The removal van won't come until next week, according to Dad.'

And now they sat at the large kitchen table, just the three of them. The dining room furniture had been stacked up, moved to a corner, and during this final weekend together they wanted to resolve whether to keep any of the pieces of furniture or ornaments that had belonged to Ilsa or whether Jonathan should either store some or simply sell or discard. He didn't particularly want to keep a lot, he'd said. He and Alea had bought a house in Beaconsfield and they were going to furnish it with some of their existing pieces, Alea's as well as his, and with new.

'Where's Alea?' Eliza asked. 'Aren't you going to introduce her to Mark?' She turned to Mark, 'I met her of course when I came over to sort the notebooks.'

'She'll be coming a bit later,' Jonathan said. 'She's arranged to see someone and couldn't cancel. Oh, here she is. That's her car.'

Jonathan got up and walked to the hall at the side of the kitchen and opened the door. A breeze came through and Eliza shivered for a moment. They heard muffled voices and then Alea walked in followed by Jonathan. She was the woman seen at their mother's cremation, then as now elegantly dressed, the woman who had whispered something in their father's ear and who had then disappeared. She was very attractive with nearly white grey shiny hair, that had been cut short and sharp, and she looked distinguished in a well fitting motley grey suit with a perfectly ironed white shirt and wearing high-heeled black shoes. As if she'd just come out of a board meeting, even though it was Saturday. Eliza wondered where Alea had been, and at the same time felt the anger again, the helpless fury at a hurt that somehow connected with her mother. Who was this woman? Had she been the cause of all of Ilsa's unhappiness? Had her father had an affair with this woman when her mother was still alive? Was that why they'd been quarrelling? And if that was the case, how dare she be here and pretend to them that she and Jonathan were just an ordinary couple talking to Jonathan's children?

'It's lovely to see you again,' Alea said to Eliza and kissed her on the cheek. 'And of course, it's lovely to meet you as well

Mark.' Mark stood and awkwardly held out his hand, rather than offering his cheek.

'Am I too late for dinner? I'm sorry I was held up. I'll just go and change into something more comfortable.' Alea kicked off her shoes and took from Jonathan a small weekend bag that he brought in from her car and disappeared with it out of the kitchen and up the stairs.

Later, after Alea had returned and joined them at the table, their conversation meandered somewhat; they talked about living in London, in the north of England, and in Germany and about Stephan living in Singapore, how they'd all dispersed. Alea talked about some books she'd read recently and authors she admired, Boyd, Maggie O'Farrell, Colm Toibin, but it was clear that neither Mark nor Jonathan had read any of them and Eliza politely agreed or disagreed with her views. Then Gerry came in and soon after Eliza and Gerry left and Mark went up to his room, called Samantha and said, 'my family is just fucked up. You have no idea.'

*

How did you deal with loss and then with secrets and past histories of your parents that were unravelling in such a callous and horrible way? All Eliza wanted was to get on with her own life and wished she could close the Pandora box she'd so eagerly opened. How stupid had she been, why was she so keen to absolve her mother, because that's how it felt, but to absolve her from what? Ilsa had hardly committed a crime, had she, even if she'd had a secret love affair and even if that meant she couldn't have been as blameless in the deteriorating marriage that she, Eliza, now suspected? Why would she try to resolve something that was clearly now irresolvable? And why would she let her parents' past and their family history take over her life now? Gerry was becoming impatient with her, she could tell, he said she was obsessed and it would only make things worse. They'd have to get on with their own lives, he said. She was not her mother and couldn't live their lives, and it was too late now to try and resolve her mother's life for her. 'As far as I'm aware, you never bothered about your family that much before, you always said you weren't that interested,' he said. He added that she'd been much more preoccupied with her own life, with her work, her friends, with her expectations and when these fell through, for example when she discovered that Tom had been cheating on her, she'd been totally absorbed with her own miseries and difficulties. He was right, of course.

Once Gerry had entered her life, it was only on very rare occasions, that she'd confided in Ilsa. At first when she moved in with Tom, Ilsa had always been available when Eliza rang or on rare occasions would drop in. She had drifted away though and had felt less in need of her mother's company, had been too preoccupied with her own day to day life in London, with starting a career, with Tom. Moreover her mother had a very busy life herself, and in addition had become more and more concerned about Anthony.

Shouldn't she just remember and cherish her memories of Ilsa as the loving and caring mum of her childhood and teenage years, and get on with her own life now, as Gerry urged her to do? What would Ilsa have wanted her to do? Had Ilsa been in a bad place when she died? That was the hurtful thing, really. To think that her mother had been unhappy at the time she died, that she'd been in the middle of something that now would never get resolved and that no one had been there for her. Wasn't it therefore up to her, Eliza, now that she was aware of that, to resolve it for her, to rescue her somehow, if only to let her rest in peace? But how could she do that. This really was an idiotic notion. The darkness around her made her feel claustrophobic and the brain whirling around inside her skull, went into overdrive. She was sleepless now.

She got up from the bed, careful not to disturb Gerry who was fast asleep, having pulled most of the duvet to his side of the bed and clenching it tight under his chin as if it would try to escape and fall off if he let go. He was breathing heavily, groaned and then lay still again. She tiptoed to the ensuite bathroom. The hotel room was only small and she nearly fell over a pair of shoes, Gerry's, suppressed an 'ouch, what the …' then rebalanced and carefully opened the bathroom door and shut it behind her. She flipped the light switch next to the door and her face stared back at her from the mirror above the whiteness of the sink, she looked pale, her hair unkempt, blue rings under her eyes. She grimaced at the image in the mirror, took a deep breath and leaned over to drink some water straight from the tap, although there should be some bottled on the side of the bed, but she didn't want to try and find it in the semi-darkness of the room, where standby lights of TV and a greenish tinge of the smoke alarm made sure it was never completely dark, even though the curtains were shut tight. Her mouth was dry even after she'd rinsed some more and spat the water back out; she shouldn't have had that third glass of wine. The taste in her mouth was awful and she wondered about her breath. She picked up the mouthwash and rinsed, spitting out the green bubbles that slowly drained down into the waste pipe.

The previous night, Alea had come down in some loose fitting trousers and a casual shirt that she wore over her trousers, with flat sandals on her bare feet, in a perfect get up as if she was about to go out again, instead of dressing down for the night. Her toenails were purple, the same colour as the varnish on her fingernails, and she wore a single gold bracelet

138

and a gold chain round her neck. She brought in a whiff of something fresh and expensive.

Eliza couldn't help but feel slightly intimidated by this woman who looked so immaculately groomed and self-confident, unlike Ilsa who would always have something of the harassed working woman, hair that needed combing, or a jumper that was too casual to be called smart. In contrast, Alea exuded a self-confidence and charm as if nothing could ever upset her or stop her from taking what was rightfully hers. She owned the world and its inhabitants, Eliza suspected, which included her father. She had carefully pushed back her hair, and smiled at them all before she sat down next to Jonathan.

'Looks deceive,' Gerry said later. 'I bet she has huge hang-ups. Don't trust that perfect façade.'

Perhaps he'd simply said that to ward off her, Eliza's demons, knowing her, aware that she had been badly impressed.

She turned off the bathroom light and went back to bed, curled up behind Gerry, pulled some of the duvet cover away from him and pushed it round her back, and eventually fell asleep again, Gerry's warmth and safety comforting her.

*

They got up early, went down for breakfast and then Eliza left Gerry at the table with his laptop and papers, already engrossed in some kind of conversation that involved a lot of humming and hawing on the phone. She walked the short distance between the hotel and her father's house, the house that wasn't her home really, never had been, where she'd only come to stay the odd weekend or a short holiday, always sleeping in one of the rooms that had a medley of her childhood possessions and those of Mark's and that had all but become a guest room. She walked around the outside of the quiet house and let herself in through the backdoor, which was unlocked.

A strong smell of coffee greeted her and Jonathan pulled out another cup from the cupboard as a welcome 'I suppose you'd want one too?' He looked sleepy and unkempt, wearing an old grey cottony dressing gown that barely reached his knees and his hairy legs stood in a pair of blue tattered slippers. 'You're up early,' he said. 'Want some coffee? Had breakfast yet?'

'Thanks Dad.' She took a cup of black coffee and held her hand over it when Jonathan tried to pour milk from a green top bottle that he took from the fridge. 'No milk, black first thing in the morning,' she said. 'Only had a small tea with breakfast.' Had he already forgotten that she always drank black coffee? Or perhaps he'd simply never taken much notice.

'I'm going to take up some for Alea,' he said, preparing a tray with coffee and toast, putting butter in a small glass jar, and a dollop of marmalade on the plate. 'Help yourself if you want breakfast, I'm going to shower first.'

'Dad,' she said to his back. 'We didn't talk last night. Not after Alea came in … What do you want me to do with mum's papers?'

'I've left a shredder in the room,' he said. 'The alternative is to burn them in the garden, but perhaps better not, it's windy, and I don't want to burn the place down.' He laughed, it sounded forced. 'I've already emptied the drawers with her financial stuff, accounts, letters, etc. I'll also take her computer and will clean it. Don't worry about that. I expect there will be photo's and once I've cleaned it you can have it.'

'So, all that's left are her work papers. What about her books? Are you taking them?'

'You take whatever you want, books, CDs and DVDs. You can also take her small telly; Gerry's kids might like it. It's quite new. She hardly ever used it. The same with her clothes. Can you go through them, keep whatever you want to keep and pack the rest in boxes for charity? There are stacks of boxes in the garage. The removal people left them for us for personal stuff. They'll come and pack whatever is left over at the end of the week.'

Still, he didn't mention the one thing she wanted to talk to him about, and then she didn't have the courage to mention it. It was there, hanging between them, Anthony's shadow wrapped in hurt and bad feelings.

'What happened to Anthony?' she blurted it out despite herself. 'What happened between you and Anthony? What was it with mum and Anthony and you?'

'We'll talk about it later,' he said. 'I'm going to take up this breakfast now.'

Tonight there will be Alea again, she wanted to say, and I don't want to talk about mum with Alea. I don't know her.

'Alea will go out to see her sister, this afternoon I think. She'll have dinner with her, won't be back till late,' he said, as if reading her thoughts. 'Mark will help me with tidying out the garden sheds and the garage. He said he might want to borrow or have some of the tools. I've got far too much stuff and won't be able to store it all, besides I'm not inclined to even hang up my own paintings anymore, we'll use a firm to help us. Mark and Samantha want to buy a house in Germany and Samantha wants a garden. I gather that in Germany men especially are expected to be wizards in DIY – that'll be a challenge for Mark.' He laughed. 'Always had two left hands, as far as using a drill and other tools are concerned.' He carefully balanced the tray on one arm, opened the kitchen door and went through. She heard him whistle as he went up the stairs. She balled her fists, took in a deep breath and slowly exhaled. She should have done some of her yoga exercises that morning. She counted, inhaled deeply and then exhaled in three short puffs. Sod them all.

*

Eliza picked up her cup of coffee and followed her father up the stairs, went into Ilsa's room and quietly closed the door behind her.

Halfway through the morning Mark came in. Eliza was sitting on the low coffee table with a pile of papers next to her, going through files and papers clipped together in some kind of order. It was amazing how much stuff her mother had stacked away in this room, which was really quite large. There were two deep wall cupboards with shelves and there were boxes neatly labelled, containing the research she'd done for her dissertation, there were boxes of photographs, boxes with lesson material for different years and going back over a couple of years. Had she never thrown anything out? Why had she kept all that stuff? Her whole life could be arranged using these boxes and the dates. Her desk drawers were all empty and these must have contained the financial stuff her father talked about, but the work room furniture Ilsa had bought for this room contained extended units that were arranged underneath the large windows of the west wall with a large central heating unit underneath the north facing windows, where you looked out over the side of he house. It was a lovely room, even though it was now in a disorganised state with papers strewn over the floor, cupboard doors that stood open and boxes on chairs and on the floor. The blinds were drawn back and so were the creamy curtains, pulled back as if a skirt tied at the waste. Rays of sunlight showed up the dust whirling around and she opened one of the windows, slightly, to let in some air. It was early May and she heard the birds busying themselves in the garden below and in the trees around the garden. Jonathan

142

must have hired a gardener, as the grass had recently been mown and the flowerbeds looked tended even if she could not see much in the way of new shrubs or flower arrangements or plants. That had always been Ilsa's job. She'd loved pottering around in that garden, had redesigned the back garden and spent a lot of time and money in nurseries around Norfolk. Jonathan had never been that interested, just wanted to sit out there with a glass of wine. Eliza wasn't sure if he even trimmed some of the hedges himself or if someone came in to do all the hard work for them. Ilsa wouldn't have been able to do all that as she'd had her job, even if it had only been part-time. She'd never committed to full-time, not even after Stephan had left and there were no longer children to look after. 'Too old now,' she'd said, 'to commit myself to full-time work when there is so much to do here. I want to keep up the garden myself, and I want enough time to sit in it with a book without being disturbed.'

And of course, there had been no need for her to work, really. Jonathan earned plenty, and moreover she and Marja had inherited a tidy sum from her father when he'd died. He'd been quite well off it seemed, although you couldn't tell from the way they'd lived, her grandparents. Eliza only vaguely remembered the rather cramped house, the heavy furniture that had never been replaced with something more modern, something new, the frugal, if healthy meals they ate, her grandmother who could neither drive a car nor invested in other luxuries, except that towards the end of their lives they'd gone on a couple of cruises and she'd been completely overawed by the luxury of it.

When you thought about it, it was hardly surprising that Ilsa had been a bit strange sometimes, the way she was brought up. And then she'd got pregnant and she'd married Dad and Mark had been born when she was only just twenty-one.

As if he knew she was thinking about him, Mark walked into the room. 'Still at it?' he asked. 'It's nearly lunchtime; I think we should go out to that nice little restaurant in the village. They do Italian I think.'

'You know that Mum was only twenty-one when she married Dad,' Eliza said. 'And she left university because she was pregnant with you. Why didn't she just finish her degree at the time?'

'You mean why didn't she get an abortion,' Mark said. 'Well, they must have been in love, Mum and Dad, otherwise they wouldn't have got married. Would they? And if they hadn't been and Mum had got an abortion then I wouldn't be here talking to you. Not a very nice thought actually.'

'She was always against abortions,' Eliza said. 'She didn't believe in it. Some kind of Catholic thing, the sanctity of life, even though she wasn't a Catholic at all. It must have been her parents, grandpa especially. He wouldn't have condoned it, I'm sure, and Mum, I think she was always a bit afraid of him. I'm sure that when they found out that Mum was pregnant, Dad was told he had to do the right thing by her. That was the way it was with them, despite the fact that the world had just witnessed the roaring sixties and the so-called sexual revolution. They were never part of that.' She stopped, then said as an afterthought, 'I'm sure.'

'Well, no use trying to figure that one out now. She never talked about it.' Mark said. 'She must have wanted children because she had you not long after me. Then there's that gap before Anthony was born. A good five years. That seems a long time, as if they changed their mind about having only two children. She must have wanted more.'

'Well, yes. Unless something else happened, which it clearly did. Dad says he'll talk some more about all that tonight. I feel like a child. I'm not even sure that I want to know any more. I just want to remember Mum and perhaps we should just get on with our lives, don't you think?' She shoved some of the papers into the shredder and the noise of the machine drowned out the bird songs that had come in from outside.

Mark didn't answer, didn't say 'well, why didn't you think of that before?' As she would have in his place, surely, but turned away and said before leaving the room, 'I'll call the restaurant and tell them we'll be there in half an hour. Ok?'

Eliza nodded at Mark's back, picked up another pile from the floor and continued to feed lesson plans and notes in her mother's illegible handwriting into the hungry shredder. She grabbed a pile of letters in envelopes. Her father must have missed these and without glancing at addresses or stamps, she continued with her destruction of what just a week ago she would have checked for more information or clues. Mark had been right, and Stephan. They were both angry with her. Neither was her father pleased when she told him what she'd suspected. 'Why don't you want to remember the good things?' he'd said. 'It's all history now, water under the bridge.' And they were right, of course they were. She needed to get on with her own life, her own family, just as Mark was and just as Stephan did, the old family was dead, history.

*

The restaurant owner had reserved a large round table for them near the window and Eliza watched the deserted road outside. Cars stood parked along the road. Coming up, she'd noticed a few of the shop fronts boarded up with to let signs on long poles next to them but here business was brisk despite the recession.

They had come in two cars, Jonathan with Mark and Alea whilst Gerry and Eliza drove up in their own car even though their hotel was only just up the road. Eliza said she was too exhausted to walk and besides she hated walking in the rain. She didn't want to drink anyway, and would drive. Alea, it seemed, was not going out after all, and Eliza couldn't help but raise her eyebrows.

'The elephant in the room,' Jonathan said, when they were seated and the waiter had taken their orders. 'It's a pity Stephan isn't here as well. I'll talk to him and I'm sure you will too.'

Eliza made as if to say something but Jonathan stopped her. 'Just let me talk, and then you can say what you have to say. Alea knows about everything I'm going to say, and I hope you don't mind she has come too. She's part of my life, has been for a long time. We're all grown ups.'

Eliza swallowed.

Mark nodded, 'of course.'

'Your mother and I went through a bad patch, around 1977. Well, a lot of marriages do, but it helps to explain perhaps what happened. Even though I didn't know it at the time. It all came out of the wash pretty soon.' He looked at Alea, who, Eliza noticed, put her hand on his knee as if to encourage him. She smiled at him, then drank some water before picking up her glass of wine, which she held as if mesmerised by the colour, or perhaps by the glass, whatever it was because she stared at it intensely before she took a careful sip, savouring the taste and clearly enjoying it.

'Eliza here found a notebook of your mother's in which someone called Hans is mentioned. Hans was the father of Anthony, I'm not Anthony's father and so he was your half brother, rather than a full sibling. But we'd already established that.'

Mark stared at him. 'Did Anthony know? Did you know all along?'

'I really don't understand. Why did you never say anything about this?' Eliza asked. 'Did you not know at first?' She said it as if the possibility had only just dawned on her. She looked at Jonathan, and repeated, 'You didn't know?'

Jonathan shook his head. 'I didn't know straight away, however, your mother confessed to having had an affair. It was only after we got back together, well, a long story, however we decided that we didn't want to break up the family. I moved back in after a brief break up and Alea ...' He looked at Alea and she nodded. 'Alea was still married and at the time we thought ...' he hesitated, then continued, 'Well, anyway, both of us decided for our own reasons that we wanted to go back to our respective partners. So your mother and I agreed that we wanted to have another go. You were small and despite our earlier disagreements we wanted you to have both your parents around. And yes, she told me about her affair with Hans but also said that it was finished and that Hans had gone back to his own country, The Netherlands I think. So we made a pact, got back together, even though I knew that the child she was pregnant with might not be mine. It was kind of hard, but then I was not squeaky clean myself and in a way was just as much to blame as she was, if you want to talk about blame. Just unfortunate that she clearly hadn't taken her precautions.' He smiled a crooked smile. 'Both Alea and Hans were out of our pictures for a while. I've always loved Anthony in the same way I loved the two of you, and later Stephan. It's complicated. It wasn't until just before Anthony went to University that it came all out in the wash, and we told him. It seemed like a good time, and honest of course, only he took it really badly and your mother and I had started to drift apart again, we couldn't make it work, never had, really …'

The waiters came round with the food, asked if everything was as they wanted it, did they want more wine or other drinks? Eliza realised that she was desperate for a glass of wine, despite her earlier insistence that she wouldn't drink and asked Gerry to pour her some, held out her empty glass. 'Just the one,' she said.

The enormity of what her father was telling them, confirming her suspicion, started to sink in. They hadn't been the perfect couple, the parents who had stuck it out together, unlike so many others, the fathers and the mothers of friends, who had divorced, who no longer lived together, but where children had been ferried from one to the other, just like Gerry's children, although they had been looked after by their grandparents most of the time. She suddenly felt a pang of guilt about what she was doing here; really she should help Gerry make sure that they were happy, that they had a good childhood that would nurture them for the rest of their lives.

Mark shook his head as if to deny what Jonathan was telling them. 'So you find out that one of your children isn't yours, yet you stay together. Why? She had cheated on you and I just cannot imagine that you'd just turn round and say, oh well, that's ok, I'll just pretend he's mine.'

Jonathan shook his head. 'I don't think your mother was really hundred per cent sure herself at the time, when she found out she was pregnant, although she suspected. Hans was married and was only in England for a six month sabbatical. His wife and children were back in Holland, he went over for odd weekends. But Ilsa and I, well we decided for our own reasons to have another go at our marriage, we wanted it to work. And then Anthony was born.'

'And then he was killed,' Eliza said.

'Yes, Anthony died. I think that for some reason or other your mother ended up blaming me for that. I think that was because I said she should tell Anthony that I wasn't his father. And of course Anthony went off the rails after that. I think she felt we shouldn't have told him, or that we should have gone about it differently, but I ...'

'What!' Eliza and Mark said at the same time.

Eliza stopped put her knife and fork down, unable to swallow the food. She wanted to get up and leave. She didn't really want to know any more of this. Why had she insisted on trying to find out the so-called truth? What was all this? Her mother couldn't give her side of the story, could she? She'd been very unhappy these last few years, and she, Eliza, always imagined that this was because she suspected that Jonathan had an affair. How ridiculous it all was, and how sad and painful and, yes, shabby. She hated them, for a second, their sordid affairs and lying existence, their make-believe happy family, all of it, she hated it.

She looked at Gerry who pulled up his shoulders, slightly, as if to say, 'look, don't ask me.' He picked up the second bottle of wine that the waiter had put ready on the table and started to fill up everyone's glass again. Eliza covered her glass with her hand. She didn't want more wine, she didn't want anything apart from getting up from the table and walk out, drive back to their home in the north of England and forget all about it, wrap it back up in the past and pretend she didn't know any of this. It was time to start thinking about her own life, pick up the threads, and make the most of what she had with Gerry and his children. This was sordid, surely.

'I'm not sure that I want to know anymore,' Mark said. 'You don't owe us an explanation, or a justification of what you do or how you live, or how you and Mum lived.'

Jonathan grimaced. 'I know I don't, have to explain, I mean. However, you are my children and you asked me. I don't want to create a rift over something that is well in the past now, and that has no bearing any longer.'

He meant that they were dead now, Eliza thought. Neither Ilsa nor Anthony would be able to give their account, to express their feelings and hurts and perhaps misunderstanding. But surely, they were owed respect, dignity, even forgiveness? Her face felt large and hollow. She forced herself to take a deep breath, forced herself to count to three before saying anything, before responding.

'Have you got any more of Mum's diaries?' she asked. 'Have you destroyed them? Was there anything in there you didn't want to come out?'

Jonathan shook his head. 'I've destroyed all her personal letters and papers, I told you that. There is no need to go over them. Besides, I don't think she would have wanted them to be read by us, not by me nor by you. She would have destroyed all of her personal effects if she'd had inkling of what was about to happen to her. I know her that well; for her sake, for your mother's sake, let it all rest.' He put both is hands flat on the table and looked at her. Was he angry now? Of course he was.

'But don't you get it? I'd like to know why Mum was so unhappy, what were her reasons?'

'Sometimes it's better not to try to rake up everything, but to hold onto what you've got,' Jonathan said. 'You loved your mum. She loved you, all of you. After you left home, she threw herself into her work and she liked her job. She made friends here in the village. That's why she wanted to go on living here. She was finding her own way. Leave her in peace.'

'Only, she didn't have a marriage worth holding onto,' Eliza said. 'Sorry Dad, I've got a splitting headache; I'd like to go. We'll be leaving early tomorrow morning. I've sorted out most of Mum's stuff, I'm sure you can manage now.'

There it was again, for the love of her mother, for the love of Ilsa, just forget about her past. She wouldn't though, even though she wanted to. She got up, grabbed her coat from the rack in the entrance hall on the way out and waited outside for Gerry to follow her. 'We're going home,' she said. 'I've done everything I could here. I can't bear to be here any longer.' Suddenly she felt the tears come through, her face exploding and she howled. Gerry bundled her in the car and they drove up the road, into the hotel grounds, where he parked and wrapped his arms around her so she could cry all the tears she had been suppressing for so long now.

Eleven: What to Do?

The mid-May Saturday was a warm day, unusually so for the time of the year. Eliza had found some of her t-shirts and a light pair of cotton trousers at the back of her cupboard but wondered whether she should go up into the large attic to retrieve some of her summer clothes that had been stored there temporarily the previous autumn when they'd had some of the bedrooms painted. She wasn't in the mood to do any of this though.

Timmy and Joss burst into the kitchen, where she stood staring out of the window, looking without seeing. 'Will Dad come with us?' Timmy asked. 'We need to go soon. You're not coming?'

She turned round. 'Yes, your Dad is and no, I'm not coming' she said. They'd relied too much on his parents these last months, to drive them here there and everywhere and it was time they pulled themselves together, even though despite her good intentions she simply wanted to walk out, like their mother had done, and then couldn't help but feel ashamed. She hadn't been a good substitute mother, especially not these last months, she hadn't been a good partner, she hadn't been any good at anything really, even her work had not been much to be proud of. She'd gone in every morning and came back in the evening, picked up the boys from their grandparents if Gerry hadn't already done so and sometimes she'd cook a meal, at other times she'd picked up something from the take away.

Most of the time she'd relied on Julie, Gerry's mother. After her father's confession, if that's what you could call it, she just wanted to be left alone. Ilsa's death had shaken her, but what she'd learned about her parents made her feel as if she'd been cut open and left to fester.

'Come on, boys. Time to go.' Gerry, as if on call, came into the kitchen. He wore his quilted jacket over a long-sleeved sweatshirt and he looked massive, his hair still wet from the shower.

That's too hot, she wanted to say, but didn't.

'We'll have some fish and chips somewhere, or perhaps pizza, hey boys?' Gerry said. 'Don't worry about food. What are you going to do today?'

She hated cricket, hated the long boredom of it, they knew, so they hadn't even suggested that she should come and so it was agreed that she would have time to herself, go shopping, sit and read, perhaps do some gardening now that the weather improved, even though most of the time she hadn't a clue whether she was pulling weeds or emerging new plants and flowers, and it was better left to a gardener.

She really wished Ilsa was at the end of the telephone, wanted to talk to her to sort out the mess in her head and wished she'd been more in touch when she could have. Her stomach contracted and blood rushed to her face as the unease rose within her as if she was going to be sick. Had she been guilty of neglect? But then, her mother had hardly been inviting, she had pushed them, rather than pulled them, had created a distance, had clearly not want to engage in any conversation that could merit the label confidences. Nevertheless, the regret ate away at her, would not let her be and when she felt like this she couldn't find her way back into her own life and the life of the people she lived with, Gerry, his sons, her own family now, surely.

'I'll sort out some of the summer clothes,' she said. 'Mine are in the attic and I think some of yours are too. I'll check.'

After a few years with him, she still wasn't quite used to Gerry's habits and what he did with his possessions, whether they were his clothes, or tools in the garage or books and laptops and speakers and music in his study. She'd never considered it important to reorganise or to come to grips with his methodical and organised existence. She went to work during the week, someone came in to do the cleaning under Julie's supervision and when it was all done Julie would lock up again, and she sometimes left a meal she'd cooked while the house was being cleaned. Eliza had maintained her aloofness from the day she'd moved in with Gerry and the boys, not wishing to upset any of their established routines, not wishing to intrude and at the same time wanting to keep a semblance of her own private life, so she simply tried to click into an allotted place within their menagerie, as she liked to think of it. His mother Julie, who had never worked and who loved her son and other two children—a brother and a sister whom Eliza had only met once or twice—to bits and she would probably like nothing better than once more look after him; she had continued to 'take an interest' as Eliza once put it to Gerry, without rancour, more relieved than annoyed. Yet Julie had also gracefully retreated once Eliza had moved in, both of them trying their best not to interfere or intrude on the other one's assumed territory, so that it had been only much later that Eliza had realised how much Julie had done and still did for Gerry, for her two grandchildren. For Eliza it had been a happy arrangement, the last thing she wanted was to become a housebound mother and wife. She loved Gerry, loved his cheerful indifference to what other people were up to, loved his casual aloofness, which only much later she realised, was probably a long established character trait, very much encouraged by his mother's lifelong concern about her son's wellbeing. But then, as far as she knew most men were slightly off the spectrum, whether or not they had doting mothers. Eliza had wondered if this capacity of his, for total aloofness and becoming self absorbed in whatever he was doing, had been the reason for the disappearance of his first wife who presumably had been unable to cope with what sometimes might appear as callous indifference. Eliza didn't think it was callousness but rather it had to do with Gerry's unawareness of other people's expectations, a certain lack of empathy. In a way she herself was not that different, was she? She hadn't really wanted anyone's empathy, not from her mother, not when she broke up with Tom. What she had needed then had been shelter; somewhere she could be safe, somewhere or someone that wouldn't reject her. It was unclear to her even now why she'd felt so much in need of being somewhere safe, somewhere that would fill in the outlines of her existence, almost as if she still longed to be back home, a child, that was taken care of.

Eliza heard the front door slam shut and then the car rev up and Gerry and the boys were gone. She looked around her, decided to find a warm jacket and sit outside with a coffee, let the late spring sun warm her face in a sheltered spot, inhale the smell of grass, of trees and shrubs and earth that were waking up from their winter slumber. Later she would do some weeding and perhaps prepare one of the beds at the back for summer plants. She couldn't really be bothered with finding summer clothes.

Her telephone rang, loud and insistent, Maggie's number blinking at her from the screen, and she briefly wondered whether to just ignore it but then picked it up.

'Are you a cricket widow today?' Maggie's voice was full of laughter. 'I'm also off duty today. Do you fancy coming for a bit of shopping with me? I need some therapy. It's been a hell of a week at work.'

Maggie was a work colleague who had become a good friend. She had two children and worked part time in the small forensic laboratory where Eliza worked full-time. Her husband was a local GP and their son who was the same age as Jos, was also a keen cricket player and they played in the same team. Maggie and her husband took it in turns to take the boy and his sister to wherever they needed to be on Saturdays, trailing from cricket ground to tennis courts and back again. Why did children have so many extracurricular activities these days? Or was it the parents who tried to make sure that they'd not deprive their children of anything even through they both worked, or perhaps because they both worked?

'We could have a game of tennis?' Maggie's voice again, ticking off in rapid succession the various possibilities and activities they could engage in, now that husbands and children were safely out of the way and they both needed some relief from work and familial existences. Maggie never understood why someone might want to sit at home alone when there were so many things to do, when you had a rare moment of freedom. 'There's also a new exhibition at the gallery,' she said.

Eliza laughed. Maggie was good for her. Drew her out, knew when to be just cheerful and not ask any questions.

'Let's go for the retail therapy,' she said. 'We could have a coffee somewhere on a terrace, the weather is that good. I'm not feeling very energetic today.'

They met at the entrance to the shopping centre and headed straight for Bertrand's coffee place, already filling up with customers, and found a free table outside. Despite the sun it was chilly here, with a slight breeze coming round the corner, flapping the awnings that the owner had pulled down as a windbreaker. A girl came and took their orders, cappuccinos and 'a toasted tea cake,' Maggie added. 'I haven't had breakfast yet, what about you?'

They settled their orders and waited for the coffees to come, chitchatting about children, work and plans for the summer holidays.

'So, what's still bugging you so badly?' Maggie asked once they were settled. 'I know, I shouldn't ask. But it's so bloody obvious that you're not a happy bunny, ever since your mother died. Understandable of course, but it's more than that, isn't it? Something is biting you.'

It was six months since the funeral, and only a couple of weeks since Jonathan had moved; to Eliza it seemed that in the space of that six months her whole life had changed beyond recognition, as if she had transformed into a different and alien person, as if nothing from the past person she'd been would ever make much sense again. She ached for the clean memory of her mother, unsullied, unquestioned, and wished she hadn't been so self righteous and read the notebooks, pretended to have done those tests, wished that Jonathan had kept his secret to himself.

'What would you do if you found out that your parents are not at all the people you always thought they were? What would you do if you found out something that skews your memory, as if everything you've always known has suddenly become false and untrue, so that you no longer trust what you know about your own life and childhood?'

'Waaw,' Maggie said. 'You are having problems! What has brought all this about? Why wouldn't your mother be the person you remember? Even if she hadn't told you everything that went on in her life, that doesn't mean that she wasn't the person you loved and that doesn't mean that she can't be trusted.'

'It's all so fucked up,' Eliza sighed, picked up her coffee and sipped into the milky froth of her cappuccino, which left chocolate marks on her upper lip. She rubbed it away with the flat of her hand after putting down the cup. Maggie waited.

'You never knew Anthony of course, my brother who died some years ago now. I told you about him, he died in a car crash. Well, that wasn't the whole story apparently. They had a bust-up, my parents and Anthony, or rather, he created a bust-up and refused to ever see them again, did some awful things as part of his drug taking, and then went completely clean and married some religious girl, fanatically religious I should add, whose family apparently didn't want to know about any of us heathens. Well, it turns out that although Anthony was my mother's son he wasn't my father's. I'm not even sure if my mother introduced him as a cuckoo into the nest knowingly or if my father knew all along. He implies he only realised later, but that they agreed to not mention it. Can you imagine that? What a weird relationship! The thing is, it was never talked about, we children just didn't know any better than that we were a happy family of four siblings with a father and a mother who, although perhaps not exactly doting on each other, had a good and solid relationship, unquestionable. That is, that was the case until Anthony created, first by taking drugs and then by walking out, marrying into some kind of obscure fanatically religious tribe and then goes on to die in a stupid accident, that was really totally absurd, a deer on the road, of all things. After that, I think it was all downhill as far as the relationship between my parents was concerned, you could see them grow apart, something had upset them about Anthony's death that only they knew about. At the time I thought it was because they blamed each other for not having prevented that marriage, for not having prevented him from first becoming a druggy and then flipping over to the other side and become a fanatic religious person who wants nothing do to with them, with us. Now we know what the cause of all that was, he found out, didn't he, and he felt betrayed. Must have. I've always missed Anthony badly, we all have. My younger brother doted on him. It was a very hard time, but then, we had started living our own lives, away from home, we had begun to grow apart anyway. We all dealt with Anthony in our own different ways.'

Eliza stopped, took another swig of her coffee which had cooled down and rather than put the cup back on the saucer picked up the spoon and ladled it along the edges and the rim of the cup, scraping off the remainder milk froth as if her life depended on it.

Maggie cradled her cup in both hands, her head slightly to one side, listening intently to Eliza's outburst.

'You've really had a rough time,' she said. 'Don't feel bad that you're still grieving, of course you are. Your mum's death was so unexpected and no one can blame you for trying to come to terms with that. And of course your mother had a life before you were born. We don't always know what kind of persons they were, your parents. Your parents must have loved each other, they stayed together all that time, didn't they?'

'Yes, of course. What I find so difficult and hard is to rearrange my memories such that Anthony is my half brother, and my father is not Anthony's father, so my mother must have had a lover, must have been with someone who might have taken her away from Dad. Only he didn't. It's just so fucked up!'

'Isn't it better to go forward? Accept that she had a life before you all came along, and try to remember the good things about her, as you did before, try and remember her as the person who cared for you, who nursed you, who was there for you when you needed her. It won't help repaint her different from what you remember, will it? It's your memories that count, don't try and rearrange them. Your memories were good.'

They were quiet for a few minutes, then Maggie said, as if it was an afterthought that took her as much by surprise as it did Eliza, 'why don't you meet up with your brothers and talk about it all? It might help. You were always close to them, I thought. Try and talk about the good times you used to have, the good memories that you have.'

Eliza shook her head. 'Not that close, at least not any more. We've drifted apart and lead such different lives. It's as if my mother cut us adrift once we left home. My father too, for that matter. I think everything changed when Anthony cut himself off from us, his family, and that's when my parents changed. I'm still not sure when my father found out that Anthony was not his. He implied he knew all along? Did my mother tell them? My father won't say much. He's started his new life and seems almost relieved that it's all in the past now. Only, does that mean that we are also in his past and better forgotten? It makes me feel like an orphan!'

They were silent for a while. The streets became busier and there was a Saturday hum around them of couples and families and women on their own and teenage girls and the odd male shopper looking as if on the way to the dentist, then seeing the coffee shop and making a beeline for it. All the seats were taken now and the buzz around, the spring sunshine, the coatless shoppers suggested a holiday atmosphere, of life beginning anew, full of expectations and thrills.

Maggie looked around, smiled and said, 'Cheer up Eliza. Think about what you've got. A wonderful partner and lover, two fantastic step children, a well-paid job that you like, brothers who care about you, whatever you say, a father who's alive and also cares, whatever you think at the moment—he's always been good to you, hasn't he? You've got friends. Your mother did love you; you have good memories about your childhood. Cherish those memories and don't spoil them by putting a microscope over everything.' She stopped.

Eliza grimaced. 'Glass half full, eh? You're probably right, it's no good and it was stupid to dig into the past, reading those notebooks, and then do that test. I even sneaked into Dad's bathroom and pinched some hair and stole his travel toothbrush …' She laughed without mirth so that it sounded more like a moan lamenting her own stupidity. 'I need never have known. Dad need never have felt as if he was facing a jury and I can see why he refused to go into any detail. It was all too painful, had been buried long ago and I dug it all up again.'

She suddenly felt very tired. Something didn't feel right, it was as if she was hiding something, only she wasn't sure what it was that she needed to see or find.

Maggie said, 'You know that case we're working on, the dead woman in the car by the lake?'

Eliza nodded, forcing herself to listen.

'Well, it's obvious that she was killed, someone shot her in the head and we all assume it was her husband, only we need to prove that and that's why we're doing all these tests, the fingerprinting, the DNA, the blood, all of it. These investigations are to find the perpetrator and we're almost there because apart from her husband's prints there aren't any others, even though he claims that someone else came to the car and shot her, but they found her jewellery in the lake so if someone shot her for her jewellery as he claimed, then he must have decided the robbery wasn't worth it as he threw the bracelet and the rings in the water … The husband was a real fool and a bad ass and I bet it turns out that he has a lover of some kind and wanted rid of his wife.'

Eliza nodded. Of course, she was very familiar with the case, had worked on it practically every day and was the CSM in charge. What was Maggie trying to tell her? Just distracting her?

'Well, I think what I'm trying to say is that whatever your mother and your father were up to or tried to cover up, they didn't commit a crime, they didn't try to murder each other for it, neither did they divorce or have shouting matches in front of you, the children. All they did was probably make mistakes, fall in love or out of love, grew apart or whatever. At least they made a good job of keeping their marriage and their family together for the length of time you were all at home, and you had a happy childhood, you said so yourself, whatever way you look at it now.' She looked triumphant.

Eliza couldn't help but smile. 'You make it all sound so matter of fact, unemotional. That's the trouble, isn't it, we become emotional when we feel we cannot trust the people we love most. Because that is still what all this is about, whichever way you turn it. I cannot help feeling that the three of us, no the four of us, including Anthony, were fooled by the ones we trusted and that if they were able to fool us about who is and who isn't a child of theirs, so that I now have to readjust to the thought that my father isn't actually, or wasn't actually, Anthony's father, then that makes me feel very upset, for all of us but especially for Anthony. And that's because trust has been given a really bad knock on the head.'

'Well, that's what happens when parents get divorced too, to a certain extent anyway,' Maggie said. 'It took me a long while to accept my parents' divorce. I felt they'd let me down. And of course, a lot of parents stay in a bad marriage because of their children.'

'Didn't know your parents were divorced,' Eliza said. 'You've never said.'

She realised how little she knew about Maggie, outside the two of them living and working in the same town and being colleagues. They'd had a good understanding from the day they met. With Maggie she could joke about the stupidity and the loveliness of the men they were with without the other one taken it seriously and slowly they realised they were often on the same wavelength, they laughed about the same things, often reacted to news in the same way, as if they could guess the other's response before it was being given.

'Well, they were divorced. My father has now died of course. Heart attack, he was married again and my mother has meanwhile settled with her retired lover in the south of England. She brought us up single handed after my father walked out. I was fourteen. Not an easy age and I was very rebellious for a while, but my mother was like a hawk and somehow managed to keep me on the strait and narrow so that by the time I went to university I was a fully fledged monstrous girl dressed in black, with red and blue hair and piercings.' She smiled. 'I grew out of it though under my mother's distant guidance. She refused to lecture me, and that helped. And look at me now. Married to a respectable GP, two kids, a truly middle class existence.'

'Do you still see your mother regularly?'

'Oh yes, she comes to visit us here every year at Christmas and never forgets either of her grandchildren's birthdays. But then my other sister lives near her in the South and she often babysits for her. She's recently had her second baby, my sister.' She trailed, looked round for the waiter and when he asked what they wanted she ordered another two coffees.

Eliza sat back. Why had she never thought to ask or talk to Maggie about her life prior to this? She'd been so preoccupied with her own ups and downs, especially these last few months, and what was happening to her, imagining that the world would stop turning because of all her problems and upheavals, first Tom so long ago now, then the move to live with Gerry, adjusting to a family life that was new and strange to her, having previously been used to an independent and fairly selfish way of life with Tom, she had been preoccupied with the new job, meeting new colleagues and finding her way around. In between there had been the upheaval and heartbreak about Anthony, first his disappearance and then the sudden message that he had died and more recently her mother's death. She had never stopped to think about what was going on in Maggie's life, had simply poured out all her sorrows and feelings of discomfort every time they got together.

'Anyway, to get back to your parents. You just can't know everything about them. You never will. And don't forget, there are always two sides to a story, or more even. We all see things differently, and that means we will remember things differently. My mother once told me that although at the time she had felt angry and rejected by my father, she later understood that there had been fundamental clashes between them and that her own refusal to understand this difference in their characters had led to him walking out in the end. They were both to blame, if you looked for blame. But that understanding came much, much later she said and only after she was happily settled with her new partner.'

'But Anthony, he must have felt complete and utter shit when he found out, that he'd been lied to I mean. He had a right to know who his father was, didn't he?'

Maggie didn't answer but just nodded. 'Just as a matter of curiosity, what did you use to test Anthony's DNA? How did you find out that it didn't match your father's?'

Eliza shrugged, 'my mother kept tufts of hair in sealed envelopes for all of us, would you believe it. There was a box with all sorts of stuff, baby mementos, so I managed to do a low template DNA test ...' She held up her hands as if to apologise. 'I now wish I hadn't, really. It was awful when I confronted my father and had to admit I had stolen his travel tooth brush and used it to test his DNA ...'

'However,' Maggie said.

Eliza smiled. 'Of course, that hair of Anthony's was no good whatsoever as far as paternity testing goes ...'

'But that's what you told your father and the others.' Maggie said

'Yes.'

'So in reality you had no proof at all, I mean you had no definitive proof? There was really only an indication that they were not related, your father and Anthony, from general DNA testing.'

'Well, yes. But my father agreed, when I pushed him and confronted him with the diaries as well as my so-called proof, that Anthony was not his son. He assumed I'd got the evidence, scientific evidence. And he was very annoyed with me. Muttered something about letting sleeping dogs lie. In this case, leave the dead alone. But that wasn't the point, was it?'

'Well,' Maggie said, and then stopped.

'Well, what?'

'He was probably right. People are allowed to have secrets, even if they're your parents. Why stir it all up now? Why did you do it? It was his to deal with, if he wanted to.'

Eliza looked shocked. 'Wouldn't you have wanted to know? If your brother is your brother and your sister your sister, your father your father and your mother your mother? Besides, the dead no longer have a right to secrecy.'

'It wasn't about you, was it? There's no doubt about your own parentage I assume. Surely you've done those tests as you were at it?'

Eliza looked down, then defiant, sat up straight in her chair, held out her hands as if in prayer, 'wouldn't you? Want to know I mean? I really doubted all of us for a while. I didn't know what to think. Didn't know what it was about Dad that suddenly made me think there were a lot more secrets hidden behind that mask of his.'

She sat quite still, then 'Yes, I'm really his daughter and Mark and Stephan are his sons. I tested us all in the lab, one weekend when there were only a few of us around. That was after the cremation. I got samples from all of us, even from Mum, from stuff that was lying around.'

She'd filched toothbrushes and combs and taken swabs off glasses and cups, to make sure. Even Gerry hadn't realised what she'd done.

*

The train journey seemed endless, fields, barns, station platforms full with people trying to get on the train and find a seat, bags were stowed in the racks, suitcases left at the storage spaces just inside the door, too small so that people had to carry their weekend bags with them to a seat and dropped them in the aisle. Every seat on this last lap of her journey was taken.

Outside, the weather had turned sultry and warm, even though the forecast had been for rain. But this was England, you never knew and you'd better not expect one way or another.

Eliza managed to find the aisle seat she'd booked, and sat with her small satchel on her lap and her laptop balanced on top of it. That was after all the reason why she'd decided to go by train rather than take the car. She needed to finish one of her reports and although the car would have been faster and definitely more comfortable, she wouldn't have been able to think and analyse and jot down her thoughts in the way she could on the train. Besides, who said the car would have been faster? Around Birmingham there would be the usual traffic jams, which would frustrate a guaranteed speedy progress. When she arrived in Birmingham station she found that, although it had improved vastly compared to what it used to be, it was still a nightmare to find out the platform for the next leg of her journey. Not that it mattered much as she had to break up her journey anyway to hop into a taxi and go to the Forensic Science Lab for a meeting with an expert who would be able to help her with her case on the woman by the lake.

*

She returned to the station at three and caught the train to London where she changed for the train to Chichester. It was a long track, but despite this roundabout way of getting to her aunt's place, she couldn't think of a better way and it gave her the opportunity to stay the night with Aunt Marja and travel back to London the next day when she would meet with the sister of the dead woman in the car at the lake to take her DNA and confirm the family relationship. The case provided a rare opportunity to mix work with private travel, she thought.

Marja hadn't been very surprised when Eliza rang her. 'I wondered when you would get in touch,' she said. 'I wasn't sure whether to ring you or not. Is it about Anthony?'

Eliza hesitated, 'well, yes and no. I'd really like to talk about my mother. You were close, weren't you?'

'Why don't you come over?' Marja said. 'I don't think I can bear to talk about all this over the phone. It'd be better done over a meal and face to face. You used to stay with us quite regularly, as a child. So for old time's sake, just come over for a night.'

Eliza remembered the summer holidays when she would be dropped off at Marja's and 'the banker,' as they later used to call her Uncle John. Sometimes she'd be on her own, at other times Anthony would come also, or Mark, but rarely Stephan who was considered too small to be left and who usually objected violently anyway, making clear that he wanted to stay with his mother. Marja had been fun to be with, she had lots of time for them, her niece and nephews, she would take them to gawp at the cathedral, she remembered trips to the beach, a canal, and sometimes they would eat at a MacDonald's, strictly out of order as far as their parents were concerned but because of that even more attractive. How come Marja had been so available? She'd never really considered it much, just assumed that that was what aunts were for, but later realised that not every aunt would have made the time or had the energy to look after their sister's small and not so small children for a week on end.

Once, when she and Mark had been quite small, not older than six and four, before Anthony was born anyway, or perhaps it was at the time Anthony was born—she couldn't remember clearly—Mark and Eliza had been left with Marja for what seemed to her a very long time and she'd become homesick, crying at nights, she remembered that she wanted to go back home. Marja had been patient, endlessly patient even if the banker had at one point said, quite audibly, 'just take them back. Your sister can't expect us to take over from her. She got herself in this mess, didn't she?'

Marja had cuddled them, said she wanted to be like a mother for them even though Eliza knew she never could be, and had cried even louder.

Eliza wasn't sure whether she remembered all this correctly or whether someone had told her these stories, whether Marja or someone else later had instilled a memory in her, one that perhaps didn't reflect at all what had really happened. That was the trouble with memories, especially those that went back as far as early childhood, you could never be sure that you remembered correctly, it was like looking at old photographs, from the time before they were all stored digitally, from the time when only the good ones were printed and the others were discarded, where you wore your best dresses and your hair was always combed, where you looked pretty and smiled. Rarely did you find a photograph that showed you in tears or where you looked filthy because you'd messed around. That had changed of course, but you would still delete the digital photo that made you look ugly, or where your double chin showed badly, or you looked fat and had a mouth full of food.

Memories were like that, Eliza thought. You only remembered the extremes, the events that stood out, and even then they were distorted because when you asked someone else about a particular day or week they always remembered them differently from how you'd imagined them, or they mentioned something that wasn't at all part of what was the picture in your own head. Eliza wondered what Marja wanted to tell her, she'd seemed keen on meeting with her niece and she'd been reluctant to talk to Jonathan at the funeral, of that Eliza was now sure.

Marja was waiting for her outside the station and directed her to what looked like a brand new Audi. Eliza couldn't help but wonder about how well off their family still were, even though the country should be collapsing around them, according to the news. Marja gave private music lessons, violin and piano, and there was no doubt that "the banker" was drawing an enviable salary as well as income from investments. 'New?' she asked pointing at the Audi.

Marja nodded, and said, 'John's out tonight. He'll be back quite late, a meeting of some kind. We have the house to ourselves. I've made us a casserole, chicken, which I'll warm up the minute we get in.'

Eliza muttered. 'Hope you haven't gone through too much trouble, just for me. But thank you. That's very nice, I feel a bit worn out after all the travelling today.'

The house was a large detached affair with gardens all around, secluded from neighbours and away from the road. Marja showed her the guest room, 'everything's been redecorated since you were here last and we've knocked through some walls, make the rooms larger,' she said. 'Come down when you've sorted yourself, perhaps you want a shower?'

When Eliza came into the large kitchen diner, the smell of good food, the table laid out for the two of them with an open bottle of wine, glasses filled, it all combined to made her feel awkward, almost guilty. Why was she doing this? All she was going to achieve was more awkwardness, upsetting people, making them feel angry perhaps. What would Marja be able to tell her that she couldn't guess?

They sat opposite each other at the wooden table, the light dimmed and cosy. Marja chatted about her work, about a student she'd been teaching that afternoon, who was gifted and about Uncle John, who'd been sorry to miss seeing his niece over dinner as he was very fond of her, Eliza. In turn Eliza filled Marja in about the wellbeing of her two step-children and Gerry and what she'd been working on, that case of the murdered woman at the lake.

Then Marja said, as she poured another glass of wine, 'So you found out about Anthony. How did you know?'

Eliza took a large gulp of her wine, and said 'there was a note I found amongst Mum's stuff, a reference to someone called Hans and Anthony and I started to put two and two together, the little events, what happened before and after Anthony died, the quarrels between Mum and Dad, always shushed when they realised we were around, and began to wonder. Then, without me even going into details with Dad, but just pretending that I had definitive proof, a DNA test, he simply said he knew that Anthony was not his son. He was angry with me, ok. He also said they'd been unhappy he and Mum for a long time and that Mum had blamed him for Anthony's death. How can I make sense of all that?'

Marja leaned back, carefully put down her knife and fork on the plate and cradled her glass of wine, looking at Eliza all the time. 'I've also known all along. But your mother didn't want anyone else to know. I was angry with her, at first and then, well …' she sighed. 'Later, when Anthony was a toddler, Stephan was born of course and for a while it seemed your parents were happy again, and Ilsa just wouldn't even talk about anything, acted as if Anthony was in fact your father's son. She'd blanked it out, recreated a new reality in which Anthony was your full brother and that everything else was fantasy, something that hadn't really happened. It was only until Anthony found out himself, just before he went to University and he went completely off the rails, it was only then that she seemed to wake up out of that stupor that she'd created, and your Dad as well for that matter, as if she was living for real in that fantasy world. She'd blocked out that she'd had this relationship, I wouldn't call it an affair in the sense that it was something she engaged in to spite your father; for a short while your mother was madly in love with Hans, no denying. But it would never have worked, he was married you see, just as she was. And he was never going to stay in England and give up his own daughter.'

Eliza took in a deep sharp breath. 'Dad said he and Mum told him, because Mum wanted him to know. You're actually saying Anthony found out himself. How? And why? We never even talked about anything like that, he didn't, he was like Stephan and like Mark, one of my three brothers, no difference. And who was this Hans? How come he just disappeared off the face of the earth like that?'

Marja smiled, 'well Anthony was your brother of course and as far as Ilsa was concerned not any different from any of your other brothers, or you for that matter, you were all her children. Nevertheless, the relationship between your parents didn't stay on course, and for some reason or other your father exploded and said something. I think Anthony may have overheard. At least that's what Ilsa implied. Don't you remember your father going away for some six months at the time Anthony went to university?'

Eliza hesitated, 'but that was to sort out some job abroad, he was in Brazil I seem to remember and Mum couldn't go with him because of her job and Stephan and yes, also Anthony, who was still at home then and who was applying to universities.'

Marja laughed, not a merry laugh, more like a grunt. She picked up her fork and picked out some of the rice and a piece of chicken from her plate, carefully placed it inside her mouth and washed it away with another sip of wine.

Eliza continued, 'I'd left home by that time of course, I was living in London with Tom and all I know is that Anthony changed, he seemed angry a lot when I tried to talk to him on the phone and I simply put it down to 'leaving blues', you know, that teenage feeling that you're about to leave home and going off to live somewhere different and you want to make sure that no one realises how scared you are.'

'He was scared all right,' Marja said. 'No not scared, confused. When I found out that he knew I offered to take him in for while, over the summer, as a kind of passing place for him to stay until he found a room in Birmingham. This was immediately after he got his A-level results, just as well he didn't find out before he sat his exams. It was the wrong time, somehow. I still don't know what happened and how he found out in such a bad way, so that Ilsa admitted it. We'll never know, probably. They're both gone …'

'He had a right to know,' Eliza said. 'We all had the right to know.' She was silent for a while. Then added, 'Poor, poor Anthony. He was so fond of Dad, always convinced that they were two of a kind, somehow, enterprising, clever, they even liked the same films and they used to go to jazz gigs, when Dad was at home and Anthony dragged him out.'

'Your mother …' Marja stopped in her tracks.

'My mother what?' Eliza repeated. She glared at Marja, suddenly feeling protective of her mother, who was no longer there to give her side of the story. Nor was Anthony for that matter.

'All I want to say is that your mother and I fell out about this. She accused me of dropping hints to Anthony, said that I had let her down. But I swear I never did anything of the kind. I barely saw Anthony when he was doing his A-levels. Ilsa, however, was busy at the time, if you remember; she'd got her degree at long last, and found that job. Your father was all over the place and away for weeks on end. Anthony and Stephan often were alone in the house, also in the evenings when your mother was out, at meetings or simply locked in her room doing schoolwork, corrections. I don't know how or what Anthony found out after that awful quarrel between your parents, perhaps accidentally, perhaps because someone else talked. There was a lady, Jean I think she was called, that came in to clean up and do some cooking every so often, you'll know that.'

Of course she knew, 'She still looked after Dad after Mum died, when he was still living there,' but she, Eliza, was wrapped up in her own life by then, she'd moved in with Tom, was busy making an impact both at work and on Tom, she was in love with her own life, with what she was achieving and so contact with home and family had diminished, almost naturally. Once in a while Stephan might ring and say he'd want to stay a night because he wanted to spend a day in London, meeting some friends or other, going out. Stephan had always been aloof though about what he did and where he went and whom he met. She'd soon become aware that he had formed a relationship with a man, older than he was, and that he was vulnerable and she'd asked Tom to talk to him. Stupid, she should have talked to him herself. Tom had been the wrong person and Stephan had been offended and had stopped visiting them. She never found out what had happened to that relationship but at least he'd come out ok, hadn't he? She didn't really want to think about it too much. She felt ashamed, but wasn't quite sure why. Stephan thought she had felt embarrassed about him being gay, but he was wrong. She felt ashamed about herself and about her own neglect, about not caring enough. She'd been selfish, without any consideration for anyone but herself and Tom, but she couldn't tell Stephan. She'd also ignored Anthony and his strange behaviour, had attributed his going off the rails at university, taking drugs, failing exams, as a necessary transition period from being a boy at home to becoming an independent adult. It was what everyone, except she herself, seemed to be doing, going off the rails. See, there it was again, her own smugness, everyone going off the rails, but not her. And where had it got her?

She shook her head to wake herself, saw Marja peering at her, eyebrows raised. 'Sorry,' she said. 'I think I missed what you said. I was thinking.'

'I said Anthony was a wonderful person and the drug taking and mayhem were transitional stages. He had to get something out of his system. That girlfriend whom he married, Ethel, was the best thing that could have happened to him. Don't look so sceptical. She's a very strong woman.'

'You know her? You've met?' Eliza asked. She couldn't help feeling surprised and also slightly resentful. Why had Marja been in touch with this woman, what had any of it got to do with her?

'Yes, I went to see them, I've been there twice now. The first time Anthony wouldn't let me in but Ethel nudged him and said he should talk to me, that it would be helpful. She was, still is, very religious, but she's a good woman. She really loved him, and took care of him when he needed it most. Also, that story about her family not wanting to have anything to do with you as a family was Anthony's fabrication. He made it up.'

Eliza couldn't quite believe this. She herself had telephoned Anthony, she had left messages, had suggested meeting up but only received one curt text message in return, that no, it's not convenient, the rest of her messages ignored. He'd made clear that Ethel and he wanted to be left alone. She'd never had the audacity to ring his front door bell, as Marja had clearly done. Of course she should have done just that if she'd been really worried about him. She could have found out his address, just as Marja had done. Perhaps even Anthony had sensed that she'd been far too wrapped up in her own life and in reality had shrugged off his problems; her own reaction had been that of 'if he doesn't want to know then why would I insist?' After all, family members, siblings especially, grew apart, and once Mark left, and once the quarrels between Ilsa and Jonathan also had increased to become obvious to all of them, and so could no longer be ignored, once she'd left to start her own adult life, all that family business had begun to unravel.

Later, she'd often wondered whether all this happy family stuff had simply been a cosy fairy tale fabricated for them when they were children, that they had been misinformed about the sanctity of family, that it was all a big lie. Look at what had happened to them, and look a bit further, at her own attempt with Tom which had fallen apart, look at Gerry's first marriage, look even at Marja and the banker, you could hardly deny that their marriage was simply a convenient facade that fitted them both. Where were these happy families once you became an adult and took the blinkers off? She couldn't find any. Even Mark and Samantha no longer gave the impression of a happily married couple.

Marja's voice interrupted her thoughts. 'You have a lovely niece and nephew. They're still small. I think you should make the effort and meet Ethel on her patch. Anthony would have

176

come round as well, sooner or later, of that I'm sure. Eventually he would have. He was your brother, and nothing could take that away.'

So that's why Marja had been keen to see her, to nudge her along, to give her that push that she always needed in order to understand what she had to do, where she had to go, how to salvage relationships. Gerry was good at doing that, unlike Tom, who'd accused her of being selfish and arrogant, whereas half the time she simply hadn't considered his point of view, was too focused on her work, too single minded. Gerry saw what was good in her, so did Marja. They both realised that she needed nudging, that she didn't always make the links. Strange really, because at work she was the one who saw the connections between what was on an assay tray and what it told them about a victim or a perpetrator, about a DNA profile and what it led to. That was science though—there were unassailable links that could be made from assays, test tube mixtures, soil samples, DNA, skulls and bones, they all provided evidence as did fingerprints. She wasn't always as good at reading other people's minds, or interpreting their emotions, but she certainly was good at reading test results in the lab. She sighed again, wished she could just go to bed now and mull it all over in her head.

'I'm totally worn out,' she said. 'It's too much to take all in and I've got to get up early tomorrow to catch the seven o'clock train back to London. I think I need to come again, or perhaps you can come and visit us up north?' She looked at Marja, expectantly.

'Yes, it would be brilliant if you could come over here with your family, soon. I've barely met Gerry and don't really know your stepchildren, I assume that's what they are to you, even though you're not married?' She laughed. As an afterthought she said, 'I would have loved to have children. I offered to adopt Anthony, you know. When he was still little, but Ilsa didn't want to know about it. Said she loved Anthony and definitely didn't want to suggest it to Jonathan at the time.'

Had she had too much to drink? Eliza saw the blush spread over Marja's face, her eyes almost brimming and then the grin, 'Well, all that's water under the bridge now. Shouldn't burden you with all this.'

'No, it's fine. I've come to find out what my childhood was really like and I'm just stunned at what has come out of the woodworks, still am in fact.' Eliza got up and started to collect the plates and dishes and carefully placed them on the worktop. 'I'll put these in the dishwasher in a minute. I just realise that I haven't actually phoned Gerry to say that everything is ok and that I'm here with you. I left my phone on the bed. I'll be back in a minute.'

'No need,' Marja called after her. 'Just go to bed. It'll be done soon.'

Eliza rushed upstairs and saw the missed call notices before she heard the beep of the 121 service letting her know of the ten messages that had been left. She didn't bother listening to them and hit Gerry's number. It was 11 o'clock.

'Gerry, I'm so sorry. I left my phone on the bed and we've been sitting in the kitchen eating.'

*

Downstairs, Marja slowly tidied away the plates and dishes, scraped the left over casserole into the bin and turned on the dishwasher. She wasn't sure whether she should have been so frank with Eliza, but then they were no longer children and she clearly wanted to know. The front door opened and she heard John's 'hello, I'm back' before he came into the kitchen and

pecked her on the cheek, bringing in a gush of cold air with
him.

Twelve: A Holiday

It was almost July. They'd decided to go to Cyprus for a fortnight as soon as the schools broke up. Eliza wondered if it would be too hot. Before she met Gerry she never took holidays in the middle of the summer and she and Tom would usually fly somewhere warm, in October or perhaps in March, and they would stay in comfortable hotels, sometimes moving from one place to another.

This holiday would be quite different; they'd rented a villa with a pool for two weeks, somewhere near a small village on the Southeast coast of Cyprus. Eliza had not been before, but Gerry insisted she'd love it. Previously, after Gerry had split up with his wife, he'd gone on holiday with his parents as well as the children. She felt slightly worried about what this new status of being a full time 'mother' to the boys during a two-week holiday would signify, to them and to Gerry. On this holiday she wouldn't be able to hide behind a busy work schedule, or come home late so that Gerry's mother would have made something to eat and would stay until Eliza or Gerry would come home. Throughout the year, the boys had continued to treat her as their father's girlfriend, not a substitute mother, and she liked it that way. All in all she felt that they got on well, she and the boys, and she'd like to keep it that way. Every so often she would ask herself whether she'd done the right thing, moving in with Gerry and two children, even though she was sure that she loved him, and then it would seem to her that there was something wrong with her, with not wanting to take on the mother role that would have to be part of the arrangements, sooner or later.

Would a change in her feelings, and admittedly reluctance, come about naturally once they were thrown together in a villa on holiday, just the four of them, together all day long for a fortnight, doing things as a family, going to the beach with the four of them, and with Gerry and herself not just being lovers but taking full care of his children? Presumably that's what Gerry expected and every so often they'd eat at home rather than go out to a restaurant and she'd be expected to cook for them, she presumed, although Gerry liked cooking and especially doing the food shopping. He could spend ten minutes weighing up the difference between two kinds of potatoes or vegetables. Buying meat took even longer, with Gerry contemplating the difference between the cuts, and whether they should in fact eat any red meat at all. She usually ignored this and often he went out on his own to get the Saturday groceries, relying on his mother to provide the list of necessities, not Eliza.

In the weeks before and after visiting Marja, Eliza had slowly become preoccupied again with her work, she'd been to court, had given evidence, had written reports and provided explanations to the jury and the court in general for what they had found, what the fingerprints could and couldn't show, what blood type had been found where, why the shoe prints couldn't really prove anything as there were many people who wore the kind of shoes that they'd found the prints of at the crime scene. Together with her team they'd spent hours recreating the crime scene and what could and couldn't have happened, what evidence they had and what couldn't count as evidence or was simply useless, and now the trial was over and the jury had found the husband guilty and the judge had pronounced his sentence. Afterwards she was ready for a holiday, it had been very intense and she had not even been in touch with Jonathan, except for an odd telephone call to ask after his health. She'd exchanged a couple of brief e-mails with Mark and one with Stephan, brushing them off really, as they were always trying to put her off doing whatever it was that she did, and she wrote that she was busy and didn't have the time to travel to London and see Jonathan, even though Mark urged her to. Besides, Jonathan seemed happy with his new partner in his new home and as far as she could work out, he was not very keen on waking up any more demons or ghosts from the past. He'd said they'd get married, he and Alea, but privately, no family, just two witnesses, friends of theirs. So much for their own close-knit family, she couldn't help thinking, and after she'd informed Mark and Stephan, neither had bothered to get back in touch with her.

She missed Ilsa, but also realised that Ilsa wouldn't come back. She would never be able to ask her, would never be able to tell her about what she was doing, why she'd pretended to have done that test to draw out Jonathan. She'd never be able to ask her why she had been so secretive, whether she had been in love with this mysterious man, this Hans, the father of Anthony, whoever he was. She still wondered if Anthony had known but until now she hadn't had the courage or the energy to ring Ethel or even to e-mail her. She felt ashamed in a peculiar way, yet didn't want to do anything about it. Something tight and unforgiving buried deep inside prevented her from doing what she felt she ought to do: get in touch with Ethel, talk to her father, ask Stephan about his life, try and meet up with Mark. However, as none of the others took any initiative either, she let herself drift away from them, as they ignored her and each other, but it felt as if they left a great big hole somewhere in the middle with all of them walking away from it, forming an ever expanding circle with increasing distances between them, unwilling to look back. She sent a birthday card to Samantha and then to her nephew Jasper and she didn't bother to pick up the phone and talk with them. She imagined she was too busy, yet it seemed a lame excuse even to herself.

Gerry usually worked late but never failed to ask about her work, about what was going on in court, he talked with the boys when he got back, helped them with their homework although she would also sometimes sit with them and help them when they asked. She was sure that they grew closer as a family. The boys began to trust her and told her stories about what was going on at school, what some of the teachers were like, they made her laugh when they imitated one of their teachers when he was angry, but she also managed to look concerned and she'd say that it wasn't right to make fun of teachers, that they had a hard job. But they clearly felt that she was on their side, and that she was one of them.

In the week before their holiday, Marja telephoned and asked 'have you been in touch with Ethel? I'd like to visit her again, but before arranging this I wondered if we might go together? I know it's a long way to go, but don't you have to be in the south of the country sometime soon? Perhaps you could combine it with a visit to your father? It's his birthday at the end of August.'

Eliza explained that they were going away; she hadn't really thought about Dad's birthday and had been very busy. She imagined Marja's smile at the other end of the line, 'Well,' she said, 'think about it. Perhaps you can all go to London for a weekend, the kids can visit the Science Museum with Gerry, it's good for them. You and I can make our visit.'

Eliza wondered about Marja. She always had these plans, as if it was all so easy. It was clear that she never had to work a full time job with a family, kids that had to go to school and couldn't just swan off. No, that was mean. Marja was simply a woman who undertook life, rather than have it lived for her. Nothing was ever too much. And she clearly had not made the choice to be childless, so that was unfair.

'I will,' Eliza said. 'Think about it, I mean. And I'll put it in the diary and talk about it with Gerry; perhaps he can combine it with work. He often goes to London for meetings, although head office seems to have issued a new ruling that people must travel less and do more of their talking over the Internet. All cost cutting.'

'Tell me about it,' Marja said. 'John's salary hasn't gone up for a few years now and bonuses have been cut down. But I guess we shouldn't complain. He could and should retire really, but then he wouldn't know what to do with himself.' She laughed, but it sounded mirthless, a bit scathing. 'Anyway, he'll be sixty-five soon and won't have a choice. They'll make him go then, if not before.'

'Well, I think it's a good idea, to go over for Dad's birthday. I've not been in touch with him much these last months. And you're right about Ethel; however, I think I should e-mail her first so that at least she has the opportunity to politely decline. Have you got her details?'

Marja read out the e-mail address and gave her the telephone number for good measure.

'It's Ethel Barrowcliffe,' Eliza said. She sounded surprised and then added, 'Of course, she has our surname through marriage with Anthony. Strange to think that I don't even know her yet.'

She wrote down the details in her address book, she would transfer them to her phone later; she could never work out how to enter names or numbers whilst talking.

'Yes, Anthony never changed his surname, although Ilsa must have told him his real father's name. I suppose he never had the time to do that. I don't know if he would have wanted to anyway. I do wonder though if his real father wouldn't want to know that he has two lovely grandchildren.' Marja said. 'Of course, I know who his father is, but I promised your mother I wouldn't interfere … Anthony never asked me.'

Eliza wondered about her aunt's thinking and approach. Had she even considered that Anthony might not have wanted to know? But perhaps he had known who his real father was, this Hans. Surely, he'd been the man at Ilsa's funeral? She didn't say out loud what she thought and instead chatted aimlessly about where they might stay the night, perhaps a hotel near Dad's new place, rather than London, would be a better idea if they were to combine the visit to Ethel with his birthday? Would they travel by car or train, and should they inform Mark and Stephan of their intention to visit Dad, perhaps make it a surprise party for him? They agreed that Eliza would tell them and then Eliza said she really had to go as she'd promised to cook a meal and she hadn't even started yet.

While she put together the meal she thought about Ethel, how she'd managed these years, what she did or whether she was a full time mother and housewife who looked after two children on a pension or on benefits. She tried to imagine Ethel as part of a close knit religious community, with lots of relatives and support, but she couldn't be sure. Wasn't her father well off though? In that case he'd probably provide for his grandchildren, but didn't Ethel also have four or five siblings? Why had she never bothered to find out more about her sister in law, because that's what Ethel was, why had she simply accepted the initial message, she couldn't remember if it was from Ilsa or from Jonathan or perhaps even from Mark, that Anthony wanted to be left alone and that his new wife's family had no desire to get to know them as they disapproved of non-God-fearing folks? How could she be sure that she hadn't simply made this up as she had had no real contact with Anthony, but had only interpreted what she'd been told? For a split second she thought that after all Ilsa couldn't be trusted, but then shook it away, no use to be bitter about things that may be mere imagination. And who was she to judge Ilsa or Jonathan or Anthony? The real truth was of course that she, Eliza, had been far too busy worrying about her own life, about Tom and then later about whether to move in with Gerry, about what to do and what not to do with her life, with her jobs, her own miseries when her world seemed to collapse around her. When all that happened, Anthony had not really figured in any of her thinking anymore. He'd become a background figure, someone who had a role in her past life, a life that increasingly resembled more of a fairy tale than reality, even before Anthony's death, and then her mother had died.

She looked out of the kitchen window and reminded herself to tell the gardener that they were going to be away and that he should come in a few more times to keep the flower beds weed free, do some pruning, cut the grass, if Gerry hadn't already done so.

*

The holiday house on the coast of Pissouri was much better than Eliza had dared to hope for. At least there was enough space for them all, to retreat if they wanted to. Upstairs there was a master bedroom with a kind of ensuite, which really was just a shower cubicle and a toilet off a walk-in wardrobe, and there were two further bedrooms for the boys with a large family bathroom in the middle. Joss and Timmy quickly decided that they would sleep in one bedroom and then use the other to dump their stuff in and to make into a playroom. The downstairs open plan kitchen-diner sitting area was split level and comfortable with a couple of large sofas in the TV area on the higher level and a large dining room table and a kitchen area with all the comforts she could wish for at the other, lower end of the open plan area; and there was a washing machine, a dishwasher, even a microwave. She sighed with relief, worried that what she had let herself in for might have been a kind of camping holiday. Off the kitchen was a door, which opened to a staircase that led to the garden below with swimming pool, toilet and shower. The boys, having decided on the room they wanted to use as their bedroom, changed into their swimming trunks and ran down the stairs to jump into the pool even though it was eight o'clock in the evening, getting dark already, and they really should find somewhere to eat. Gerry smiled at her, held her tight and whispered, 'See, it's not all bad. We'll have a lovely time here. And you can relax and enjoy yourself. Forget work and your family. You deserve a break.'

She was surprised at the concern that came through in his voice. Had he noticed her reluctance? Gerry took their suitcases upstairs and lifted them onto the double bed, 'Go on, get into your bikini and have a swim, I know you want to. I'll dump all this in the wardrobes. Then afterwards we can go out again. The village main street and the beach are only a ten-minute walk away and we can eat there. Restaurants should be open till ten at least.'

She enjoyed every day of that holiday, even the cooking and the shopping and all thoughts of Ilsa, of Anthony, of Jonathan and of her work on the murder case, of everyone back in

England became hazy, a backdrop, and slowly they lost their focus. Instead she laughed out loud with the boys, she lay in the warm sand on the beach under parasols to protect them from the heat of the sun, and together the four of them swam back and forth to a small rock a couple of hundred metres away, where they'd sit and rest in the hot sun before swimming back. Perhaps having children wasn't so bad after all, she could cope. In the evening they drove up into the main village and had meals out on the small square that filled up with locals and tourists, or sometimes they just strolled along the road into the village to one of the restaurants along the beach. One day they drove to Nicosia, leaving early in the morning and Eliza marvelled at the Venetian wall that separated the new from the old. The boys were fascinated that they had to show their passports and walk through a tunnel-like corridor to the Turkish part of the city with quaint tourist shops that had dummy models outside dressed up in garish and colourful garb to welcome potential customers; then they walked to the large imposing mosque that was cool and quiet inside with carpets and golden opulence. She wondered what it would be like to live on Cyprus, in the southern half of course, but decided that it would be too hot and she would rather live in the England she knew than move to a place that had, as far as she could tell, an uncertain future with the Green Line division as well as the uncertainty of the euro across the Euro countries, which included Cyprus.

Gerry said that a lot of people, many of them English, were trying to sell up their properties bought in better times, but faced great difficulties. No one talked about potential Middle Eastern unrest that might affect them, but she felt a reserve and unrest underneath the holiday atmosphere. They went into Paphos and the boys had their photos taken on the rock where

Aphrodite rose up from the sea. She preferred to stay in and around their villa, wander to the local shops and the beach and let the sun burn through her skin and sizzle her brain so that all the unease and unhappiness of the previous year slowly burnt away and her body began to feel strong and energetic again with all the swimming and the walking. At night they lay naked in their bed and hoped that the closed doors would prevent any noise travelling from their bedroom to the boys' rooms and Gerry said, 'I want to marry you. If you want a child, let's have another child.'

She had to think about that, she said then, but when he said the same the next night as they lay gasping for air in the sultry night and after an orgasm she couldn't remember having reached with Gerry before, she said yes, but that she wasn't sure yet about wanting a child. She had delayed it for so long that having children seemed almost unnecessary now that she was going to be the stepmother of two boys anyway. Would they really want to threaten the balance they had begun to establish and now that the boys had begun to trust her? There was also her career; she was loath to give that up or to threaten her future job prospects. She'd never had maternal instincts, she said, but she was lying. At the time, when she was still with Tom, she'd realised that Tom had wanted children and she had suppressed her own slight yearning because she'd wanted to make a career. She'd been reluctant to give in to what she considered to be an illusion at the time, that having a family was part and parcel of being a couple, but she had not wanted to give in to it, not for herself.

She no longer felt uneasy in the same way as there was no need to confront herself or her partner about this question of having a baby, she was just enjoying the sex and wanted to keep her independence, her job, as she was more reluctant than ever to give up who she was, Dr Eliza Barrowcliffe, the woman who was renowned for her skill as a forensic scientist in the small team around her and further afield.

She said then that she would want to keep her own name, she didn't want to become Gerry's appendix. He looked slightly hurt when she said that but she added quickly that she thought it would be good for the boys, to get married, to have the security. She wondered briefly how getting married would make them feel more secure than they were now. How they would ever forget their own mother walking out on them. She pushed away all her doubts, wasn't it time to move on?

The next day Gerry told Joss and Timmy that they would get married and they'd have a big party, probably next spring. Eliza watched them but there was no cloud or shadow on their faces, they shouted 'hurray,' almost as if relieved, and ran to the pool, jumping off the edge and splashing the water wide across the sides, smiling and shouting 'we'll have a party'.

After they returned home an e-mail arrived from Ethel saying that she looked forward to seeing Marja and Eliza in August and that any Saturday towards the end of August, including the Bank holiday weekend, would be fine.

*

For Eliza's birthday, just after their Cyprus holiday, Timmy and Joss bought an expensive looking box of chocolates, beaming at her when she opened it and smiled at them. She never ate chocolates and she wondered why they had bought her this, she was a stickler for a healthy diet. She put the box aside, unopened. When the boys had left the room Gerry asked, 'can't you just open the goddamn box and offer them around?'

She looked at him, surprised. 'But you know I don't eat chocolates. And they know that as well, don't they?'

'That's not the point,' he said. 'They've gone out and bought you a present from their own money and without help from me and you barely acknowledge it. You just put it aside and they're upset.'

She then wondered briefly if that really wonderful holiday they'd just had as a family was in her imagination; that she'd misinterpreted all of it. However, there were too many other things that she needed to deal with and one of them was meeting Ethel.

Thirteen: Jonathan

It was Jonathan's birthday. He and Eliza were in the kitchen of his new home, Gerry and the children were outside, where Alea was doing something or other in the garden before they would go to their dinner appointment with Ethel and her children.

Jonathan repeated Eliza's question, after taking a short time to mull it over, and looking away from her into the garden beyond, almost savouring each word, 'What happened? Why?'

'Perhaps I shouldn't ask,' Eliza said. 'Children shouldn't ask. It's just ...' she shrugged. 'It's just, Gerry and I, we want to get married. I really feel I need resolve some of this first though, there's something not quite finished in my life.'

'Well, congratulations,' Jonathan said and he smiled. 'I'm really happy for you. Gerry's good for you, you can see that. That's as good a birthday present as any.'

She wondered if he meant it, if he ever meant anything nice he said to her nowadays.

The laughing voices of children rose up from the garden and then died down again. Somebody shouted and a ball rolled across the lawn. She looked away from the kitchen window at her father. 'But that doesn't answer my question. You see, I've been thinking and thinking about Mum, about her life, about who she was. And ...'

He held up his right hand as if trying to stop a car in the middle of a road. 'Don't go there,' he said. 'You cannot live her life, you cannot change anything. And don't think that she had a sad life. She didn't. She had her secrets. We were happy, in the beginning. None of our lives are perfect, no marriage is perfect. I'll tell you something. I have thought about it too. Of course I have. About what happened. About what happened to us. It's best if you leave it alone now. Your mother is dead. Leave her in peace.'

He got up and switched on the coffee machine. 'You want one?'

She nodded and he made the two black coffees in silence. 'Help yourself to sugar or milk, if you want.'

She shook her head.

'I don't want you to go over the past, our past, forever and ever. You've been doing that, as if you have to resolve a crime before you can move on yourself. I know it sounds harsh, but you've really got to get on with your own life. Tom was a mistake perhaps, although I liked him, and so did your mother by the way, nevertheless it almost seems to me that you are scared to make mistakes that other people have made, as if you've got to mend something that isn't even broken, just grown out of shape, become slightly damaged over the years, inevitably so.'

'Is that what you think? That you and Mum became damaged, became worn out over the years? What hope is there for any of us, if that happens and if it is inevitable? And you think that's normal.' She looked furious, raised her voice, picked up her cup and banged it back down on the table, some of the coffee spilling across the wood.

'No, calm down. I'm probably just expressing myself badly. You know, your mum, Ilsa and I, we were children of the sixties really but with the hang-ups of the stifling fifties. What happened then, that kind of change in attitude and culture didn't really come to us naturally, that change in expectations of what couples were about, about relationships, no, it didn't really come to most of us until the seventies or even eighties. It took time to get used to the idea that we no longer had to live the lives that our parents had lived, the marriages that they had, the role of women, all of that. It only dawned on us gradually even though we were fully part of it. It's just hard to remember how things used to be. We were rebellious, tried to get rid of all of the stuffiness that our parents were part of. Also, there was a sexual freedom that confused some of us. I think your mother more so than me. We made mistakes, definitely.'

He sipped from his coffee and looked at her over the rim of his cup. She saw weariness in his narrowed eyes that wouldn't give up their secrets and she looked away again, towards the garden where the boys were visible now, sitting on the lawn, pushing a ball across at each other. From beyond she could hear Gerry's voice and then the higher voice of Alea, sounding like a question mark. Alea walked into view, wearing garden gloves and holding a small spade, pointing at the ball, said something, raised eyebrows. Eliza looked away from the window and repeated her question, 'so what happened? Why?'

Jonathan shook his head, 'Just wait, and let me tell you my own way, will you? I can see that you want to know. It's too easy to say that we both had an affair, don't look so surprised. Lots of couples had affairs, have affairs still. We did. It's much easier to admit when you know that you're both as guilty as the other. Now that I know. I had an affair first and thought Ilsa didn't know and then clearly Ilsa had an affair that I knew nothing about for a very long time. But all that happened in a context, things aren't as black and white as you want them to be. You've never been any different. I suppose that's why you've become the scientist, the one that meticulously digs up

194

all evidence and then draws her conclusion in black on white.'
He laughed as if to soften his criticism of her. Because that's
how it felt; she was being put in her place. She suppressed the
annoyance she felt, swallowed and carefully picked up her cup,
sipped slowly, screwing her eyebrows together. 'Go on.'

'Your mother was a very attractive woman and also very
clever. I was madly in love with her, even if we didn't always see
eye to eye about our political beliefs, I guess she was much less
interested in the wider world affairs than I was at the time, but
then few girls that I knew were, except some at university, and
Ilsa wanted me to get on with my studies. Our really serious
mistake was that we both thought it quite acceptable that she'd
give up her studies; yes both of us did, so that I could become
the breadwinner. That was old-fashioned, even at the time, in
some circles anyway, but our families, even most of our friends,
we all thought that once there were children, the women would
look after them, even if she didn't stay at home all the time and
had a part-time job.'

'Well, what's changed,' muttered Eliza. 'Most women still do
most of the muddling through.'

'Anyway, my job took up most of my time, I earned a good
living, but I failed to see Ilsa's unhappiness and I admit that I
became slightly irritated by what I saw as her dullness, her
inability to be the sparkling woman she once was. She became
obsessed with ordinary household things, I felt. She was always
going on about feeling tired, being stuck at home. I was guilty
and I admit it, but we both lost something, Ilsa didn't try very
hard to be interested in what I was doing and expected me to
throw in my weight with you and your brothers, be there whilst
at the same time there was little time for the two of us together.
The usual story I guess.'

'So you had an affair, at one point. Who was she? Was it Alea, even then? Did mum find out?'

'No, it was just an affair, a fling, it didn't last, but it showed me that it was possible. To be unfaithful. And Ilsa needed never know about it.'

'So why are you telling me? What happened that Mum became so unhappy, that she nearly chucked it all in, that it nearly broke up your marriage?'

'That first fling, as I said, made it seem easy. It happened whilst I was at a conference for work. Everyone seemed to be at it …'

Eliza felt the anger well up again and told herself to stay calm, after all, she'd insisted to know. What was it with men, even her own father, that made them think betraying your partner, her own mother, or simply lying to them, was ok, as long as it saved the pretence of a happy marriage? She closed her lips and realised she must look exactly like her father did when he was angry, the same pencil mark for lips, the slight redness in her face. She swallowed then took a deep breath. Perhaps it wasn't such a good idea after all to interrogate your own father. Perhaps it was better not to know any of this. Perhaps she should stop him. Fold it all away, back into the cupboard.

He seemed oblivious now to her qualms and it was as if a hidden stream had been unleashed, as if he had been mulling this over for years and years without being able to talk about it with anyone. Not even Alea? She wondered how much Alea knew any of this, whether she was aware that he'd been an unfaithful husband, well before she came along. She really shouldn't have to know all this, but it seemed the only way towards the truth about Anthony, about Ilsa and the son conceived by another man. She shivered slightly. How had Ilsa kept all this to herself? How had she been able to continue in a marriage that was so clearly broken? What was the pact between Ilsa and Jonathan? Or was it as simple as this that Jonathan had loved her above all else and felt protective because guilty?

She put her hands over her eyes, as if she wanted to obliterate what she saw, rubbed her forehead and then looked at her father. 'So why did Mum have a child that wasn't yours? And why did you stay together? Have you known all along that Anthony wasn't your child?'

'No, I didn't. I didn't know. I only found out later, much later. Your mother kept it secret. She never told anyone, except perhaps Marja, but I've never asked Marja about this. I couldn't. Anyway, by the time I found out, and by the time Anthony found out it all fell apart. Anthony fell apart and then he died in that awful accident.'

He slapped his hand flat on the table, angry, helpless. He scrunched up his face. She could see that he was upset and despite herself wanted to hug him, but he warded her off with his hands flat, arms outstretched. 'No, leave it. I'm ok.'

'When was that?' She nearly whispered, couldn't bring herself to speak out loud.

'When he finished his A-levels. I don't know what made him do it. Perhaps it was a kind of joke. You used to talk about these tests that you learned to do, as part of your studies, these DNA tests and paternity tests. He had one done, as a kind of a lark I think, as part of a challenge with friends, but also because he must have thought about it. He took my toothbrush, I remember wondering whether I'd forgotten to bring it back from one of my trips, then confronted me with the results. How on earth he got them done I don't know, perhaps you do?' He suddenly looked at her, suspicious.

She held up her hands, shook her head. 'I had no idea. Honestly Dad. I do remember we used to laugh about it, partly because the four of us, we were all so different, we still are, we even look quite different but perhaps the most striking difference between us, yes, that was Anthony ... We teased him, Mark and I, but then we teased Stephan also, fallen off the wagon, we used to say ... But it was never meant seriously.' She stopped then said 'and of course I was studying all this at the time and Anthony must have picked my brains. Only I cannot remember him doing so, not openly.'

Eliza calculated: Anthony must have had that test done in 1996 when he was doing his A-levels. They'd only just started to use the PCR, the polymerase chain reaction, technique; they would copy small fragments of DNA, which you could take from any part of the body and the process was pretty quick. Nowadays they could of course carry out extended DNA tests and heritage could be traced down the paternal or maternal lineages through Y-STR or mitochondrial DNA tests. And that included tracing the paternal side of someone's family, from father to son. It's what she claimed to have done, only she hadn't really been able to get hold of Anthony's Y chromosome, had she, even though she pretended to. She would have had to have access to an autopsy report, or to hairs that included the root, and she hadn't dared request that, afraid that Jonathan would have been informed and refused the request.

The year that Anthony was sitting his A-levels Eliza was doing her PhD at University College London and she was about to move in with Tom, who at twenty-eight was five years older than she was, and who had already establishing himself as an art historian. He had written a best seller and taught full time at the college where she did her PhD. They'd met, as so many of those accidental encounters, at a friend of a friend's house, a party that she'd been dragged along to by her roommate and where Tom was because he was the brother of the hostess, his older sister whose husband had decamped with their au pair and she had been left with their child, a precocious three year old. Both Tom and his sister were well-off, had been left a generous allowance by rich grandparents and despite her abandonment the sister appeared quite on top of things and continued to live in the large apartment in South Kensington and regularly organised dinner parties where she would invite former university friends and present colleagues.

And so Eliza had entered that world of Tom's; highly academic, well-off, intellectual and yes demanding. Demanding in the sense that she'd felt she needed to reach those same heights that Tom and his sister aspired to even if her job had been much less glamorous and by the time she'd found her position as a lowly lab assistant in the forensic science lab in London, she'd been almost financially reliant on Tom and his generosity, never held back. As well has having the financial means, Tom also travelled regularly, usually without her, as part of his book tours, or a visiting lectureship, or simply a catch up meeting with colleagues in America or in Germany or in Italy. She had accepted it as par for the course, this was after all what it was like to be with Tom and she admired him, loved his fluency, his knowledgeability and the glamour that became increasingly attached to his name. She simply had not the time to care much about her own family, had happily abandoned the often moody atmosphere that she had recently found at the house her parents lived in, no longer her home. She had vaguely realised they quarrelled, that there was a disagreement, a loss of love or even an increasing acrimony that had wiped out all previous good feelings and even attachments.

When Anthony died she'd been upset, of course she had been, and was heartbroken when she realised that even at the funeral they had not really been welcome, had stood apart from his unknown wife's family, her small child and her large belly that indicated the next one was due any time, with her father and mother supporting her in her visible grief. It had been a truly awful time for all of them. She remembered how Stephan had stood there quietly, tears running down his face, how Mark had stood white-faced but dry eyed, clenching his hands in front of him, how Jonathan and Ilsa had stood slightly apart, as if an invisible wall had been erected between them, through which they could not or would not communicate, how Ilsa at one point slightly moved as if she was about to fall and how Jonathan had gripped her elbow and had held it there until the service was over, how at no point any of Anthony's wife's family had looked at them, but how at the very end they had walked up to them and they had extended a hand in condolences to Ilsa, but had not really looked at Jonathan. She still felt sickly when she thought about it and wished that the photographic images could be deleted from her brain, that she would simply forget how bloody awful that funeral ceremony had been. What happened afterwards she couldn't clearly remember, she'd not wanted to talk to Anthony's wife or family, it had seemed incongruous, totally out of place, to start an acquaintance at such a horrible occasion. She had pulled Tom with her, away from the place, and they had driven back to London in near silence, except that Tom had said Anthony's wife had seemed a nice woman, very young still and quite pretty, as if he'd expected her to be some kind of an ogre or an unkempt religious harridan, after the few comments that Eliza had made about her, in the past.

*

Jonathan hailed her back into the present when Alea came in, 'Come we'd better get ready, Marja will be here any minute now. I understand you've invited her along?' He raised his eyebrows into a question mark. The children came in after Alea. They were shouting at each other and Gerry pulled them back, told them to be quiet. It sounded as if there had been a fight of some sort, but Alea just smiled, 'Yes, we'd better get ready. It's nearly six.'

Marja had arranged to come by train and would meet them at the restaurant. They had booked into the local hotel and Marja and Eliza would drive south the next day, to meet with Ethel. Neither Mark nor Stephan had been able to come over to celebrate their father's birthday, but that had not really surprised Eliza. It was hardly worth travelling all that way just for a meal out and it was not as if Jonathan had been hugely enthusiastic about the idea in the first place. She suspected that he'd probably much rather spend an evening out with Alea, and not have to drag up old hurts or to be reminded of everything that had been left unsaid between them. He and Alea had been to Germany recently to see Mark and intended to go to Singapore for a short holiday, stopping over in Dubai and perhaps carrying on for a week in Australia. He'd always been a keen traveller and Alea was just as eager to fly off around the world, unlike Ilsa who'd preferred to stay in England. Alea had plenty of money from a divorce settlement. Her previous husband had been a wealthy if unfaithful man.

'We've arranged to see Ethel tomorrow,' Eliza said. 'Although they have church services it seems, she's happy to see us late afternoon. It does seem a bit crazy now, this arrangement, but Marja thought it was a good idea …'

'You must do whatever you feel is best,' Jonathan said briskly. 'I'm getting changed. We're booked for seven.'

Eliza realised that she would not get any more out of him, not today, not ever probably. He was done, he wanted the past to close down and he wanted to live and enjoy his life with Alea. They were very fond of each other, she thought, as she saw them exchanging a few glances and smiles. She felt a twinge, it should have been Ilsa, happy like this, even if she couldn't find anything against Alea, really. Except that her father clearly was in love with the woman and seemingly had already forgotten about Ilsa. No, that wasn't fair. She was unfair, trying too hard to hang on to the past, to uncover things that were probably better left were they where, events and lives lived that had nothing to do with her, as Gerry kept telling her.

Fourteen: More Emails

Eliza looked at the blank message box on the freestanding monitor that she had attached to her laptop computer, and then firmly pulled the separate keyboard towards her and wrote:

Hi both. Gerry and I are getting married next spring and I want to make sure that both of you (and your family / partners of course) will be able to be there with us. It won't be a huge affair but we haven't seen each other for such a long time, not all of us together anyway, that I would really love it to be a kind of family reunion as well as my wedding party. I will also invite Ethel and her two children, your half nephew and nieces ... Is that what they're called? Anyway, they're family! I think she will agree to come. I've been to see her a few times now and it's been good. It's time you met up with her and show your uncle faces to your other half of the family! Dad and Marja will of course be there, but before we fix the final date I want to make sure that both of you are ok to be there. How about a May weekend, say Saturday 17ᵗʰ May 2012? Once you confirm (please soon!!!) we will send out the official invites.

Love you both, Eliza xx

Hi Eliza

That's great news! Congratulations. Yes, I will put 17th in the diary and nothing else will come between us! Sander delighted to come as well.

Best, Stephan.

Hi Eliza
Well done and congrats. We'd be delighted to accept. 17th is fine. We'll make it a holiday week—kids will love it!
Best wishes. Mark and Samantha x

Hi Ethel. So glad you and the children will be with us on the 17th May. The date is fixed now. Marja will of course be there as well, so we won't all be strangers for you. I think Dad would like to meet with you before the wedding. Are you ok with this? Perhaps it's time to bury some of our hatchets? I would love to come and visit you sometime next month. Perhaps we can arrange for a meal out with Dad and Alea and you and me? If we make it a Saturday lunch you could perhaps bring the children along as well? Let me know.
Love and best wishes, Eliza x

Dear Eliza, Thank you for inviting me and the children to your wedding. Of course, we'd be delighted to be present at your ceremony and reception. I'm happy to meet your father if he would like that. As you know, I've been in touch with Anthony's real father, or rather he has been in touch with me. Anthony became aware of who he was only shortly before he died and therefore never met with him. I think my children, our children, should know who their grandfather is. I hope that your father is aware of this. I understand however if he doesn't see any reason to meet the children or me. I have not explained to the children the situation, just implied they have two grandfathers, that Anthony's first dad was lost for a long time. They're too young to understand.
Yours, Ethel

Hi Ethel. I spoke with Dad over the phone, he says he'd still very much like to meet with you and so I've arranged to come south next month, I have to be in London on the 19th for a meeting and could travel to you early the next morning. Aunt Marja will probably come as well. Would you book a restaurant for all of us? Alea will come with Dad and I will travel back with them after our lunch.

Love Eliza.

Hi Ethel. It was great to see you and the children and it was nice to see how well they got on with Dad and Alea. I am well aware now that the non-communication between Anthony and us had little to do with you and that you tried hard to persuade him to keep in touch with us. I so wish I had cottoned on to everything sooner and been in touch with you before it was too late. It's really very sad and I can honestly kick myself now for not having tried harder to speak with Anthony at the time. I don't know what went through his mind. You've been very good for him, and I'm sure that if Mum had known all of this, she would have been happy. In hindsight, a lot of heartache was so unnecessary, if only we had been braver and communicated. You clearly loved Anthony and perhaps I'm right in saying that you still do. That is such a relief. I very much look forward to seeing you at our wedding, let's stay in touch.

Love Eliza.

Eliza wondered about what she'd written in that last e-mail, hesitated but then hit the send button anyway. It was better, this conciliatory tone, letting go of the past and coming to terms with it. At first their lunchtime meeting had been stiff and unnatural, Ethel barely spoke and with stern facial expressions kept the children in check. They were clearly brought up strictly but then Alea seemed to manage to get through the barriers, by indicating that she knew quite a bit about Ethel's father's company, she had provided some kind of management training to staff in a branch in the north of the country, and in fact had met with her father to set up the training. Ethel visibly relaxed, and Jonathan was drawn into the conversation when it turned out that he had worked with the sister company in the States, where her father's brother was in charge, Jonathan had provided some software or other.

They sat round a large round table in the busy Italian restaurant on the main road of the small town. The waiters took their time with their orders and although Marja and Alea asked for some wine with their food, neither Ethel nor Jonathan drank, 'Driving,' Jonathan said and 'I don't drink,' Ethel said and asked for sparkling water. Eliza said she would drive back, or at least part of the way and therefore wouldn't drink either. Marja and Alea took their time choosing a bottle of wine and this seemed to cement a kind of friendship between the two.

Ethel explained, 'I'm the part time HR manager in my father's office here in the South. The local office doesn't really require a full time person, too few people, unlike elsewhere in the country. That is just brilliant as far as I'm concerned and my father is much happier having family members in key positions.' Eliza felt relieved somehow; at least Ethel was not on the dole. She wasn't sure why she had expected that Ethel would have been a full time mother, or housewife. They had never talked about it, her parents, her siblings, or even Marja, but then they had never really shown that much interest in the person Anthony had married, had been devastated that he had staged a full separation from his own family and had implied that it was what his new in-laws wanted.

'You've always worked?' Eliza asked.

Ethel simply nodded, without elaborating.

Their food was delivered and once they had all started to eat, they were even able to talk about Anthony. Ethel said, 'The children miss having their father around, although of course my father and also my brothers are very good to them.'

Eliza realised she had no idea how many siblings Ethel had, whether they lived nearby, whether they had families of their own, nothing at all. She looked at her father, then at Marja and suspected that Marja was aware of some of the relationships, of Ethel's extended family and who they were, but she kept herself aloof. Before the food was brought to the table, Marja had pulled out colouring books and pencils from her large bag and played with them, then once they had their food in front of them, helped Ethel, handing them their forks, spreading and tucking their napkins around their necks, handing them their glasses to drink some water and generally answered all their questions and listened to them attentively.

Alea on the other hand listened intently to the conversation with Ethel and once in a while nudged it along, when a longish silence threatened.

'Of course, neither of our two children have really known their father. Anthony died in 2004,' Ethel swallowed, then continued, almost as if determined to get it all over with, to lay it all bare, what they'd missed, who she was and who Anthony had been, a father. 'We were both very young still, and Noah was barely a year old and I was pregnant again, with Kyra, our daughter, when Anthony ...'

Eliza also felt tears welling up but blew her nose and took a deep gulp of the glass of water. 'It was the most awful time of all of our lives,' she said.

'I am truly sorry for all that happened,' Jonathan scraped his throat. 'Anthony was so angry, had been angry for a while. We were all in bad places.'

Alea put her hand on his arm, which shook slightly. 'Perhaps we shouldn't go into the details here,' she said. 'Not with the children around. Too many things happened, it was a freak accident; no one could have foreseen that or done anything about it. No one was driving too fast, no one was drink driving, and no one fell asleep behind the wheel. It was simply a deer, a boar really, crossing the road in the dark. Who could have done anything about it?'

There, Alea had said it with all of them present. She'd exonerated all of them, she made sure that they could all carry on from here on, not as if nothing had happened, but making sure that there was not a guilty party, that life had conjured up a calamity that had thrown them all into disarray, but it was through no fault of their own.

Eliza felt grateful and looked at Jonathan who had become quiet and at Ethel who had turned to wipe Kyra's mouth. Kyra was a lovely six-year old, in a pretty blue and white dress, her dark brown hair long and held together with a big bow on top of her head. She looked seriously at the grownups. 'Are you all sad?' she asked. 'I thought this was a party. You should be happy.'

They all smiled at her in unison, and Eliza said 'of course we are happy. We are happy because we are here with you and with Noah and with your mum and we are happy that you're going to come to my wedding party next year.'

All in all it had all worked out and even Dad was clearly relieved that the initial contact had been made. Still, Ilsa should have been there of course, just as Anthony should have been there, it should have been Ilsa smiling at her grandchildren, a happy Ilsa, not the depressed and despondent woman she had been that last year of her life, perhaps even longer; Eliza didn't know, couldn't be sure. She would always carry that with her, that accusation deep inside her that they had all let her down, even if through no fault of their own perhaps. But still, shouldn't she, Eliza, if no one else, have tried harder? Shouldn't they all have tried harder? Then again, she wondered what they could have achieved, how they could have made life different for her. After all, it had been Ilsa who had chosen to conceal the truth about Anthony and that had come to haunt her later on in life, you could hardly blame that on her children, or even on her husband, although he had been the cause of it all indirectly.

Eliza shook her head as if in denial, she'd never untangle all of it, life was just that, uncoordinated, often unfair, often muddled, but then they all carried on, trying to make the most of what they had and what she had to do now was give some direction to her own life, organise her life with Gerry and take responsibility for that, including trying her best with his children, change herself to become a mother for them? She still wasn't sure that she wanted to.

She picked up her laptop and walked with it to the sofa, sat down and started another e-mail:

Hi Marja, I think it's time that you let me have the contact details of Hans? Ethel said that he had contacted her and I think that she has met him. Surely it was you who informed him of mum's death and not Ethel? Love Eliza.

She pressed the 'send' button.

There, again you had it. Was she meddling? Was she making clear how much of a busybody she was? All she wanted was a clear picture of who her family were, and what was real and what wasn't in her past. If Anthony was her half-brother than she wanted to know who it was that her mother had been in love with. She assumed that Ilsa had been in love; otherwise surely she wouldn't have chosen to keep Anthony? What was she thinking?

Fifteen: Mark

Mark wasn't exactly happy about Eliza's discoveries and never-ending interference in what he said was digging up a past which, as far as he was concerned, should be left were it was, as it was, not being poked into with a dirty stick, with her endless moaning about needing to know. As a small child he'd loved his mother unreservedly, like any ordinary boy would who had a loving and caring mother like his had been, and during his teenage years he had just as unreservedly rejected her, but that had more to do with his own hormonal dissonance than with anything specific that Ilsa might or might not have done. At least he never considered that she had been to blame for his abominable crudeness and rejection of her for a brief period of time, not later anyway. At the time of course he'd been horrified by her being feminine, so young that some people had asked if she was his older sister. Imagine that. He'd been embarrassed, thought there was something wrong with her, she'd been too sexy somehow, she'd been too provocative sometimes at least in the eyes of a thirteen year old, struggling with who he was and was developing into, a boy with regular nightly hard-ons, hairs sprouting everywhere, a voice that sounded ridiculous even to himself. He'd grown out of that idiotic behaviour quite reasonably, he now thought and subsequently, as an adult, he had a more measured respect for her and that included his unconditional love and acceptance that she was his mother and that they had a bond that would never be severed, maybe become less fierce over the years because of distance in lifestyle and in geography, but she would always be there as the first woman he'd ever loved; his shock at her death had been immeasurable, he'd felt near giddy when he took that telephone call from Jonathan, and a glass had shattered in his brain, the shards hitting every single inside part of him, coursing through his whole body. Until that telephone call, it had simply never occurred to him, had not been anything he had thought about very much, that she might die and no longer be there. After all, she'd been relatively young still.

As a child he'd considered himself to be singular, encouraged by his father's praise of him and his mother's devotion. She'd been a very young parent, he realised later, maybe that's what explained her extraordinary energy and determination to make the best of her children, she'd used clear and precise language with him and with his siblings, she'd never had recourse to baby language, he seemed to remember, and always told them to try again when they'd failed at something, the reading, writing your name in full for the first time, learning to ride a bike, climbing a tree, nothing daunted her, and always she was there to encourage them to get on with it, 'you can do it.' Was that why they had all become such successful people? He, Mark, was a senior director already in an international company, Eliza a specialist scientist in a forensic science lab, Stephan the high earner in Singapore? But not Anthony though, Anthony had failed, had failed them all, not just himself. He'd gone haywire first and then had walked out and not finished his studies and become a loser, as far as he, Mark, was concerned. Anthony had always been a disruptive element, had always caused disagreements, the slamming of doors, shouts between his parents, insolent friends, books thrown on the floor, hushed conversations late at night, and of course his father going off for months on end, and even though he claimed it was business, he, Mark knew better and had watched how his parents' marriage descended into a war zone and he had always blamed Anthony for this, well before Anthony had apparently discovered that he wasn't his father's son, according to Eliza at least. He'd prefer to leave it all well alone, and he wanted to remember the mother he knew, rather than the one now being discovered by Eliza and who might not completely fit the picture he had in mind. He and Anthony had always been at loggerheads, unlike Stephan who had always adored his middle brother. Yes, Mark had been singular also in that respect. Had he been jealous because of his mother's obvious devotion to Anthony and had he slowly begun to realise that, as far as his mother was concerned, Anthony might even have been more special than he had been?

He grunted and looked up and around. There was no one else in the kitchen diner and, still watching the closed door that led to the hall, he picked up the newspaper as if guilty of an unobservable crime. It was only this last year that he had started to dwell on these things and it was so unlike him, before all this happened, to sink back into this morass of old feelings and memories, that he wasn't sure how to deal with, they just kept cropping up in his head. He knew what had caused this last attack of irritation at the world and his family. Although he'd answered in an upbeat manner to Eliza's wedding invitation, he didn't really want to go there, didn't want to become involved in the expanding family saga, the wife of dead Anthony, this Ethel, and Anthony's children, the reconciliation bit between Jonathan and Ethel. It made him feel slightly nauseous, all of it. At times he still experienced that out of air feeling, a kind of nausea, that had pushed him of balance, when

Jonathan told him over the phone of his mother's death, and this sickly feeling had wormed deep in his belly.

'Isn't it amazing,' Samantha had said. 'You know, your father and Alea having met with her, with Ethel. Eliza emailed to tell me it had all gone really well.'

'I'm not particularly looking forward to this wedding and this so-called family dinner,' Mark said. 'It's all really quite sordid, isn't it?'

'What. Why?' Samantha's voice shot up an octave higher. 'What's bugging you now? Isn't it better this way? Everything out in the open, at long last some answers and closure, and you've got another sister-in-law whether you like it or not, and a nephew and a niece you knew nothing about. Even if Anthony wasn't your father's son, he still was your mother's son, so he was still your half-brother, nothing murky there!'

'Well, it's hardly going to make a difference to our lives, is it? What use is it to drag all this up, both they and us would probably be just as happy, if not happier, if we'd left all this where it belongs. It's in the past. Imagine what Dad must be going through. Besides, we're forgetting about Mum in all this so-called excitement. She should be at that wedding, not Alea.'

'Oh honey, you're still grieving, aren't you?' Samantha put her hand on his arm, leaned over towards him and kissed him lightly on his forehead, as if he was a child that needed consolation.

He pulled away, got up and walked over to the coffee machine. 'Want one?'

Samantha shook her head but wouldn't let go. 'It's all right to grieve for your mother, you know. You can do both. I also miss her but I'm sure she would be the last person who'd have wanted you to reject Ethel. She loved Anthony and was hugely distraught by him walking out the way he did. She never got over it, and that's so sad, I mean, that she will never know that you've all reconciled with Ethel and that you'll be seeing Anthony's children.'

'Oh, come on!' He violently pulled the coffee machine forward and it nearly dropped over sideways, hiccupping over the uneven granite surface. 'This is all so much rubbish.' But he wasn't quite sure why it would be rubbish. He simply did not want to, couldn't reconcile his own feelings with what had happened, and so he wouldn't accede to Samantha's reasonable conjectures. He was aware of his own rigidity but still wouldn't help her, didn't want to cooperate with her or with Eliza or with his father, for that matter. He shook his head as he took the coffee cup from the machine, the smell suggesting that he should be somewhere else, not in the middle of this awkward conversation, but at work perhaps, or in a coffee shop, somewhere safe, unruffled. He shuffled backward from the machine as if it was threatening him, then said, 'No,' without finishing what it was he tried to deny. He sat away from Samantha in the chair at the opposite end of the table, again smelled the coffee, and tucked in his upper lip then said, 'I simply find it all very unpleasant. But of course, we'll go to the wedding and we'll be civilised, if that's what you're afraid of. Not going I mean.'

Samantha pressed her lips together, her face tightening. 'Now I think you're being downright silly. What on earth's the matter with you?' She felt cold suddenly. She forced a smile, which told him more than words, what she thought of him right there and then.

She got up. 'It's time to get the children. I don't suppose you feel like going? They're at Ann-Marie's, a birthday party.' He didn't respond. 'Well, I really hope you're going to work yourself through this stew you've created in your head.' She slammed the door behind her.

This was the nth time over the past year when out of nothing they'd ended up quarrelling or being mad at each other. He blamed Samantha for being short tempered all of a sudden, while she said he had become morose and impossible to live with, forever with his head in work or grumpy about something, usually his family. She was right of course, but he blamed Eliza and her interfering holier than thou attitude and the way she was trying to involve all of them, the whole family to become engrossed in her quest for unearthing their real mother. He was utterly and totally sick of it. And why wasn't Samantha on his side? For Christ's' sake, Ilsa had only been dead for just over a year and here they all were going to celebrate weddings and discoveries of additional relatives without a thought about her. No one had even thought to bury or spread her ashes properly yet, unless they'd gone ahead without him. He felt his stomach contracting at the thought and for a split second felt he might implode.

*

When Mark was twelve and Anthony just five they had their first really serious disagreement, if that's what you could call it. Really, Anthony could hardly be accused of being deliberately nasty to Mark, their mother had explained to him, but he had shaken his fists and clenched his jaw so that Ilsa had become quite concerned at the violence she detected in his, Mark's response. 'Darling, what's wrong? Anthony is your little brother, he really didn't mean anything very bad by going through your books or by looking in your drawer. All he's doing is trying to imitate you, his big brother. Don't you understand?'

No, he hadn't understood, still could feel the nauseous sweat of his clammy hands with which he'd tried to strangle Anthony had not their mother come in and prevented this act of brotherly murder.

Anthony had gone through some of his favourite books and marked pages with a pen, a red pen, crossing out whole lines and even tearing up one or two pages. Was that trying to imitate him? He would never have done anything of the kind, his books were sacred, so were the notebooks he kept in his drawer and the special pen his father had once given him, his compass, the pencil box with twelve different kinds of pencils ranging from very soft to HH and then in the corner of the room his very special drum set, that he'd received last Christmas and Anthony had gone in and made the sound that had caused him to run up the stairs and grab him with both hands and shout at him, his fingers firmly round his neck 'I'll kill you if you ever touch my stuff again.' Anthony had stood, bewildered and with tears slowly replacing the glimmer of pleasure in his eyes and he had run out of the room as quickly as he could after their mother had come in.

Ilsa had tried to talk reasonably with him, tried to convince him that these angry outbursts were unnecessary but his father that evening had exploded and hit him hard, a smash against his ears, then had looked as shocked as Anthony had, he had looked at his own hands as if he couldn't believe what he had just done and said, 'oh my god. I'm sorry. I shouldn't have hit you. That was wrong of me.'

From then on, they'd been enemies, he and Anthony, always at loggerheads. Anthony at first seemed only to avoid him, trying hard to keep well out of his way, ignoring him, hiding behind Eliza, behind Stephan, making sure almost that they were rarely alone together and he definitely never entered his room again, nor did he try to touch any of his stuff, not even if it was lying around in the room downstairs, or in the hall or out in the garden. Had it been the age difference? He didn't think so, after all, he rarely had trouble with Stephan who was even younger than Anthony, rather he'd always felt protective towards Stephan, his baby brother as he called him, there was a ten year gap between them and when he had that first bust up with Anthony Stephan had been a toddler, fast asleep for his afternoon nap whilst their mother had tried to enjoy the quiet rainy Sunday afternoon lying on the sofa with a book in her hand. He couldn't remember where his father had been, out somewhere although he'd come back home for dinner.

He was sure this bust up with Anthony and his mother's reaction had also been the beginning of his teenage rebellion against his mother who hadn't understood how disagreeable Anthony was, who had always defended him, saying he was only little and that he, Mark, ought to know better, being seven years older than Anthony, only a baby in comparison.

Later, once he'd gone to university and lived in his own digs with fellow students he'd put it all behind him, and on his weekend and holiday visits home and on the rare occasions that both he and Anthony found themselves in the same room together without anyone else present, he'd acted as if nothing had ever happened between them, as if it had never been part of their childhood, the teasing, the superciliousness, the underhandedness of his action and the pure hatred he had felt. Similarly, Anthony had learned to ignored him and walked around him as if around a glass bauble that if touched would shatter into thousand pieces of shards that might injure him. Then Mark met Samantha and had fallen in love, recognising in her something his mother had also had in the distant past, when he was still a toddler, a singular attention just for him, as if he was unique, could never do any wrong. He was sure Sam thought he was extraordinarily clever even though she herself graduated with first class grades all round whereas he got a second class degree, even if it had been an upper second one, but then she said that his subject had been so much more difficult and demanding that it wasn't surprising. Samantha had been open and so without any maliciousness at all that he had felt it rubbing off on him and he had decided to bury the hatchet with Anthony and with some of the other people that he had disliked, his Aunt Marja, some of his friends even if he would never have admitted it. He had become more human, more approachable and so he had been able to re-establish the closeness with his mother who had very much liked Samantha, he was sure.

Eliza had known all of this, surely. She had been part of that same childhood even though she now acted as if theirs had been the perfect family. Of course they hadn't been, perfect families didn't exist, whatever she imagined. She'd chosen to remember only the good things. Surely she'd been aware of their father's frequent and long absences in their lives? The au pairs and cleaners and other helpers, once Ilsa had decided to go back to college and try and get her degree after all that time? Mark had never quite understood what had driven Ilsa, especially as their father had clearly earned enough money for them to have a comfortable existence, they were never short of anything, so why would she want to get a degree and a job? Again, Samantha had put him straight, had explained that his mother was clever and had felt undervalued, that she must have been eager to make up for lost years, that, perhaps even, she hadn't just wanted children and look after them, but had wanted to do something more with her life. Of course, he'd understood that by the time she'd actually got her Masters and

Teaching Certification and subsequently a part-time job, but not when he was a child and had to fight his siblings for the attention he considered to be his birthright.

*

He decided to ring his father to ask him straight out what his intention was, whether he was going to let Eliza do whatever she wanted to do at her wedding, make Ethel part of the family, and did he expect that he, Mark, would contribute to this whole banal exercise, adding to it with an acceptance speech of some kind. Were there going to be speeches or would everything be low-key? He could of course ask Eliza directly but he was reluctant, afraid that she would try to pull him in even further and God forbid, ask him to give a speech. He wouldn't.

Jonathan picked up his phone after two rings, 'Mark. Is anything the matter?'

'Not to worry Dad. Everything's fine. Just ringing to touch base in connection with Eliza's wedding. We've all had a few e-mails I gather but I wonder if you know anything more regarding the procedure?'

'Procedure? What do you mean? Your sister's getting married. It's not a board meeting!'

Trust Jonathan to make fun of him.

'No, I don't mean it like that. Anyway, how are you? How's Alea? Are you well settled in your new house?'

'Hardly new, son. We've been here for a year now and yes, we love it here. Time you came for a visit perhaps?'

'Perhaps we can stay over for a couple of nights when we're in England for the wedding? Mind, there's four of us and you may just feel a bit cramped. We can always stay in a B and B nearby and see you during the day ...'

'Of course not. We have plenty of space, two guest rooms. I don't suppose the kids mind sleeping in the same room in single beds? Alternatively one can sleep on a camp bed in one of our workrooms. I haven't downsized much, really. You should know. Both Alea and I like our own space when it comes to it.'

This was going nowhere. Too long a conversation for two mobile phones in different countries, paying a huge bill just for exchanging inanities wasn't his intention.

'Dad, ok, that's fine. We'll stay with you. But I'd really like to know if you're ok with all this pulling in of Anthony's wife, the wife we weren't allowed to meet as far as he was concerned, and his two kids and with all that digging of Eliza's ...' He stopped, not sure about the silence from the other end. He waited, 'Dad? You still there?'

'Well, yes. I'm still here. I'm not sure what you're trying to get at, what you're trying to say? You think I'm upset or something. About Ethel? Or about Anthony? Or perhaps about you and Eliza as well? Oh, and for good measure, Stephan of course.'

Typical, he was sarcastic now. Just like he used to be, even though he'd managed to hide it these last years, at least hadn't shown that side of his character very much to his grown up children after they'd left home. Rather, he'd ignored them but something must have bitten him about Eliza's stomping into his private affairs, otherwise, why would he say this?

'Oh, forget it. I just thought you might be uncomfortable with all of this. I am, for sure. Why can't Eliza just get married without all these extras? She needn't involve all of us in her own quest, surely.'

'Son.' Again this address, he could hear the way he was trying to fend him off.

'Mark. I don't think it has got anything to do with any of us. This is Eliza's wedding. It's her choice to want to come to terms with a past that she's only just discovered. Unlike you perhaps, Eliza loved Anthony. So did I for that matter. You didn't, you never liked your brother and I don't quite know why not. It's not as if he did you any harm. And whatever you think, I am not upset at Ethel being there, nor about the fact that Anthony left behind two very nice and well brought up children who think I am their grandfather, and in a way I am. Not genetically of course, but you are aware of that by now.'

'Ok, I get it. Anyway I've got to go now, have a meeting in ten minutes. Bye Dad.' He carefully pressed the exit button, closed the flap of his phone and put it on his desk in front of him, stared out of the window. None of them were even the slightest bit interested in what he thought of it all. His father hadn't even mentioned Ilsa and he, Mark, had forgotten to ask about her ashes and what had happened to them.

Sixteen: Stephan

S tephan had always been the baby of the family, the baby-brother, the baby-son, the toddler to be indulged, the child to be spoiled and the child who was so very fond of his brother Anthony. He had adored Anthony, had wanted to go with him when he went out, had wanted to be like him, Anthony, his big brother and friend. Mark had always been too far removed, too distant, unapproachable, and slightly fearsome when he got angry or was annoyed, especially with Anthony. By the time Stephan sat his GCSEs and then his A-levels, Mark had long gone, as if he was not really part of them anymore. Also, things had changed at home of course, his mother was working, Anthony would often pick him up from his tennis lessons or from a friend's place because their mother hadn't come home yet and their father would sometimes be absent 'for work' for weeks on end in far flung places, but as he had always come back Stephan had never been unduly worried about any of that. Anthony had been close to him in age, there was only three years difference, enough to make sure they had different friends and rarely interacted in school or tennis or music lessons, but not so much difference that they didn't often play together at home as children, and he had followed Anthony around like a puppy and Anthony had loved him in return, of that he was sure. So had Eliza, but Eliza was a girl and therefore different. Eliza giggled, laughed and played with other girls, she was good at tennis, he had to admit, almost as good as

Anthony was, but she played with other girls and they kept themselves separate even though she and Anthony had a similar sense of humour and would often laugh out loud at something that he didn't understand or was not allowed to hear, 'you wouldn't understand' or 'go away, you're a baby still.' That would hurt, but he also realised that they meant no harm and that they got on with each other. Mark had always been a bit of an outsider, Stephan was sure that Mark thought that when Stephan and Anthony played or shouted, that this was childish and well beneath him and whereas Eliza would look at them good-humouredly and would tease them, Mark would press his lips and turn his back, pretend they weren't there.

*

Stephan carefully packed his suitcase, six sets of underwear, socks, five long-sleeved shirts that would need ironing all over again once they came out at the other end, his toilet bag, a pair of jeans and a pair of expensive twill cotton trousers and t-shirts, a couple of jumpers and a sweatshirt, clothes he could never wear in Singapore and that were only taken out of the cupboard for trips to Europe. It could still be quite cold in May, he knew, and he wanted to avoid having to buy more jumpers or sweatshirts once in England. He got out his suit and rather than carrying it by hand he decided to fold it, if necessary he would have it pressed in England. He'd had a new one made, light grey, and knew he looked good in it. He stroked the material, which felt soft and warm, and he held it against his cheek, just because he loved the feeling.

Sander's suitcase was already packed, stood ready in the hall. He had to attend a meeting that morning and would come back after lunch when they would take a taxi to Changi airport. Their flight was an early evening one and they would try and sleep all the way so that the jet lag wouldn't hit them too badly, when they arrived late afternoon the next day, the eight hours difference was a real pain, he knew from experience.

Eliza's wedding was in five days' time and first of all they were going to stay a few nights in London with friends, hire a car and then would drive up north the day before the wedding. He wanted to avoid spending days with his relatives, Eliza would be too busy, Jonathan now had his own life with Alea and he didn't think they would want to put up him and Sander and so he hadn't asked.

He frowned, a message from Jonathan came up on the screen of his phone that lay on the table, 'When are you flying / arriving? Mark and family to stay with us for a few days before the wedding, would you and Sander like to come and see us afterwards? Where are you staying?'

Typical. To come with this so late in the day, when they'd all but finalised all the arrangements. He wouldn't answer straight away but consult with Sander first. They were bound for The Netherlands after the wedding, but they could of course always delay for a day or two. Sander's parents wouldn't mind and Sander just wanted to spend a few days in his birth country to catch up with some old school friends he kept in touch with. Afterwards they were going to spend a well-deserved holiday on the beach in the south of France. 'Want to introduce my partner to everyone I know,' Sander had said and nudged Stephan.

He felt he could not avoid Eliza's wedding but he would have liked to avoid it altogether. Of course he was happy for his sister getting hitched at long last, but what had been so wrong with Tom and what was it about Gerry that she found so attractive? When they met for the first time at his father's house for Ilsa's funeral Stephan had been slightly mystified. Why on earth would his sister want to shack up with a guy who was so clearly dull, compared to the much more flamboyant Tom with whom he'd had some quite good conversations and who was so very knowledgeable about everything to do with art to be watched, enjoyed and felt in London, and who was well-known and had lots of friends. Gerry had two kids, what on earth did Eliza think she was getting herself into, he'd wanted to ask her, but refrained, after all, they were living such different lives nowadays that it was hard to imagine that once they'd been quite close and she'd been his big sister who'd looked out for him. He was touched when he remembered how she had told Tom to talk to him, and Tom of course had told him that it had been Eliza who'd insisted on it, that she was worried about the company he kept, that she wasn't worried or upset about him being gay, but that she'd wondered about some of the men they'd seen him with, they'd looked down and outs, not trustworthy, perhaps and he, Stephan, was still so very young. They'd had a couple of drinks in the pub, Tom and he and Tom had more or less said that he trusted Stephan's instincts and that if he was in any trouble, ever, or if he needed someone to talk to, Stephan could always knock on his door and he'd be there for him. Otherwise, it was up to him how he led his life, they'd all made their own mistakes in their student days, part and parcel of the learning curve and he was sure that Stephan was bright enough to look after himself.

Yes, Stephan would have liked it had the groom been Tom, not Gerry. He and Gerry had hardly exchanged anything but some politeness during that week of Ilsa's death and cremation. He couldn't help feeling that Gerry was an intruder, someone who diminished Eliza somehow. But who was he to say? He closed the suitcase with a bang and turned the lock shut. They travelled first class, had fiddled it such that they both would attend some work meetings the first few days in London so that the trip could legitimately count as a business trip, Sander had even arranged some business in The Netherlands, but Stephan had refrained, partly because he wasn't quite sure who to contact there. He did have some business relations in Paris and wondered whether perhaps he should go there for a few days, arrange something. Madness, why arrange more work; if it came to it he, Stephan, would pay for the trip in full for both of them and be done with it. After all, they weren't poor by any means, but with Sander it was a lifelong habit of counting and balancing the books, whatever books they were and he worked it all out to his advantage in minute details. Stephan wouldn't be surprised if he even managed to swing it so that the night in the hotel in the north of England would come off his expense account somehow. He smiled. It's who he was, Sander, 'my Dutch Calvinist upbringing,' he'd say, 'watch the little ones and you'll be rewarded in heaven, or something like that'. Not that his parents were religious, at least Stephan hadn't noticed.

Once they'd visited Sander's grandfather, quite old now but still living independently, in an old grand house in one of those well to do places near The Hague somewhere. He had a housekeeper and refused to move into something smaller or more convenient for family members who felt they had to look after him. He spoke little English, partly because he was quickly becoming forgetful and could not remember individual words and so Sander provided a near parallel commentary in English for Stephan's benefit.

They'd had lunch prepared by the stern looking housekeeper and to Stephan's surprise everyone round the table was quiet and bowed their heads before they started to eat, the grandfather saying a prayer out loud, hands folded firmly in front of him and it was only after the very audible 'Amen' that everyone picked up their knife and fork and started to eat. Even

227

the meal had been the strangest he'd ever come across, they'd eaten slices of bread with knife and fork, layering them with thin slices of ham or cheese and when he glanced sideways Sander had winked at him.

Once or twice the grandfather looked over at Stephan and said 'Ja, ik was in the oorlog …'

'He says he was in the war' Sander explained, but then the grandfather gave up and turned all his attention to cutting up his food in small pieces. Under his breath Sander said, 'He cannot really remember what he wanted to say about it, more and more is becoming unavailable to him.'

Later he said, 'he's too old to change anything, this is how he's always lived and he hasn't got much longer to go, so we indulge him, although he can be a bit over the top at times. I'm actually surprised he's let you come, although I don't think he's aware what we do, at least he wouldn't even consider it!' Sander grinned. 'He would be horrified. No, I'm sure that he's been told that we are colleagues or friendly colleagues, or something like that. I've never enlightened him anyway, not worth it.'

Stephan wondered about this and how the grandfather must have been one of the very few still alive from that time. Even his own parents couldn't remember anything about the Second World War; however, in Holland someone always seemed to know someone else who could remember.

Thinking about it brought his thoughts back to Tom, because Tom had sometimes talked about someone who'd been in the RAF during the war, an uncle of an uncle or perhaps even his grandfather and Stephan wished he'd paid more attention even though all this time he had never quite lost touch with Tom, not after he and Eliza broke up. He could meet up with him and ask a few more questions so that he could have a conversation with Sander's grandfather, if he was still compos mentis, that is.

Tom wouldn't talk much to him, Stephan, about what had happened between him and Eliza although he had implied that he thought he'd been a fool and that you couldn't undo anything as stupid as what he had done, because trust had gone as far as Eliza was concerned. As far as Stephan was aware, Tom had not started another long-term relationship. He e-mailed Tom to let him know that he and Sander would be in London and could they perhaps meet up for a drink? He added, as an afterthought, 'Eliza getting married '.

Now the telephone vibrated in his pocket and when he looked at it he saw the text message from Tom, 'When's Eliza getting married to that jerk?'

Poor Tom.

*

The taxi dropped them off at the entrance to Changi airport terminal and after having dropped their cases off they would saunter through the passport and security checks. Having residence cards helped beat the longer international passports queues. Once inside they would look at gadgets or perhaps even some of the expensive clothing or luggage in the smarter outlets before having a coffee and going on to walk through the boarding gate. Stephan still thrilled at the sense of importance and power it gave him to be waved through the first class channel by a smiling man or woman 'sir, this way please', which kind of confirmed that they had really made it, he and Sander, and that some of that bullying he had suffered in the past was history, this was his two fingers up to that, as far as he was concerned.

'Tom wants to know when Eliza's getting married. I just texted him the date,' Stephan said as they lifted the suitcases on the band.

'Why, is he going to try and stop it or does he want an invite?'

Sander hadn't actually met Tom as yet but knew about him and the break up of the relationship with Eliza.

'Not sure actually, I texted him the date anyway. We'll be seeing him the day after tomorrow, for a drink. You'll like Tom; he's a great guy, and very interesting. What he does, I mean.'

Glamorous and smartly dressed tiny eastern looking girls in their twenties and casually expensively dressed men of various nationalities walked past them, then a Chinese family looking worried and upset when they divided into two at the security barrier, the man and two teenage boys going forward, looking backwards and smiling, the woman with a small girl in her arms, staying behind, both of them crying. Then they were gone and were overtaken by other groups and disjointed emotions, single businessmen walking at a pace trailing a wheelie bag whilst looking at mobile phones, or talking into little microphones dangling on earphone wires below their chins, middle aged couples looking as if out for a break or a holiday, middle eastern women with headscarves, however, very few women wore chadors, not here in Singapore; Chinese, Japanese, American, Asian, European languages, all speech transformed into warbles of incomprehensible noises, some exotic smells lingered and others came and vanished, all within that oppressive airless and bright lit space that had become one of the many manifestations of human existence, not unique to Changi airport. What was it about airports and masses of people travelling all over the world all the time that seemed to suggest the world was in constant turmoil and upset, they were places where you saw raw and floating displays of heartache, rampant lies, bitterness, happiness, unease, indifference, tears, smiles, concern, expectations, and so many other variations of human expressions on so many different faces of so many ethnicities in an even distribution across the thousands of faces shifting in opposite directions.

Sander was distracted though by messages on his phone and once or twice said, 'Shit' under his breath before directing his attention to Stephan and to what Stephan said, 'I wish she wouldn't marry that jerk either, I'd much prefer having Tom as a brother in law. Mind, we'd hardly see them anyway, so I suppose it doesn't really matter.'

'Family, eh?' Sander said, absentmindedly. 'Listen, I need to make a call to the office, someone is screwing up badly. I can't leave it.'

Stephan nodded, 'that's fine. I'm just going to deal with my last e-mails too, before we board. Let's have a coffee.'

They worked without talking amidst the noisiness, which formed its own shield against interference of particular sounds. It's what they were both good at, this ability to distance yourself from everything going on in their immediate environment and to focus on what needed to be done. At last Sander looked up, 'Done,' he said. 'Let's go and find the gate, it must be about time to board.'

*

Upon arrival in their London hotel there was a message from Jonathan and Stephan looked up at Sander in disbelief, then laughed, 'We've got to go and see Tom,' he said, 'asap.'

Seventeen: Girls' Night Out

Eliza woke up with a shock and looked at the strange surroundings before remembering that she was in a hotel room and that Maggie was snoring lightly in the twin bed next to hers. Light filtered through the sides of the drawn curtains and she looked at the clock on the bedside table. Eight o'clock. Her head pounded and her mouth felt as if she'd smeared it with glue, a rather horrendous tasting glue.

Blurred images of a long and rather alcohol laden meal with Maggie the previous night twirled around in her head, and the pleasant battering of a sauna prior to that. Much good that treatment had done, the sauna and also the massage she now remembered, the treat she had looked forward to so much. How stupid to then go out and have so much wine with their meal that both had nearly fallen over when they got up from the table to find their room. They'd staggered into the lift like two eighteen year olds that couldn't keep their drink, and she hoped that no one had witnessed their rather inelegant departure. She felt her face, her eyes and realised that she hadn't even taken off her makeup, although she distinctly remembered attempting to brush her teeth before she'd collapsed on one of the beds. Something had upset her, had made her feel bad. They'd had a girls' afternoon and night out, prior to the wedding, she and Maggie, but then something had happened, what was it? Then she remembered the text message halfway through the meal, from Tom of all people.

'Don't do it.' It said. 'Don't get married. I'll come and rescue you.'

'He's mad,' she said out loud when she read it and Maggie raised her eyebrows.

'Hey, no telephone, no text messages, just you and me having girlie chats. That's what this day is supposed to be about. Switch it off and put it in your bag. Didn't even know you had brought it to the table. I left mine upstairs in the room.'

But Eliza couldn't help herself. Not now, not after she'd read that message. She hadn't been in touch with Tom since she'd left him, not for five years. She'd severed all contact, had deleted his messages, the ones that he left during the first few months of their separation, had wiped him off her LinkedIn account, off her Facebook account (family and friends only), had even deleted every single e-mail message without reading until he'd given up trying.

Now she'd opened the message not recognising the number and had read it before realising that it was from Tom, who though it appropriate somehow to text her that she shouldn't get married. The cheek of it! Must have been Stephan who'd told him, she knew Stephan still saw Tom, he'd implied as much without being explicit about it. But that was Stephan's business.

'Oh go on, then.' Maggie said. 'I can see that it's something you want to talk about now. That you're upset.' She'd already drunk half a bottle of red after the two gin and tonics pre dinner drinks at the bar, and was beginning to slur slightly. Eliza was trying not to keep up with her, had stuck to only one gin and tonic and was still on her first glass of wine. Maggie clearly needed a get away as much as Eliza had wanted to be away from Gerry and the children for one day before the wedding, to reflect, she'd said to Maggie, to prepare and to just have a good old girls' night out. Prepare for what she wasn't sure as nothing much would change in their living arrangements, it just had seemed a good idea to do this, a girlie thing, something she'd rarely indulged in all her life and Maggie had been up for it.

They'd talked about their lives, as she could only do with Maggie, had confessed to boyfriends they'd slept with before getting into a serious relationship, Maggie before she got married and Eliza before she moved in with Tom. Then after Tom she'd had a few 'sordid encounters', she'd called them and Maggie had giggled after the second gin and tonic, 'explain?' she squealed, but Eliza wouldn't except to say that 'they were drunken encounters, once or twice when I was mourning Tom and wanted to prove to myself I didn't really need him and that I could get on with men quite well, thank you very much. Stupid of course.' Then she'd met Gerry, serious Gerry and they'd developed a long term relationship and she'd felt safe and they would get married even though she'd have to accept having his children although previously she'd never wanted any because she'd wanted a career and was convinced that she wouldn't be able to if she was distracted by babies. As they were talking and laughing and giggling, she got more and more confused and started to become entangled in her own thoughts that wouldn't come out as proper sentences, definitely not well strung together. 'Can't have it all, can we? Careers, family, well you know.'

Maggie shook her head. 'Of course you can have both. I have both. Well, my salary may not be quite as high as yours as you're more senior than I am, but so what? I have two lovely children and wouldn't miss them for anything in the world.'

'See, 'swat I mean.' She definitely slurred now as well. 'You regret not being as senior as I am, of being held back. My mum was the same—she never got anywhere she really wanted to be.' Eliza frowned. Then something else occurred to her, unrelated, 'Ethel's coming to the wedding too, Anthony's wife?'

She looked down at her phone as if it was an alien object. There was a message from Tom of all people, Tom who'd have liked to have children she suddenly knew quite clearly. She didn't and then he'd gone off and had affairs with other women, some of them no more than girls in their early twenties, when he went on his lecture tours. In fact, she didn't really know whether there had been more than one but in her mind the thought had taken root and as Tom hadn't denied anything she'd moved out in a huff, 'I cannot live with someone I cannot trust,' she told him when he simply wouldn't either deny or confess anything, only repeated how sorry he was and 'it was a mistake, a mad moment.'

What was it she'd wanted from Tom, having him all to herself but refusing to have children with him? Had he decided that perhaps it was a good idea to split with her so he could look somewhere else for a wife who would be a mother of his children too? She had always refused to think about this possibility, but it now hit her in the face. What if she, and not Tom had been to blame for their breakup?

'Why's he texting me now? After all these years?'

'He clearly doesn't want you to get married to someone else. Perhaps he's been waiting for you to break up with Gerry and go back south.'

'He's mad. Gerry and I are getting married in five days' time. Does he really think I would just call it all off because he says so?'

'Well, would you?'

235

Maggie's question shocked her more than Tom's message. She could have laughed it off, if Maggie had let her, but Maggie looked at her curiously, put her head in her two hands, elbows on the table alongside her plate, "Giraffe position," she thought, remembering her yoga classes and then she did the same, copied Maggie's position and took a deep breath into her nostrils, held it and then let go.

'You're kidding me. You don't seriously think I would cancel my wedding at this late stage, would you? Think of Gerry, think of his poor children, first let down by their own mother and then by me. I couldn't do it, even if I had a single grain of doubt. But I have no doubt. I love Gerry and Gerry loves me, we have a future together. This is what we both want.'

'If that's so, then everything's fine.' Maggie said and picked up her knife and fork again, carefully balanced some vegetables on the back of her fork and pushed it into her mouth.

Eliza then said that she imagined Maggie's mother standing over her and telling her to eat properly. But Maggie wouldn't let go, wouldn't be distracted, frowned,

'Why are you so disturbed by that message then? You look as if you've seen a ghost.'

She really was mad, Maggie, if she thought that Eliza would even contemplate doing what she suggested, she wouldn't even think about it. She pulled at her shirt, a shiny silky affair, creamy and loose fitting over a lovely tight black skirt with a long slit at the side. She didn't usually dress this glamorously, but had felt the need to show herself to the world as the chic and elegant woman who would be married shortly, someone in full control, who had a successful career and now would even have a ready-made family, looked after by the husband's mother. She stopped in her track. Looked after by others? Wasn't this whole set up slightly odd? Wouldn't Gerry take for

236

granted, well she knew he did, that she would slowly but certainly take over as the mother of his children? What was she thinking? Her husband's mother in full control of the household, the children, the cleaning, and everything else that kept a family together whereas she, the wife and step mother continued to keep well away from everything that would make her responsible or put her in the centre of that family. She didn't really want to know, did she; she wasn't prepared to be wife and mother all at the same time. She didn't really want to build a genuine partnership with Gerry, but would rather continue to be, what, his girlfriend, uncommitted? What was he to her? A carer? A brother? What on earth was she thinking? They made love, didn't they? They had plenty of sex, ok nothing out of this world, but good enough to satisfy her and also Gerry she imagined. It wasn't as it had been with Tom, but there had been a kindness and consideration that she clung to, giving her the opportunity to hide even if she never felt very passionate.

'Oh fuck,' she said and looked up, held up her two hands like a begging bowl.

'What.'

'Oh fuck, fuck, fuck.'

She replaced her head in her two hands with the elbows on the table and bit her upper lip violently so that it drew blood.

'Have some more wine,' Maggie said. 'It'll stop the bleeding. It's alcohol.' She was truly tipsy now but at the same time looked very concerned. She put out a hand with a tissue she somehow found in her bag after much searching, 'here'.

'So sorry. I don't normally use bad language, my mother would send us upstairs if we did.' Eliza smiled warily now.

'Why did I look at that telephone? He's a bastard, doing this to me. Making me doubt this way.'

'Well, he may only just have found out. Isn't he going to see Stephan when he arrives in London?'

Yes, of course, that was it. Stephan didn't have much time for Gerry that was clear when they met. And Gerry had kept at a distance with all her family, had tried hard not to interfere with anything or upset anyone. Or had he simply not been that interested? Why was she doing this to herself? Why was her brain like a tangled clump of wool, and loose strands of different colours, not helped by the wool being saturated with alcohol? She took another large sip from her wine.

'I'm going to have to call it off, don't I?' Her face turned red and felt lumpy as she swallowed hard to keep from crying.

Maggie got up, stumbled and then pulled up a chair next to her, put her arm round her shoulder and pushed her head onto it. 'Oh come on girl. Have a good cry. Perhaps it's all just pre-nuptial nerves and you'll be perfectly all right tomorrow. We've overdone it a bit with the wine and all the exertion today. You're tired. Perhaps this wasn't such a good idea after all.'

'You think so?' She was crying now, blew her nose heavily into the serviette that Maggie held up. The waiter started to come over to their table then changed his mind, turned and walked away. She heaved again, a heavy shudder but then straightened up, 'going to the toilet, wash my face,' she mumbled and tiptoed on her stockinged feet to the ladies' room, forgetting that she'd kicked off her high heeled shoes under the table and became only aware of this when she closed the door behind her and stepped flat feet onto the cold tiles of the brightly lit room. She really was an idiot. What was she doing? Who was this disgraceful woman with distorted face looking at her from the mirror? She heard the door behind her open again and then close and Maggie stood next to her smiling into the large and wide mirror over the row of washbasins, holding up a shoe in each hand, 'you looked quite funny,' she said. 'Thought you might like to walk back in there without attracting attention further. Come, wash your face and then take a deep breath. Let's talk this through. Drink some water.'

*

They refrained from drinking more wine throughout the rest of the meal and had a coffee, but by that time Eliza said she felt so clear headed now that she'd need a nightcap, something really strong that would send her off to sleep without fail. The waiter brought two brandies and they warmed the glass with their hands, sipped carefully. They talked and talked, taking it in turns to try and work out what Eliza really felt for Gerry, whether she was making a huge mistake or whether all this was really no more than an upset caused by a sudden memory of what she'd had with Tom; after all, that would never come back, Eliza said, it never would. Tom had cheated on her and was untrustworthy, Gerry was reliable and would give her the kind of life she wanted, safe, living in a pleasant town where she had good friends, a good job, all the amenities she could wish for, and on top of that with a man who loved her very much, of that she was sure.

'I should have thought of all of this before, I should have thought all of this through and I shouldn't have read that stupid message from Tom.'

*

But now, in the early morning in a hotel room with drawn curtains and a yellowish light that spread from the bedside table lamp across the greyness of the sullen environment of twin beds that had hostile side tables and with a hefty wall desk that supported a large widescreen TV and with small armchairs that were too dainty and small for the room, she was awake, even if with a drum set in her head and a taste of thick glue in her mouth. She gulped down the glass of water that stood on the bedside table, got up, refilled the glass with a fresh bottle from the tray on the large desk along the opposite wall, which she also drank and then walked to the bathroom where she looked in the mirror and realised she was still wearing the smart blouse which now looked as if it had been retrieved from the rubbish bin. What a mess, how could she have let herself go like that, this was supposed to have been a sophisticated dinner at a spa retreat with her best friend and colleague, what was the matter with her? And Maggie, she hadn't been any better, but thank God they were friends and they would laugh it off together once she woke up.

She slowly undressed letting her shirt, her panties and bra drop on the floor of the bathroom, turned on the shower and stood under it with the water enveloping her, rinsing off the smell and the horrible thoughts she'd had the previous night. She shampooed her hair and lathered herself with the expensive bath cream from one of the little samplers and then once more stood and let the water wash her clean. She stood for a long time, then turned off the tap, wrapped one of the large white towels around her, and with her hair still dripping wet walked back into the bedroom, shook Maggie by the shoulder and said, 'I'm going to call it off. I'm going to call off the wedding. It's a mistake.'

*

There would not be a wedding, not yet, anyway. Family members were in disarray, friends telephoned each other and asked what on earth had gone wrong, some flights could no longer be cancelled and hotel bookings had to be cancelled, Mark blamed Samantha although even he himself wasn't quite sure why he blamed her, Caroline and Jasper couldn't understand why there would not be a wedding and looked shocked when their father slammed a door in their faces, Jonathan said he'd always suspected that Gerry was no bloody good for Eliza and that he'd never understood why she'd been in such a hurry to give up everything in London to move in with 'a man who lives in the north and who has two goddamn children, while she, Eliza, has always professed she never wanted to have children', and why, whilst he was at it, had she split from Tom who'd wanted children, that had never been a secret, and then moved in with a dull-witted man who had two ready-made ones? Stephan and Sander on their second day in London had a drink with Tom and asked him whether he was aware of what had happened, but Tom looked surprised, then said, 'oh my god', and disappeared into the men's room whilst pulling his phone out of his jacket pocket and he began to key in frantically even before he'd shut the door behind him; Stephan raised his eyebrows to Sander and said they could perhaps go over to Jonathan's sooner so they could fly to Holland as initially planned and carry on with their holidays, no point cancelling any of that, then said 'But we really need to see Eliza first, where is she?' Aunt Marja rang Ethel to tell her the wedding was off and Ethel said 'poor Eliza, what's happened?' Her two children were as mystified as Mark's children as to why they would no longer go to this wedding party which they'd been looking forward to for such a long time now, and Maggie who, that same day that Eliza had decided she wouldn't marry Gerry after all, had taken it on herself to inform as many people as possible about the cancellation, Maggie wouldn't tell anyone where Eliza was, although everyone assumed that she knew perfectly well. Eliza had disappeared after she'd had a tearful and miserable face to face with Gerry in their very own kitchen, looking at Gerry who had turned white and then tried to hug her but she wouldn't let him after which he'd growled at her and had become angry, saying she was the lowest bitch he could think off and Eliza had been thoroughly shocked at the emotional reaction and Gerry calling her a bitch.

She'd run up the stairs, filled a suitcase and grabbed her laptop bag and had dropped the case down the stairs, pulled it outside and lifted it into the boot of her car and without looking back she'd disappeared, out of the street and hadn't told Gerry where she was going. The children had looked out of their upstairs window at her car driving away and they'd crept downstairs to see their father slumped over the kitchen table with his head in his arms. Gerry called Jonathan who said he had no idea where Eliza was, she hadn't turned up at his place, and Gerry got in the car and drove to Maggie, who politely refused to let him in because she was just on her way to work and said she would call him that evening. She said she was sorry, very sorry, and that Eliza seemed to have some kind of a breakdown 'I don't think she ever got over her mother's death and just suppressed all that stuff about her parents and Anthony and I think she's suddenly realised that she needs to come to terms with a lot of things before she can commit herself to anything.' She sounded pathetic, Maggie thought, all psychoanalytical, but then she did think that she was right about Eliza. Eliza had not been herself, had been running around and organising and trying to put back together a family picture that had shattered when her mother died and she'd discovered that she'd been trying for years to build her own life on that of the imaginary perfect marriage of her parents. Or something like that. Maggie didn't want to say all this, after all, Eliza had sworn her to silence and said that she would turn up again when she felt ready to face her family. She wouldn't go back to Gerry's house, but she would contact Marja and see if she could stay with her for a while. Marja was the only person she could trust not to let her down and who would not rush her into anything.

No one thought to ring Marja, at least not at first.

Eighteen: The Netherlands 2013

Flares of mist hung over the unfamiliar Dutch countryside that was flat but not empty and every time a patch cleared you could see farmsteads dotted about fields, an odd warehouse with large lorries and small cars parked around the ghostly contours, then a cluster of houses as if someone had started building a new village but thought better of it and finally Eliza drove through the small village she was aiming for and which came with a butcher, a supermarket, a few deserted outdoor terraces, an ice cream parlour, closed it seemed, all built alongside the main road and the cycle paths where women carelessly pedalled along, balancing shopping bags in baskets hanging from their handlebars and children in seats on the back carrier; a pregnant woman cycled along with a child strapped in one of those backseats and who stared as if in a trance at the cars passing by, its face cold and white. The very British satnav female voice told her that this road, that had come off the motorway some five miles back, would take her to her destination. It was three in the afternoon. Hans had agreed to see her, 'come for a tea, at about half past three,' he'd said in clear English but with a faint Dutch accent.

Eliza reminded herself once more to stay on the right hand side of the road when she came off the roundabout and entered a housing estate, houses neatly laid out, small front gardens, clean pavements, tidy front doors and small cars parked along the length of the road; a few houses had dug up their gardens and created car parking spaces, roads led off to yet more streets with yet more identikit houses but her satnav instructed her to stay on this road and then announced 'you have reached your destination'. She carefully parked in a space between a small white Ford Fiesta and a black Volkswagen, both old but very clean.

She had driven straight from Amsterdam airport to the address that Hans had emailed her and she had booked a hotel for on her way back, near Utrecht, before she would drive to the airport the next morning. The timing was bad, she thought, she should have caught an earlier flight, arranged to meet Hans for lunch and catch a flight back that same evening. He hadn't been very forthcoming though, said he didn't like to go out for lunch and preferred to see her in the afternoon, anything earlier was inconvenient.

When he opened the front door she saw the man she had spotted at her mother's cremation ceremony, and understood why he had been reluctant to a meal out. Instead of being slightly stooped but tall, he was now bent over and holding himself up on two crutches, not long enough for him, with his right leg held in front of him 'I broke a leg,' he said, pointing at the visible rigidity under a too long pair of jersey sweat trousers, just the tip of his foot sticking out, whilst standing on his left socked foot in an old sandal. He shuffled sideways, 'come in.' The house had a slightly stuffy smell, the smell of stale cigarette smoke, of unopened windows and she assumed that he lived alone, he and his wife divorced 'a long time ago,' he had said on the telephone. But he didn't say whether that was the wife he'd been married to when he had his fling with Ilsa in London, so long ago now.

'I'm so sorry,' Eliza said. 'This is really inconvenient for you. Why didn't you say?'

'Don't be silly. Come in, it's nice to have some company. You must be Eliza.'

He held out his right hand, pressing the crutch between his upper arm and side and grabbed her hand and shook it quite firmly. 'Come in,' he said again. 'Perhaps you can carry the tea tray from the kitchen to the front room. My daily has put everything ready for us, she was here this morning.'

*

Hans and Ilsa fell in love when they met at university, when Ilsa was finishing the degree that had eluded her when she'd become pregnant with Mark. Hans was a guest lecturer. 'She was pretty,' he said. 'In a serious kind of a way and also, you know, very mature. Of course she was mature. She was an adult student, not an eighteen year old.' He laughed as if what he said was quite funny. 'I didn't know at first that she had children, you and your brother, but I did know she was married. She was, you know, not happy with her husband, your father I assume. She said that he was a cheat. But she had great plans, would get her degree and become independent once she had a job.' He rattled on as if he had decided beforehand that he was going to let it all out, but only the things that he was willing to part with. He sounded slightly scathing and she had to refrain from interrupting him.

Eliza wondered how much of what he said was true. How could Ilsa not have mentioned her children, pretended that she was not a mother? She, who had always seemed so devoted, in her own way.

'Of course, I found out she had children, quite soon afterwards, but then, you know, it was too late.' He had a faint smile on his face but seemed to check her out first, to see if she would approve or whether perhaps this was not so funny after all. She was not sure she actually liked the man, but she had

246

come this far and wanted to know what had caused such havoc in her mother's life, and in theirs, her family's, wanted to discover who her mother had been, what she had been, outside of their own family unit, hidden from them. She wanted most of all to understand what had caused her own uncertainty and misgivings, imagined that it had been due to something that had passed from her mother to her.

'Go on,' she said. She swallowed. Had Ilsa denied that she and Mark existed? Had she denied her own children?

'Go on,' she said again, when he stayed silent. Then, hesitating at first but quickly resuming his full speed monologue, he said

'Well, you see, she said her husband was a domineering man, she used that word, domineering, and that he never allowed her space and that she wanted to divorce him once she knew how to earn her own money. Our relationship developed, well, for as far as it did. I didn't think at the time that she wanted anything more than a fling outside of her marriage.' He had that same slightly crooked smile again and she wondered what her mother had seen in this man, whether he had been like this when he was younger or had become disillusioned and grown old savouring his youthful dalliances, surely, he had had more than just one? You only needed to look at him, this was a man gone to seed, she thought, feeling malicious all of a sudden. She hated him, hated his casualness, the absence of any guilt or concern, the self-satisfied smirk on his face. Or was that an attempt to hide something, to make it seem as if he had almost forgotten that time in London, that she'd woken him up from a slumber and that he was as uneasy about what had happened as she was?

He explained that he'd been in England on a work permit 'England wasn't in the EU then, and you still needed to have a job if you wanted to live in that country. But I never intended to stay anyway. I had a job at the university in Nijmegen, one of the oldest universities in The Netherlands, and I was only in England for six months, a kind of guest lectureship with the university. I never planned to stay longer than that.'

He hesitated, looked away from Eliza out of the window across the road at the windows that were haunted black eyes in the evening dusk, no living creatures visible, no lights switched on inside, deserted to all intends and purposes, until a woman came, opened one of the front doors and one by one lights were switched on, and then curtains drawn so that only a yellow glow vouched for occupancy.

He's so old, she thought, he has aged much more than Jonathan has, even though he cannot be any older, or is he? Gone to seed? Again she wondered what her mother had seen in this man. Had she been smitten for all the wrong reasons, had realised it and that was why she'd never left Jonathan or her children, but instead, when she discovered she was pregnant came back home and to her senses and made Jonathan believe she was pregnant with his child? Did that mean that she was carrying on with Hans whilst still in full sexual relationship with her husband? Oh shush, she shook her head. What did it matter now?

It was as if he read her thoughts. 'I didn't know she was pregnant. Truly. She never said.'

'How long?' Eliza asked

'Well, as I said. I was only in England for six months. It was only during that last month of my stay there that we ... that Ilsa and I ... and then I went back to Holland, you know. She said she didn't want to break up her marriage; that she had realised that nothing could come of our relationship, it was too complicated. She knew that I was also married, had a daughter;

still have a daughter of course. She's about your age I should think.'

Did the daughter know that she had a half-brother? Eliza didn't ask. 'When did you find out, about Anthony, about my brother, I mean?'

'I kind of suspected two years later when I was in England again. Of course, we'd kept in touch, only intermittently, just a friendly Christmas card, exchanged addresses when she moved to Norfolk later. She wouldn't see me again though, hung up the phone when I suggested we'd get together. Said it was not right. But later I found out from friends that she'd had a baby, another child and that the timing fitted in with our affair. She would never tell me though. And then, of course, later, when Anthony found out that Jonathan wasn't his father Ilsa e-mailed me to say this, to tell me. I agreed to a DNA test. She knew of course all along, women know these things. I was divorced for the second time then, my daughter grown up, a son who wouldn't see me and who stayed with my second wife. We have lost touch altogether now. I was happy actually to find out I had another son. It didn't work out though. He didn't really want to see me at first, I offered to come to England, but he didn't want to know. Later, yes, when he had children. I think his wife insisted, said he would be happier if he knew his father.'

Again, he stared out of the window. 'And then he died. Ilsa e-mailed me, and it was all gone ...'

The dusk came down quickly, the room felt gloomy and he lit another cigarette, inhaled deeply and bent over to the side of his chair and switched on a reading lamp. He sat in the halo of the light, casting shadows against the wall and she suddenly felt sorry for him, for his life where everything must have once seemed so brilliant and promising and which had then evaporated like the steam of a switched off kettle, dissipated into this mundane existence in a small village in a flat country, where he was living alone in a small house on an estate, however well kept, thinking about a past that had once been so promising. She was running away with herself. She didn't know any of this, she just assumed that he was lonely and had no one but he'd had a career, surely.

'Of course, you want to know what I would have done if I'd know ...'

She wasn't sure anymore that she did. What difference did it make?

She heard a key turn in the front door, a woman's voice *'Hallo papa. Ik ben het.'*

'My daughter,' he said. 'She's bringing the shopping on her way from work. She's a teacher.' He sounded proud and suddenly happy.

*

They didn't resume their conversation where they'd been interrupted. He didn't repeat his question and she didn't ask him, not after Ann-Marie had introduced herself, and Hans had introduced her 'the daughter of an old friend of mine in England,' not after Ann-Marie had stacked the fridge and the kitchen cupboards with the shopping from her bags, chatting all the time, switching over to a very respectable English when she realised that her father's guest didn't speak any Dutch, happy to show off her fluency, not after Ann-Marie had offered to make more tea but also said that she needed to get home before her own children came back from the school in the town, not after she'd closed the door behind her.

After Ann-Marie left, Hans got up and said he was tired; not only had he broken his leg but he'd also had trouble with headaches and tiredness after the fall from the ladder, a stupid accident, cleaning out his gutter. Eliza apologised, got up and said they could perhaps talk again, over the phone, but she also knew that neither Hans nor she could see the point of that.

'Have you been in touch with Ethel?' she asked before she closed the front door behind her.

'Yes,' he said. 'Once I get better I will try and visit. They are my grandchildren after all. But I haven't really yet talked about any of this here at home, not with my daughter. She doesn't really know about any of this. And I'm not sure that Ethel is very keen …'

She wondered why he and his wife had divorced.

'I've had three wives and three divorces,' he said, reading her thoughts, again with that crooked smile. 'It all gets a bit complicated.' Then he carefully closed the door behind her and she stood on the front door stoop, inhaling the damp but clean evening air. She drove in the dark, the roads crowded with people going home from work, the motorway a slow long queue of cars, with drivers switching lanes haphazardly if only to escape the boredom of looking at the back of the same car in front of them, until she finally reached her hotel. She telephoned Marja, 'you're quite right. There's nothing more to find out. But it's done, I'm done. I'm going to let Mum rest. And Anthony of course. I'm flying back tomorrow. Let's talk about where we will scatter Mum's ashes. He doesn't have to be there. I don't want him to be there. I'm sure Mum was done with him.'

Nineteen: For the love of Ilsa

'Surely we should scatter her some place that she used to love going to? And that's the beach, especially the Norfolk coast. She was very fond of taking us there, usually when the summer season was over, in autumn or during the Christmas holidays. She used to love marching us along that coast, said it was good for us. Of course, by the time we were teenagers we'd refuse to go with her and she often went on her own, got in the car, took her wellies and would come back blown through and cold but happy. Remember?'

'You mean to say that you've kept this urn all this time without telling us?' Stephan sounded incredulous. They were talking on Skype without the video on, just the telephone, Stephan always said he hated that gimmick, staring at each other over long distance, he'd rather use just the 'communication bit' and that worked fine, much better in fact, there was always interference when you tried to have visuals as well. It meant that she could move around the kitchen and prepare food whilst talking to him. She had no idea what Stephan was doing.

'What are you doing?' she said. 'Have you packed your bags? I'm really excited. A wedding after all!' She was able to make a joke of it, thank God.

'Will Tom come with you or do I have to invite him separately?' Stephan asked.

She frowned mockingly, but then realised that Stephan couldn't see her and said, 'Of course he's coming with me, you're inviting me AND partner I assume?'

It was good being able to joke about it all, good that the air had cleared, that the stiffness between them had gone and that she could once more talk with Stephan the way they used to, before Anthony and then Ilsa died.

'Have Mark and Samantha patched up a bit?' Stephan asked. 'I just can't make head or tail out of his reactions. He's avoiding me, that's for sure, always busy, travelling here, there and everywhere. Doesn't even answer my e-mails anymore.' He sounded petulant now.

'He'll be fine. Samantha told me that they have made up, that they've decided to have another go. They've just been through a very bad patch. These things happen. And of course he'll be at your wedding. It's a great excuse to get together again after all this time.'

*

Stephan and Sander's wedding ceremony went by without a hitch. They were all there, almost all there. Sander's grandfather had declined when he realised his grandson was marrying a man, not a woman, although he claimed that he couldn't travel, he was too old and he had sent a card with his best wishes and also a cheque for an undisclosed amount, neither Sander nor Stephan would say, but Sander's mother murmured something about having gone soft in the head, '£20,000 to buy a carpet', she whispered to Eliza during the ceremony. Otherwise, everyone appeared to be there and Eliza wondered whether it was part of the curiosity value of a gay wedding that no one could resist the invitation which both Sander and Stephan had generously distributed to family members as well as their university friends and colleagues. Stephan's family was complete, even Jonathan's twin sister Diana turned up, dressed as if she was going to a country house ball, and Jonathan's younger brother Robert with a wife who was at least fifteen years younger than he was; Aunt Marja and Uncle Banker were there and so were Mark and Samantha and the kids; Jonathan and Alea and Eliza and Tom arrived together although they hadn't planned it and Tom quickly whispered to Jonathan, definitely winked at him, said that he and Eliza were thinking about getting married too, but not yet. Ethel and her two children arrived shortly after; she and Eliza saw each other regularly now that Eliza had moved back to London.

Jonathan stood up and looked at ease when he made his speech. He said that Stephan's mother Ilsa would have been so proud of him and would have loved to witness this wedding of her youngest son,

'Her favourite of that I'm absolutely sure. Not that this diminished in any way her love for her other children. And we all miss Anthony of course and would have liked him to be here. Let's drink to Stephan and Sander, to Ilsa and Anthony and to all of you of course, all of the two families.'

*

'What happened to Gerry?' Samantha whispered to Marja, later when they had cheered to Stephan and Sander as they left the hotel in their hire car for the airport, off to one of the Greek Islands to 'celebrate in style'.

'Not to worry,' Marja said. 'I don't think he was too upset, said he had realised that his lifestyle wasn't for Eliza but had hoped that getting married would somehow or other make her feel better about living in the North and accepting his two children. I keep in touch with him, well, I always do, don't I?' She smiled. 'As a matter of fact he'll be getting married soon anyway, to his former sister in law, a younger sister of his wife who's always been smitten with him and who was dead set against him marrying Eliza.'

Eliza looked at them, raised her eyebrows at their burst of laughter and then turned to Tom. 'Let's go. I've promised Stephan I would scatter Mum's ashes after the wedding. She's been here all the time.' She pulled the vase out of a large handbag that had stood on the table when the speeches were made and held it up.

'She's been here with us all this time. Tomorrow we'll lay her to rest, at Holkham Beach.'

About the Author

Corri van de Stege was born in The Netherlands where she attended secondary school before moving to England and completing a philosophy degree at University College London and an MA at the University of Sheffield. She lives in rural Norfolk in the east of the UK, and after a successful career in education and as a management consultant she is now a full time writer and book blogger. *Half the World*, a memoir of living in Iran before and during the 1979 revolution, is her first book and *Notes on Anna* is her debut novel. *For the love of Ilsa* is her second novel. She is also working on a collection of short stories that she has been writing over the years. The author is a keen traveller and with most of her family and friends living abroad there is always an excuse to take a trip somewhere.

For the Love of Ilsa and the author's other books can be bought in eBook and print from Amazon, Barnes & Noble, and other online and physical bookstores worldwide. Further information

can be obtained from the author's site and blog on
http:www.corrivandestege.com

Now you are at the end, the author hopes that you have enjoyed
this book and would welcome any feedback or questions on any
aspects of the story, characters or settings. Please support the
author by providing a review on Amazon, Goodreads, Twitter
or any other favourite book site or social media

Twitter: http://twitter.com/corrivandestege
LinkedIn: https://www.linkedin.com/in/corrivandestege